Xenofall

The Wasteland Chronicles, Volume 7

Kyle West

Published by Kyle West, 2014.

This is a work of fiction. Similarities to real people, places, or events are entirely coincidental.

XENOFALL

First edition. June 27, 2014.

Copyright © 2014 Kyle West.

Written by Kyle West.

10 9 8 7 6 5 4 3 2 1

Also by Kyle West

The Wasteland Chronicles
Apocalypse
Origins
Evolution
Revelation
Darkness
Extinction
Xenofall

Watch for more at kylewestwriter.wordpress.com.

Thanks for sticking with me for seven books, 1,800 pages, and 450,000 words. It's been an incredible journey, and here's to many more.

Chapter 1

"On my mark," Makara said. "Move up the rise. And stay low."

The surrounding fungus emanated an ethereal glow, and the air was warm and sticky. Our squad sat with backs to a large boulder. Stilted trees twisted from the xenofungal bed. In the distance, a crawler shrieked.

"Go," Makara said.

Makara and I, along with four other Angels, advanced up the hill at a crouch, the fungus squishing beneath our boots. *Perseus* hovered high in the clouds, piloted by Anna and ready to descend at a moment's notice. We were in the Great Blight, after all; things could change in an instant.

Three meteorites had fallen near 3:00this location in Central Texas, and Makara wanted to inspect them up close. The one we were after had impacted not two hours ago, but Makara wanted to investigate all three. So, she had split us into three teams – Samuel and Ruth led one, while Julian and Michael led the other. Makara and I headed this one, and Grudge had come along for additional support.

At last, we made it to the top of the hill. Below, the Blighted valley spread, glowing in the night. A thin stream wove between the hills, its flow and gurgle audible even with distance. Judging by its quick flow, it was water rather than *Radaskim* ichor. In the center of that stream was a large boulder, out of the center of which radiated a molten glow. Steam hissed from the rock's sides where the water touched it.

"There it is," Makara said.

She raised a pair of binoculars enhanced with night vision to her eyes. I wished I could get a look, but I had to make do with my own eyes. Xenotrees grew thick on the stream's banks and alien chirps echoed in the hills. The clouds hung low, blocking starlight, though the bioluminescence of the vegetation provided ample light.

Makara lowered the binoculars. "Can't see a damn thing. We'll have to get closer."

Grudge grunted. "Sounds like a bad idea."

"Maybe," Makara said. "But we're not finding anything out up here, that's for damn sure."

"Maybe we should give it a bit more time?" one of the other men asked.

"No," Makara said. "The time is now."

The wind blew, warm and humid, like the exhalation of a beast. Being in the Great Blight was like being inside a living thing. That suffocating feeling went beyond the physical; it was like a thousand eyes watching your every move. The longer we remained, the more the *Radaskim* became aware of our presence.

It wouldn't be long until Askala noticed us as well.

The meteors had fallen all over America, and maybe even all over the world. We were investigating the ones in Texas because they were far from our usual action, and hopefully, less likely to draw Askala's attention. All the same, we still had to get in and get out soon.

My thoughts wandered to Ashton. It had been a day since his death, and we had done all the grieving we had been allowed – which was very little. I felt he would have known what to do about these meteorites, and probably would have had some theories about what they were.

"Alright," Makara said, lowering her binoculars. "We've been looking down there for two minutes now, and nothing's moving." She paused a moment before giving a nod. "If anything jumps out at us...shoot first."

Then, Makara walked downhill at a crouch, the rest of us following suit.

The glow of the fallen rock brightened as we advanced. It was about the size of a small house, and it was hard to imagine something this large falling from the sky without completely obliterating this valley. The boulder emanated a pink, molten glow that cast the valley in dancing light. I didn't think any of us expected the meteorite to be so big. Perhaps the fungus had padded its fall somewhat, or maybe it had impacted at a low velocity.

As we advanced, I could see that downstream, the water radiated a pinkish light that seemed to come from the meteor. The pink riddled the stream, contaminating the water.

Slowly, cautiously, Makara stepped onto the stream's bank. Water wrapped around the glowing rock, rushing past.

Grudge joined her, holding out a hand to touch the rock.

"Don't touch that," Makara said.

"I wasn't going to," Grudge said, defensively. He paused, feeling the surrounding air. "It's warm. Hotter than a stovetop."

"Doesn't surprise me," Makara said, frowning. "I don't get it. What's Askala trying to accomplish with these things?"

The Angels around her were quiet. She looked directly at me, so I racked my brain for a theory.

I pointed to the river. "Well, there's obviously something in this rock. Whatever it is, it's getting into the water. Maybe it has something to do with that?"

Makara watched the glowing water downstream. She lifted her radio.

"Bravo, you have a copy?"

Samuel answered. "Yeah. We're by our rock now."

"And?"

"And nothing. It's still glowing from its re-entry, but there's nothing around here." He paused. "Crazy how such a small thing could do so much damage."

"Wait," Makara said. "You said *small?*"

"Yeah," Samuel said. "Probably the size of a watermelon or something. Crater's as big as a football field."

Makara looked up at *our* rock, the size of a house, which had no discernable crater or sign of impact. She was silent for a moment.

"Are we in the right place?" she asked me.

"Should be," I said, pointing to the giant rock. "You can see it glowing. It definitely fell, maybe at a low velocity. Still, you'd think there'd be more of an impact than just splashing into a stream."

"Maybe it was here all along," Grudge said.

We both looked at him. He gave a shrug, pointing to the center of the rock.

"Only that one part of it is actually glowing. Maybe this giant rock was here before, and *it* was hit by a smaller meteorite."

Makara and I inspected the boulder more closely. It was cracked, right down the middle, which I assumed had happened from its initial impact. But Grudge was right; if this entire thing *had* come from space, it would have laid waste to this area for miles around.

"Grudge is right," Makara said. "Most of this thing was here before. It was hit by a smaller meteorite, which caused it to crack. I guess the contagion spread to the rest of the rock, along with the stream."

"Makara," Samuel's voice came. "Makara, you there?"

Makara raised the radio again. "Yeah. Just trying to figure things out."

"Ruth's on the line with Julian right now. They've found something."

The radio sizzled to silence, until Julian's voice came out.

"Makara?"

"Julian. What'd you find?"

"We're by the lake now, Point Charlie. The meteorite must have fallen into it, because the whole thing's changing color. It's not water, either. It's that icky crap."

"Changing color, how?"

"Not color, really," Julian said. "It's just...getting brighter."

"What do you want to do?" Grudge asked Makara.

Makara held up a hand, quieting him. "We'll meet you over there, Julian. I'm converging all teams at your location. Point Charlie, you said?"

"Yeah," Julian said. "We'll stay put."

"If anything happens," Makara said. "Call Anna and alert us all. We'll meet at extraction."

"Copy that. Try to hurry. It's spreading fast. Twenty feet or so a minute, if I had to guess."

"Copy that. We'll be there soon. Over and out."

Makara switched frequencies.

"Samuel, we're converging on Point Charlie. Head over, stat."

"Copy that."

At last, Makara switched over to Anna's line.

"*Perseus*, stand by for further orders. All teams are converging on Point Charlie, so let's use the Charlie extraction point we picked out earlier."

"Copy that," Anna said. "Things are quiet up here. Haven't seen any more of those things falling, and the infrared shows nothing outside the natural heat of the fungus. You should still be good to go."

"All the same, stay alert," Makara said. "It's been quiet down here, too."

Too quiet, I wanted to add, but I kept my silence.

"Be careful, Makara," Anna said.

"Advise me of any changes," Makara said. "Over and out."

She attached the radio to her belt, then withdrew her handgun. She gave one last glance at the split boulder before turning back to the rest of us.

"Let's go."

She headed back to the western hill, and we followed.

***

We left the valley, crossed the hill, and entered a thick stand of xenotrees. Point Charlie was through these trees and beyond another ridge. Samuel and Ruth would make it there before us, so Makara set a quick pace. The trees and the night were silent, yet all the same, it continued to feel like we were being watched.

When we passed the last line of trees, we took to the ridge. When we crested the rise, I looked down to see the bottom of the slope meeting with the shore of a massive lake, filling an entire valley with pink, translucent ichor. About one-third of the way into the lake, the liquid glowed *especially* bright, a neon pink with a silvery, metallic hue. Tendrils of the brightness expanded outward, claiming more of the lake's surface.

"Come on," Makara said.

At the bottom of the incline, twelve or so people stood, masked by darkness. We descended the slope, heading for the shore. Once we were close, I recognized Ruth, Michael, Samuel, and Julian. All of them were staring at the lake. Together, we watched the lake in silence. No matter how far the bright glow spread from the original point of contact, it kept its original luster.

"Theories on what this is?" Makara asked.

"The meteorite landed right in the center of that glowing section," Julian said. "We got here soon after that."

"I know that," Makara said. "But what is it *doing?*"

"Maybe one of us should go for a swim," Ruth said.

Julian guffawed. "After you."

One of the Angels picked up a nearby rock. Michael swatted it from his hand.

"Bad idea."

"Is it even safe to be standing out here, in the open?" Ruth asked.

"Yeah, we should get going," one of the Angels said.

"We *need* to find out what this is," Makara said. "Otherwise, this was a waste of time."

"I'd rather waste my time than die," Ruth said.

"We're staying," Makara said. "Nothing's attacked us yet."

Ruth shrugged. "There's nothing around for now, but..."

Grudge pointed across the lake. "Don't speak so soon."

"Down," Makara said.

Everyone dropped to the ground. Makara raised her binoculars to her eyes. Samuel and Michael followed suit with their own pairs.

"A crawler," Michael said. He scanned the far shoreline, seeking additional threats.

"It's going in the lake," Julian said, staying focused on the crawler.

Now, even I could see it. The crawler entered the shallows on the far side of the ichor lake. Its form was shadowed, silhouetted against the glowing pink of the ichor. The crawler paddled, slowly, across the lake toward the glowing section that was still spreading.

"That's a long swim," Ruth said.

Makara dropped her binoculars, allowing them to rest against her chest, held by the strap.

"There's more," Michael said. "Look."

Michael was right. Two, and then three more crawlers, appeared from the xenotrees bordering the far side of the lake. They slid into the ichor, almost *floating* in the direction of the iridescent glow. The original crawler was now halfway across the lake.

"Yeah," Makara said. "We need to fall back."

She rose at a crouch, the rest of us following suit. Together, we turned and headed up the slope.

"Makara," Anna's voice came. "We have two Behemoths heading for the top of the hill."

Makara reached for her radio to respond, but paused when a massive shadow, darker than even the night sky, materialized on the hilltop. A moment later, another large silhouette appeared beside it.

Everyone fell to the ground. I knew we wouldn't go unnoticed for long; with the glowing xenofungal floor, those monsters would see us eventually.

"Two Behemoths," Makara said, nonplussed. She lifted her radio. "Anna? Can you take them out?"

"Standing by. Acquiring targets..."

I glanced over at my shoulder back toward the lake. *Hundreds* of crawlers were now entering the lake's ichorous surface, which was now frothing and bubbling like a witch's brew. They paddled with their spindly legs toward the radiant ichor, now covering almost half of the lake. The first crawler had made it there and was now bathed within that glowing liquid. A deep buzz thrummed from the lake, in even pulses. The strange sound made my hair stand on end. The crawlers' glowing white eyes no longer just focused on the lake – they scanned the hills, searching...

"They know we're here," I said.

One of the Angels suddenly screamed, bolting to our right.

"Quiet!" Makara hissed.

But it was too late – something had caused the man to become unhinged. The Behemoths at the top of the ridge, once silent statues, sprung to life. They charged for the fleeing man. He continued to scream, leading the Behemoths away from us.

"Anna," Makara said. "Fire."

"They've disappeared behind the hill," she said. "I'd have to leave the extraction point."

Makara said nothing as the man continued to run and scream. Several crawlers appeared from the shoreline, cutting off his escape path. He swerved right into the mandibles of a waiting crawler. His screams were shrill and bloodcurdling.

The Behemoths caught up with the fleeing Angel, joining in the carnage.

"They're gone," Makara said. "We need to move."

We stood and ran up the hill full speed. The hum of the swarm behind intensified as Makara lifted her radio.

"Anna. On our way to extraction."

From the ridge top came two more crawlers. With twin shrieks, they charged toward us.

"Fire!" Makara yelled.

Men in the front knelt, unloading their rifles into the approaching monsters. Other Angels remained standing, focusing their fire on the lead crawler. The monsters stumbled to a stop under the hail of bullets.

From the sky, *Perseus* descended to the top of the hill, its landing lights scanning the ridge. From the lake below, crawlers had gathered and were now scuttling uphill. Meanwhile, we ran past the crawlers that had taken the bullet fire, continuing to shoot at them as we passed. One made a feeble attempt to pounce on a passing Angel before going still.

We reached the top of the rise. On all sides, the glowing fungus revealed the crawlers ascending from the lake below. *Perseus* was now landed about fifty feet away. The boarding ramp extended.

We ran toward the ship as the crawlers pressed in from behind. Once there, we ascended the ramp in a line, Makara staying at the bottom and ushering everyone on board. She took a few shots with her handgun at the approaching mass of monsters.

Once in the wardroom, I looked back out to see that Grudge was still running from the swarm, three crawlers clipping at his heels.

"*Grudge!*" Makara yelled.

She took a few shots, but quickly ceased her fire upon seeing how close those shots came to hitting Grudge. When he was still twenty feet from the boarding ramp, the lead crawler leapt mightily, the sharp tips of its legs stabbing Grudge in the back and bringing him to the ground. His face contorted in pain. The other crawlers tore into his flesh, and he let out a horrible, cracked yowl.

There was no way he would survive. Makara ran up the ramp and into the hold. As soon as the door slid shut, *Perseus* lifted off and the boarding ramp retracted.

We lifted into the air, all of us sitting on the deck to avoid falling, until we were far out of range of Askala's swarm.

"He's gone..." Makara said, obviously shaken by Grudge's death.

"There was nothing you could have done," Samuel said.

I hadn't even noticed that he fell behind. None of us did in our mad dash to escape. All I could feel was shock and disbelief. How would the few Suns who remained take the news, back in Los Angeles?

The angle of the ship soon evened out, and I found myself still lying on the deck.

"Everyone else alright?" Makara asked.

"We lost Bates, too," one of the Angels said.

I assumed he was the man who panicked and ran.

Makara nodded, and now that the ship had stabilized, everyone began to stand. Makara lifted herself from the deck, brushing off her clothes. It was hard to tell what she was thinking.

"I know it's not easy, losing people," Makara said. "Grudge will be missed. Bates, too. But we've learned something valuable about the *Radaskim* today. *Something* was going on with that lake. I don't know what it was, but it seems important."

None of the men said anything. It wasn't easy to brush aside death like this and focus on the mission. I could tell it wasn't easy for Makara, either. All of the original gang lords of Las Vegas were dead, and Grudge had been the most helpful one of them all. Without him, we would have never survived the Community in Bunker 84.

Now, we didn't even have a body to bury.

"What's the plan now?" Julian asked.

"We're heading back to base," Makara said. "We might have to come back here, later, to see what else we can learn."

"I'm not going down there again," one of the men said.

"We won't be able to take more samples that way," Samuel said.

"You got something?" Makara asked.

Samuel raised a vial of glowing, pink liquid. The men shrunk back at it. I didn't even notice Samuel taking the sample; I was probably too focused on the crawlers.

"I tried to get some of the ichor that was glowing a little brighter," Samuel said. "The contaminant introduced by the meteor should be in here."

"So, what do we do with that stuff?" Julian asked.

"I need to analyze it," Samuel said. "There were labs and a database of xenoviral strains in Skyhome, but that's gone, now. The only other place with extensive research laboratories is Bunker One."

"*No,*" Makara said. "Absolutely not."

"I don't like it either, but we have no other choice," Samuel said.

"Maybe we do," Ruth said. "Askal or Quietus might know something about the contaminant. Askal was the one who pointed us here, anyway."

I had no idea if the *Elekai* could tell us what this was, but it was better than risking our necks in Bunker One. We barely escaped that place the first time.

"We're not far from the Xenolith," Makara said. "It wouldn't hurt to check."

"Yeah," I said. "It's worth a shot."

Makara nodded. "Let's head there, then."

It was already past midnight. I knew the men would be ready for their bunks back in Los Angeles, especially after a night like this, but we needed to learn what we could. Those meteors falling, and the lake changing color and the crawlers bathing in it...we couldn't just ignore that.

Anna entered the wardroom from the bridge. "Holding a party without me?"

It took her a second to recognize something was off.

"Grudge is gone," Makara said.

"What?" she asked.

She looked around the wardroom, as if she were going to find him here. When she didn't, she looked at Makara.

"He was caught by the crawlers while we were running here," Makara said. "He didn't have a chance."

Anna nodded, her face pale. It wasn't an easy death, and it was enough to make even Anna queasy.

"We're heading for the *Elekai* Xenolith," Makara said. "We're hoping the *Elekai* can help us figure out what was going on at the lake."

"Right," she said. "Makes sense. I can have us there in under an hour."

As Anna returned to the bridge, Makara faced everyone in the wardroom.

"We'll only need a few people to go in there. The rest of you can get some rest."

Makara left for the bridge as they talked amongst themselves. I could only think about Grudge and his horrible demise. It seemed almost unreal that it could happen so suddenly, and it was a reminder that everything we did was dangerous.

I could only wonder when the next death would come.

Chapter 2

We landed at the Xenolith thirty minutes later. Anna, Samuel, and I were the only ones going inside.

We left the ship behind and went down the familiar path into the Xenolith. Before long, we stood before the ichorous lake.

"Askal?" I called out.

The surface of the ichor was calm and still. Askal, along with other dragons, was off somewhere else. All the same, I heard Askal's response resound in my mind.

Elekim. *You have returned.*

From one of the further caverns, Askal swooped across the lake. His wings outspread, he glided above the surface of the ichor and settled on the shoreline before us.

We went to one of the impact sites, I said. *The meteor seemed to change the* Radaskim's *ichor. You know what might be going on?*

Askal blinked. *I have no idea,* Elekim. *Show me what happened.*

At Askal's request, I transferred my memory of watching the crawlers enter the lake. I felt Askal's unease heighten at the image.

I don't know what it is, Askal said at last. *It can't be good.*

We brought some of the ichor back. We were hoping you could tell us what was in it.

And you brought this here?

Yes. Is that bad?

There was a long pause, but at last, Askal answered.

No. The ichor will not harm us. It is only…distasteful. He gave a flutter of his wings. *These meteorites – did they fall elsewhere, or just in this lake?*

I assume they've fallen all over the world, or at least in the Great Blight.

Samuel and Anna were both looking at me, wondering what Askal was saying.

Perhaps there is some new power in the lake, Askal said.

What power?

You ask me, Elekim? *I know not. But perhaps we can read the contents.* He paused. *Set it on the ground.*

"He wants the sample on the ground," I said.

Samuel nodded, placing a vial of the glowing ichor at Askal's feet. As Samuel backed away, Askal extended a long, sharp claw to pull the vial toward him. He lowered his head until his nostrils were right above it. He gave the vial two hard sniffs.

"What's he doing?" Anna whispered.

I shrugged.

Then, Askal chomped on the vial, cracking the vial and spilling the *Radaskim* ichor all over the fungus. Some of the ichor was absorbed by the fungus while Askal lapped up the rest with his tongue.

Askal! I said. *What are you doing?*

The dragon looked at me, his white eyes glowing. *With luck, I might discover its contents this way.*

You're risking your life!

Askal stood on his haunches, waiting a moment. All the *Radaskim* ichor was gone – either absorbed by the fungus below or eaten by Askal. He closed his eyes, as if in meditation.

What are you doing?

Askal didn't respond. He merely sat there, eyes closed, waiting for...something.

The three of us exchanged confused looks until, a moment later, Askal opened his eyes again.

It's a new strain, he said. *A new sickness.*

A new strain? I asked.

Yes, Askal said. *There are additional codes...instructions. These strains will change the* Radaskim *as we know them.*

Additional codes? I asked. *Like what? There's more than one strain in there?*

New evolutions are imminent, Askal said. *I...cannot say what they are. But if Askala's swarm is entering that pool, they are probably doing so all over the Great Blight. When they are exposed to the new ichor, the* Radaskim *will undergo a transformation.*

What kind of transformation?

That's all I can say, Elekim. *The codes are like another language to me, but I can sense that much.*

"What's going on?" Samuel asked.

Samuel and Anna had missed the entire exchange, so I had to bring them up to speed.

"Askal thinks it's a set of new evolutions," I said. "The ichor contains new genetic codes to modify the *Radaskim.*"

"How so?" Anna asked.

"He doesn't know," I said. "But something big is coming. We just need to figure out *what.*"

Samuel and Anna went quiet, thinking. Over time, the virus evolved to become more dynamic, adaptable, and more able to create bigger and deadlier monsters. At first, the xenovirus had only affected microbes, bacteria, and relatively uncomplicated life forms.

Just thinking about this progression made me wonder – what could be next? Or were the new strains only going to affect the forms of *Radaskim* xenolife already present?

I turned back to Askal. *Is there anything else we should know?*

Askal looked at me. *I've told you all I can. I will think about this,* Elekim, *and see if I discover anything more.*

I nodded. *Thank you, Askal.*

Perhaps Quietus may be of more help.

I realized Askal was right. If there was anyone who knew about what the *Radaskim* might be planning, it was probably her. After all, she *had* been *Radaskim*.

"We need to talk to Quietus," I said. "You have any ichor left, Samuel?"

"Yeah, I managed to collect a few vials before we evacuated."

"Good. Let's go find her, then."

***

We found Quietus in one of the back caverns, sitting alone on an island in the center of a small pool. Two xenotrees with white bark grew from the island, but Quietus towered over both. She had a way of dwarfing everything around her. As we swam into the cavern, her white eyes turned upon us. She unfurled her dark wings, stretching them, before folding them back.

We reached the island and emerged from the ichor. I craned my neck to look at Quietus. Despite her now being *Elekai,* there was something still a bit chilling about her. Dark. Her white eyes blazed as she glared down at us.

Quietus, we need your help.

Doubtless – otherwise, you would not be here. I feel your trepidation, and do not fault you for it; indeed, it is well-placed. Still, perhaps I may be of use to you. How might I aid you, Elekim?

I tried not to let Quietus's preamble unnerve me, so I went on with what I was going to say.

The Radaskim *have sent meteorites crashing into the Great Blight. One of them crashed into a lake of ichor, which made it change in color.* I paused, as Quietus watched with glowing, white eyes. *The crawlers swam into the lake, and Askal thinks a new set of evolutions is imminent. What do you think?*

Quietus made a strange sound in her throat, almost like a chortle. Anna and Samuel looked at each other.

You deliver the ichor to Askal, who knows nothing, Quietus said. *But leave none for the First of the* Radaskim? *Before I could assist you, I would need a fresh sample.*

"She needs some of the ichor," I said to Samuel.

He reached into his pack, withdrawing a vial of pink, glowing liquid. He walked forward, laying the vial on the fungus in front of Quietus.

Splendid, Quietus said. *Let us see what horrors my Mother is brewing.*

As Askal had, Quietus broke the vial, letting the pink ichor loose. She lapped most of it up with her tongue, taking care to avoid the shattered glass. The rest was absorbed into the xenofungal bed.

Quietus stretched her neck, closing her eyes in contemplation.

Ah, she said. *A fine draft. These are old genes, genes not seen in millions of years. I was young when I first learned of these. They are from the First Reapings,* Elekim. *Though I am still* Elekai, *in my soul, some small, dark part of me sings at the ruin these codes confine.* Quietus opened her eyes, gazing at me levelly. *The Dark Mother fears you,* Elekim.

Why does she fear me?

Askala is ruled by fear, Quietus said. *After all, she herself rules by it. You forget,* Elekim – *even Askala is a thrall of a lord more ancient and terrible. But thankfully for you and this world, he is far off yet.*

The fact that there was something *worse* than Askala out there was more than unnerving.

My Mother's webs are intricate, and the Radaskim *have hidden paths that even I, Quietus, know not. I have tasted the ichor, and this I know: the expansion of the* Radaskim *swarm shall quicken. But do not despair; there is still time to fight, though that time is little. There are three days until the final battle, until this final evolution is complete.*

I looked into Quietus's featureless, white eyes, chilled to the bone. Three days, and we still didn't know what we'd be up against. More than ever, the fight seemed impossible, and I was tempted to despair.

Quietus's head lowered, until it was right in front of mine. Each of her eyes was as large as my face, and both of them stared at me now.

Take care, Elekim. *And do not lose hope. If you lose hope...then the Dark Mother has already won.*

Quietus...thank you.

I looked at her a moment longer before turning to Samuel and Anna.

"Let's get back to the ship," I said. "There's a lot to explain."

***

Everyone was gathered in the conference hold. Michael, Makara, and Ruth were bleary-eyed at having been woken up. The Raiders slept on in the wardroom.

Michael poured a cup of coffee from a thermos into a ceramic mug. He passed the thermos on to Anna, who poured herself a cup.

I explained everything over the next few minutes, everyone becoming more alert when I talked about how the final evolutions would manifest in three days, which was when the final attack would begin.

Once I was done, Makara was the first to speak.

"Three days doesn't give us much time. Augustus won't be too pleased."

"We really don't have much choice," Samuel said. "The facts are the facts, and Augustus will understand that."

"Did Quietus explain what the final evolutions would be?" Michael asked.

I shook my head. "Not really. The one thing she did say was that the ichor contained old genes she hadn't seen in over a million years." I sighed. "That doesn't really help us, though."

"Now we *really* have to go to Bunker One," Samuel said. "It has tons of xenoviral strains on file, so there might be some matches to the ones in the ichor. Some might even be *exactly* the same. We could crosscheck the genes, and it could reveal what we might be up against."

"Do you think Bunker One's servers are still online?" Makara asked.

Samuel nodded. "They were when we left. If not...we could see if Bunker 84 has similar research, though I doubt it does. The bulk of xenoviral research occurred in Bunker One, as we all know. Ashton uploaded most of that research into Skyhome's servers, but..."

All I could think was how untimely Ashton's death had been, and not just him – *everyone* who had lived in Skyhome.

"Bunker One will be dangerous," Makara said.

Michael shook his head. "We should think twice before going in there. These things have a way of getting complicated. With a big Bunker like that, it would be easy to get trapped in the lower levels"

"I know," Makara said, "but do we have a choice? Where else can we find out about these final evolutions? We know that they're old, but we need specifics."

"We just have to analyze the ichor, and the system will allow us to see if any of the strains are recognizable," Samuel said. "It's worth a shot. Even if it's a dead end, we'll probably come away knowing more than we do now."

Everyone looked to Makara.

"Alright," she said. "We'll get what rest we can. Take everyone back to Los Angeles and brief Augustus on the situation. Then, we'll come back to Bunker One tomorrow. Or, I guess, today. It's already 03:00."

"There's also the matter of getting the army ready," Anna said.

"That's Augustus's and Carin's field, along with Char and Marcus," Makara said. "Nevertheless, our input might be needed."

We still hadn't hammered out details for the final battle. The Angels, the Empire, and the Reapers were all working together, which was easier said than done. Even though Carin Black had betrayed Augustus, we still needed his resources and tactical know-how. Even with Augustus keeping him in check, the fact remained that the Reapers had betrayed us once already, and they could easily do so again.

For now, at least, everyone appeared to be on the same page. Without that unity, we were *all* dead.

"Let's head back, and get some rest," Makara said. "I want everyone in the wardroom by 10:00. We're going to have a busy day."

Chapter 3

We were on the ground in Los Angeles at 10:00 sharp. I still wanted a few more hours of sleep, but when would I ever *not* want that? When the world was ending for a second time, sleep inevitably took the back burner.

We headed to the U.S. Bank Tower, where we were to meet up with Augustus and Carin to plan our attack into the Great Blight. On our way there, I took in my surroundings. As I watched the people of Los Angeles filter in and out of the decrepit skyscrapers, I realized that an entire community existed here. The Black Reapers might have controlled the city, but the majority of its citizens were not members of the gang. They merely lived in the gang's shadow and had to play by its rules. I'd been told, back when I lived in Bunker 108, that Los Angeles had a population of ten thousand.

Surely, after the battle, it was much less now.

There were the citizens and there were the slaves, and it was easy to tell the difference between the two. In front of a soot-stained skyscraper, a heavyset woman thrust a broom at another, thinner woman, whose clothing had rips and tears. The woman took the broom, keeping her eyes to the ground, and began sweeping outside the building's entrance. After a few sweeps, she paused and looked up, meeting my eyes. I was surprised at how young she was, a mask of dirt darkening her hollow cheeks. But worst of all, a brand had been seared into her forehead: the number *0*. Around the brand the skin was reddened and raw.

Her gaze quickly dropped to the ground.

"We need to do something about the slavery here," I said.

"I'm not saying it's right," Makara said. "It's just a lot more complicated than it looks."

I supposed the sight of slavery was far more common to her than it was to me. I knew this world had a way of hardening emotions, but seeing one human being control another was something I'd never be okay with. All the same, it wasn't like the free citizens were just standing around; it seemed as if everyone was cleaning the rubble left behind by the *Radaskim* attack. On the side of the street, a giant pile of dead crawlers had been gathered for burning. Even a few days after the attack, cleanup was still going on.

"One thing at a time," Makara said. "Survival is the most important thing right now. I'm sure the slaves would agree with that."

I supposed Makara was right, but it was hard to stomach the injustice that existed here.

We continued on to the tower. As we neared, the crowds thinned. We ascended a set of steps to the entrance. Two Reapers with assault rifles stood guard out front, flanking each side of the entrance. They stood still as they let us pass.

We stepped into a lobby lit with torches. Shadows danced on the wide walls of the spacious atrium. The white marbled floor gleamed in the dancing light.

A long table had been set up in the center of the space. Among the few Reapers present, there were many more Imperials – purple-garbed Praetorians, grizzled legionaries, along with Augustus himself, sitting at the head of the table. Carin Black sat in the next chair over, looking at us with his glacial eyes as we entered. A small, superior smile stretched his thin lips. The yellow light of the torches illuminated his heavily tattooed arms – the serpent on his right forearm, the Grim Reaper on his right biceps, and the skull and cross-scythes on his left biceps. Behind Black stood his son, Onyx, his black eyes like pits in the firelight. He smirked.

"The Angels from on high arrive at last," Carin Black said.

"Shut up, Black," Makara said, taking a seat at the table. "Augustus is the only reason you don't have a bullet in your head right now, but from the way you're talking, it's probably full of empty air, anyway."

Black frowned, while Onyx gave Makara a death stare.

"Actually," Anna said, taking a seat next to Makara and fixing Black with a level gaze, "it's probably full of earwax."

"That would make sense," Makara said. "It would explain his propensity to not listen."

"Alright," Black said, "shut it, you dumb, stupid..."

Augustus held up a hand. "Silence!"

But Black's son, Onyx, wasn't listening. "Father, I will shoot them right now if you give the word."

Anna looked up. "One more croak out of you, toad, and it's your guts on the floor."

Everyone went silent. While I wanted to high-five Makara and Anna, the Emperor was less than amused.

"We must focus on the task at hand," he said. "I *will not* have this peace broken with these petty gibes. You make a mockery of this alliance.'"

"Alliance is too kind a word for this farce," Samuel said, also taking a seat. "But let's pretend a little longer."

Everyone else took their seats as the Reapers and Imperials gazed on in silence. I noticed one of the legionaries was Horacio, the short man who had cooked for us back in Augustus's camp. He gave a slight nod of acknowledgement before I looked at the Emperor.

"First," Augustus said, "let's all agree to be peaceable. Makara has already let me know about the evolutions the *Radaskim* are developing. I would think she, of all people, would have the most reason to set aside differences for the sake of progress."

Makara's face burned. She'd been put in her place, and she knew it, but she wasn't going to apologize.

"I thought it would be best for Alex to explain everything," she said. "He's the one who talked to Quietus."

"That *Radaskim* dragon?" Carin Black asked.

Makara gave a terse nod.

Once again, it fell to me to catch everyone up. As I spoke, Augustus and Carin listened while Onyx glowered in the background. I could tell that he wanted nothing more than to shoot both Makara and Anna dead. Even if the two of them wanted to do the same, Augustus was right. We had to keep the peace.

When I had finished explaining, everyone sat in silence, thinking.

"So, there's some new evolutions coming," Black said, "only you haven't figured out what they are yet?"

Makara stared at him pointedly. "We're going to find out. We need to take *Perseus* to Bunker One and let Samuel run his tests on the alien ichor."

Augustus raised a quizzical eyebrow. "And who'll be going with you?"

"Me, for one," she said. "And obviously, Samuel. We could use two or three more. I definitely don't want to draw attention or risk too much of our manpower on a single mission."

Carin sniffed. "Especially one that will probably fail."

"No one asked you," Anna said.

"If you really think this will help, Makara," Augustus said, "then I'll trust your judgment on the matter. You and Samuel know more about the xenovirus than I do. Just get out of there if it's too dangerous. Don't even land if it looks a little bad."

Makara nodded. "Don't worry. It's a risk, but it's one we have to take. My team and I have gotten in and out of much worse."

"Your number will be up eventually," Carin said. He didn't look the least bit unhappy at that.

"Maybe," Makara said. "But so will yours, if we end up failing. We're all in this together."

Carin shrugged.

"When are you leaving?" Augustus asked.

"As soon as possible," Makara said. "I want to be in and out of there by nightfall."

"If you need three more," Ruth said, "I'll be one of them."

Makara looked to Michael, who held up his hands.

"Oh, come on," Makara said.

"I need to use *Orion* to start moving people here from Bunker 84."

"Absolutely not," Makara said. "On moving people here, I mean. Let them stay in the Bunker for now. At least they're safe there."

"They won't be very safe without power," Michael said. "The Bunker can only run so long without a spaceship to power it. It's time that they moved here. It's the only long-term option."

Makara sighed, thinking for a moment.

"This is something we've been putting off," Michael insisted. "We need to do it. I guess they could stay in 84, but we'd have to commit one of our ships there to power the place."

"They should still have enough power for now," Makara said. "After Bunker One, we can set that plan into action, but I'm going to need you at the Bunker. It could be dangerous, and you're a good shot."

"That works, I guess," Michael said.

Makara turned back to the table. "We've got Samuel, Ruth, Michael, and me. We need one more to go to Bunker One."

"I'll go," Julian said.

Makara gave him a glance before acquiescing. "Alright. That's our five."

"What about me?" I asked.

"You're staying here," she said. "We're not risking you again. I don't know why I let you into the Great Blight earlier, but you're out of action until we're ready to attack."

"If I'm out of action, I actually *will* die. Of boredom."

Makara shook her head. "I'll take that chance."

Anna didn't even have to ask what her job was. As it was in Skyhome, she was supposed to keep me out of trouble.

"Alright," Augustus said. "Makara, Samuel, Ruth, Julian, and Michael. I think we have our team."

"I think that's as settled as it will ever be," Makara said, pushing back her chair.

"We're not done, yet," Augustus said. "We still need to plan the attack."

Makara paused, sitting back down. "Right. What did you guys come up with?"

"More agreeable now, aren't we?" Carin Black asked.

Makara's mouth twisted. "Yeah. If that's what you call it."

Carin smiled pleasantly. Well, I guessed *he* probably thought it was pleasant.

"We did a head count of my troops and Augustus's legions," Carin said. "Together, we have about eight thousand. Not a lot when you're talking about all the *Radaskim,* but far more than should have survived that battle." Carin licked his lips before continuing. "A thousand of those are my men, armed to the teeth and well-trained. Seven thousand are Augustus's." Carin gestured to Makara. "Of course, let's not forget the two hundred you've graciously brought to the table, Makara."

"You're welcome," Makara said.

"Mobilizing the men can be done today," Carin said. "We can leave the city limits by tomorrow morning and begin our push into the Great Blight. Resistance will be light, at first, but we expect it to get heavier the farther we go east."

Carin had our full attention. His tactics were the reason he rose to power in Los Angeles in the first place. As much as Makara or Anna hated to admit it, he knew what he was talking about, even if he was despicable in every other way.

"As Augustus has already said," Black continued. "The point isn't victory from this engagement – it's merely to draw Askala's forces and attention away from the Crater. I have my doubts about that. If Askala is half as smart as you guys say she is, she's going to leave plenty of defenders behind – enough to make getting inside close to suicide. But I digress..."

"Get to the point," Makara said.

"Here's the point: we still have nine nukes left in Bunker 84. We can use them to clear the way."

Now, *that* I hadn't expected.

Black went on. "We could launch the nukes at some key targets in the Great Blight. Xenoliths that seem to be communication hubs. Maybe some of the larger gatherings of swarm movements. And, right before you guys land..."

Black made a gun gesture, followed by a *pow*.

"What's that supposed to mean?" Anna asked.

Carin smirked. "Whose got the earwax brain now, girl?"

Before Anna could get her own barb in, Samuel spoke up.

"He wants to nuke Ragnarok Crater. Of course, that won't defeat Askala, but it might get rid of a lot of resistance."

"Ragnarok Crater is big," I said. "And you'd be exposing us to dangerous levels of radiation."

"Dangerous?" Black asked, with a chuckle. "We're going to be neck deep in purple blood in the Great Blight for your sake, Chosen One. Don't preach to me about danger. Besides, you're all as good as dead, anyway. What's a little radiation going to do? Might even give you a healthy glow."

"What targets are you thinking about?" Makara asked. "Specifically."

"Glad to see you like my idea," Black said. "I was thinking three, right on the Warrens. Those are the tunnels that lead down to Askala's lair, for those of you not in the know."

"We know," Anna said.

Carin went on. "It should give you guys an opening – literally. Those bombs could open up some of those passageways and make it easier to climb down."

"Or close them," I said.

"You have to pick your risks," Carin said. "It's probably better to use the nukes than to be drowning in a sea of very angry crawlers."

Carin was probably right. There were nine nukes in Bunker 84, and it'd be crazy not to use them if we could. Askala probably took over the Bunker through Elias because she feared those nukes being used. Even if we didn't bomb the Crater directly, we could still take out a lot of key targets, as Carin had said.

"It's a good idea," Samuel said. "But who would be pulling the trigger?"

Carin smiled. "Why, *you* would. I don't even trust *myself* to do that."

We all looked at Carin, suspecting some trick.

"I guess you're right, about the radiation," I said. "If we're dead anyway, what's the point of worrying about it?"

"Yeah, he does have a good point," Anna said, reluctantly.

"Glad to hear it, doll face."

Anna narrowed her eyes. "Don't call me that."

"So," Samuel said. "Nukes. A massive advance east. Anything else we're missing?"

"Oh, yes," Carin said, his smile widening. "I have a railgun."

All of us looked at each other. I had no idea what a railgun was, but from everyone else's reaction, it seemed to be a big deal.

"A *what?*" Anna asked.

Carin shook his head. "Oh, so *now* she's interested, now that she knows I have a giant gun. Typical."

"Shut up," Makara said. "Why are you just now telling us this?"

"I have a flair for the dramatic," Carin said, his blue eyes dancing. "That, and I was missing one of the components necessary to run the railgun: an incredibly strong power source. Fusion power, to be specific."

"Where do you plan on getting this fusion power?" I asked.

"Why, I was going to bat my eyes and ask all nice-like." Carin batted his eyes, looking at Makara. "Pretty please, with sugar on top, can I borrow your spaceship for the battle?"

"Why not ask Augustus?" Makara asked.

"I already did," Carin said. "He didn't succumb to my charms."

"Well, neither will I," Makara said.

"Wait a minute," Michael said. "A railgun would be *highly* useful. Carin is right. With enough rounds, those things would shoot dragons right out of the sky. The rounds fire incredibly fast, so dragons would have a hard time dodging them."

"You can find your fusion drive somewhere else," Makara said. "We'll need *both* ships to make the attack on the Crater."

"We could salvage *Odin* for a fusion drive," I said. "Or maybe *Aeneas*."

"*Aeneas* is far too big to salvage," Samuel said. "*Gilamesh* went up in flames, so that's a no-go. And *Odin*...maybe it survived the crash, but even if the drive is still functional, there's the matter of transporting it." Samuel looked at Carin. "How do you plan on moving this railgun? Where did you find it?"

"We've had it for a long time," Carin said. "It's an artillery piece that rolls on treads. A halftrack. But, like I said, we don't have the power to run it. These things fire using powerful electromagnets. First of all, I'd like to see if the damn thing *works*. I'll need one of the ships to run some tests."

"Is it worth giving up one of the ships so you can shoot down dragons?" Makara asked.

Carin shrugged. "I think so. My railgun could shoot down far more dragons than any of your ships. It shoots quickly, and even reloads automatically. A computer points and shoots, so there's no way it could miss. The rounds fly too quickly – at Mach 10, to be precise. It could rip everything out of the air in a matter of minutes."

"I'm just wondering why we didn't use this in the battle earlier," I said.

"Well, I'll admit," Carin said. "It's a *little* hard to get something that big on top of buildings. Kept in the streets, it wouldn't have gotten a good shot at anything. Besides, you guys *really* wanted to use your ship to find the old man. There were too many variables to have made it anything but a last-ditch defense. Now, if you guys had gotten here earlier, we might have had time to run the proper tests. But it's no use crying over what might have been. Let's run the proper tests now and we'll all be better for it."

Makara looked around the table, seeking other opinions. No one said anything.

"I think we should give it a shot," Samuel said. "No pun intended."

"Alright," Makara said. "We'll do some tests."

"Thanks," Carin said. "But in the end, I believe you'll be the one thanking me."

"Don't count on it."

As the planning continued, a man ran through the door. Two Praetorians escorted him to Augustus. I recognized him as the courier I'd seen briefly back in Augustus's camp.

"Are they here?" Augustus asked.

"Yes, *Princeps*," the courier said, a tall man with curly black hair. "The fleet has arrived."

"The fleet?" I asked.

"That's another thing I didn't mention," Augustus said. "My fleet, complete with reinforcing food, weapons, and supplies, has been en route for a while. I gave them orders to leave Nova Roma two months following our departure."

"That's good timing," Samuel said.

"Char and Marcus need to know what's happened here," Makara said. "They said on the radio they'd be in Port Town."

"Port Town?" I asked.

"A settlement down by Long Beach," Augustus said. "Francisco can take you there."

I was wondering who Francisco was, when the courier nodded.

"What are they doing in Port Town?" I asked.

"Booze, if I had to guess," Makara said. "And hopefully it stops there."

"It's eleven in the morning!"

"The bars will be open, because the sailors are in town," Makara said. "And it's never too early for a Raider."

I felt I was being given a pointless task, but if we hurried, it wouldn't take long.

"I guess I'll see you all later, then."

Anna and I left our chairs, following Francisco outside the building.

Chapter 4

I learned from Francisco that there were a lot of dingy bars, taverns, and brothels down in Port Town where the dregs of Los Angeles society liked to converge. In addition, Port Town itself was fairly sizeable, at almost two thousand people, which made it large enough to have its own seediness, even without L.A. feeding it from the north.

When we stepped outside, we found a Recon waiting for us on the street. We climbed in, Anna and I taking the backseat.

Francisco wove through the rubble-strewn streets. What few people were out parted as we passed. The dull red sky did little to illuminate the monochrome gray of the towering, crumbling buildings. Smoke belched into the sky from burning piles of crawlers.

After a couple of minutes, we ascended an on-ramp and drove south. The highway was clear, and what cars there were had long been pushed over to the shoulder. The cars had been stripped of any useful components long ago, leaving behind metal shells.

It was a near-straight shot south to Port Town. To the east and west, tall buildings rose. The lifeless, eastern hills marched north to south. Everything looked empty of life.

The silence stretched on, and was starting to get to me, so I decided to talk to Francisco.

"What's it like, being a courier?"

"When the Emperor has a message to carry, he needs a man he can trust. That man is me."

"Do people live this far out?"

"Most of the city is abandoned. The Reapers say they control everything, but that's only in name. The farther from downtown, the more dangerous. Many criminals live here, outside the Reapers' justice. Or so I've heard."

"The Reapers' justice?" Anna asked. "Didn't know there was such a thing."

Francisco chuckled. "Even a man like Carin must keep peace. In the Empire, the old cities are the same. They are too large to control." Francisco made a sweeping gesture toward the crumbling, abandoned cityscape. "What you see here, my friends – that is no city. It is as wild as any jungle of Nova Roma."

The rest of the trip passed in silence. On our left, I noticed a wide, concrete-lined ditch, dry as a bone. The ditch ran even with the highway for a long while before widening and filling with dull, gray water. A high, arched bridge crossed the ditch that was now as wide as a river. The highway twisted, and Francisco followed its arc, before crossing the bridge.

"Long Beach," Francisco said. "Now called Port Town by the locals."

My gaze went out over the water. Docked in one of the harbors were fourteen wooden ships, sails furled after their long voyage. A good half of the ships were large things, with three masts and meant for carrying large quantities of cargo. The other ships were smaller, but sleeker, built for speed. These ships might have been the escort for the cargo ships. Men moved on the docks below, going on and off the ships, unloading crates of supplies.

"That's a sight," Anna said.

"The supplies will be traveling north to join Augustus's forces," Francisco said. "The fleet will return to Nova Roma in the morning."

"A long way to come just to go home," I said.

"Augustus needed the supplies," Francisco said. "These waters are usually bad, so it's good fortune that they made it."

The ships disappeared from view as Francisco drove the Recon down the bridge and entered the street. We continued to drive down the avenue, each side of the street flanked by buildings that had seen much better times. Trees stood wilted and fallen in the narrow median and on the avenue's sides. Dirt covered much of the road and sidewalk. Sailors milled in and out of one the buildings, most of them jovial.

"There are the bars," Anna said.

"They should still be working," Francisco said.

Whether they were supposed to be working or not was not really my concern. I was just here to find Marcus and Char.

"Pull up here," I said. "We'll start our search at this place."

I could hear the sailors' raucous laughter, even inside the Recon. They wore baggy cargo pants and plain shirts, for the most part, overlaid with heavy jackets designed to protect from the harsh sea wind. Several pointed at us.

"Careful," Francisco said. "Port Town isn't safe. Don't be deceived, even if Augustus's men are here. Some gangs that are discontented with Warlord Black take up residence here."

"Good," I said. "We don't like Black, either."

"I'm just telling you to be careful."

"Where can we find you once we get Char and Marcus?" I asked.

"I'll be here," Francisco said. "If not here, then nearby."

We left the Recon and stepped onto the dusty street. As Francisco's Recon drove away, a group of sailors standing in front of a bar set eyes on us. Several of them smiled and catcalled Anna, despite the fact that I was standing right next to her. I wanted to teach them a lesson, but knew, in the end, it was probably futile.

Anna just ignored them. "Keep your gun showing. I doubt most of these men are carrying anything more sinister than a knife."

"A knife can still kill," I said.

"Yeah," Anna said, touching the hilt of her blade. "But mine is bigger."

Several of the men averted their eyes upon her touching the blade, but the bold ones continued to stare.

"Come on," I said. "We can start with this one."

Anna looked at the crudely painted sign hanging above the glass door, of two drunken sailors holding bottles. The door was wide open to the wind, but I could see that the glass had several bullet holes and webs of cracks.

"The Wasted Wastrel," she said, reading the sign. "Do any of these men know what that word *means?*"

"Do you?"

She shook her head. "Come on. There are probably ten other such places here. Finding Marcus and Char might be difficult."

"Let's get started, then," I said.

As the Imperial sailors stared on, Anna and I strode toward the door. The stench of ale, sweat, and smoke became stronger as we neared the building. Several men called out to Anna in Spanish. I was glad I couldn't understand what they were saying.

We pushed open the swinging, wooden door.

***

At least fifty filthy and extremely drunk sailors were crowded into an area that was about equal to the deck space of the entire *Perseus* spaceship. The interior was dim and dingy, both from lack of light and an abundance of smoke – smoke not just from tobacco, but various, questionable origins. Anything less than a yell could not be heard in this environment.

Trying to find Char or Marcus in this place, or in ten others like it, was definitely an unenviable task.

"Just work your way around the room," I yelled.

Anna nodded, and we jostled our way through the stinky and teeming mass of humanity. As we came to the room's far corner, I was surprised to hear the honky-tonk jangle of a battered piano, an old sailor mashing on the keys hard in order for the song to be heard. Several sailors belted out words to a Spanish sea chantey. If there was a regular piano player for this establishment, he'd probably been run off by the horde of sailors.

The men drank deeply from pint glasses, the brew the color of deep amber. Froth covered lips, beards, and faces. A sour reek permeated the air. I couldn't believe Marcus or Char would want to hang out in a place like this.

"I don't think they're in here," I said.

Anna shrugged off the groping of a fat-bellied sailor. I reached for my gun, but Anna slapped my hand away.

"We're here to find Marcus," she said. "Not start a fight."

I noticed more drunken men leering at Anna. I realized Samuel might have been a better companion for a task like this. I hadn't realized how full these bars would be, especially in the daytime. The sooner we found Marcus and Char and got out, the better.

We got to the bar itself, completely filled with boisterous mariners. Two men chugged from pint glasses while others cheered on.

Marcus and Char.

Anna and I watched, shocked, as our two friends raced to drain their mugs. Fists pounded on tables as batts shifted between sailors' hands. Who would win, the Alpha of the Raiders, or the Chief of the Exiles?

But at last, Marcus tipped the remainder of his mug, draining what was left of the froth, wiping his red beard in victory. His brother finished just a second later.

A roar emanated from the watching sailors, batts exchanged hands, and a second round was bought for both brothers, regardless of victory. They nodded their thanks to the jovial sailors, and began drinking anew

I stood, shocked, as Anna strode up. She laid a hand on Char's shoulder. Voices quieted as she spoke.

"I haven't seen you drink like that since the Bounty," she said.

Char turned, flashing Anna a rueful smile. "Care to join us?"

"No, but I see why you were missing your radio calls."

Both brothers looked at her, shrugged, and took another drink.

"It's been so long since we've had a drink," Char said. "As brothers. We thought one last time wouldn't hurt, before the second end of the world."

Marcus laughed, even though there was no particular reason to. I noticed his crutches leaning up against the bar. His leg, still in a cast, hadn't stopped him from wetting his whistle.

"Remember, Char," Marcus said. "The first time the world ended, we were at a bar."

"Aye, it's true," Char said.

"Look," I said. "There's been some important developments. It's probably best to rejoin the crew."

"Probably?" Char asked. Marcus giggled next to him.

"He means that this is your last drink," Anna said. "Makara will have no tolerance for this kind of thing."

"Oh, piss on Makara!" Marcus said.

Char held up a hand. "No. She's right, Marc. We've been here too long. Remembering old times, too much." Char sighed wistfully. "Much has changed on this road, over the years, but the Wastrel still makes the finest ale in Port Town."

Marcus nodded his agreement, taking a sip out of his mug. Since it was his last, he had decided to savor it.

"Don't take too long," I said. "We have a driver waiting outside."

Both men sat and drank in silence. I had officially killed the buzz for good, but it wasn't time to be partying. The entire world was on the line, and two of the Angels' most important members were drinking in a bar.

From next to me, Anna cried out.

"Let *go!*"

She pushed a burly man, but two more flanked his side. At second glance, I realized these weren't sailors from Augustus's fleet. They were probably locals.

"I was wondering where the entertainment was," the burly man said.

His two sniveling companions snickered. They had long, greasy hair and hollow eyes.

"You want entertainment?" I asked, stepping up, putting a hand on my Beretta.

The men looked me up and down. The burly man, who seemed to be in charge, answered.

"I'm not into that sort of thing," he said, with a smirk. "But Rummy, here..." He gestured to one of the men, whose black eyes danced. "He might be more accommodating."

Anna's eyes warned me not to go for my gun. If I shot these guys down, it might go badly. The entire bar would erupt in a fight, which was the last thing we needed.

"Leave her alone," I said. "Or else."

The man sneered. "Or else, what? You come into our bar, you play by our rules, kid. The Krakens rule the Port and the Krakens take the spoils!"

With this, he grabbed Anna's wrist. From the anger in her eyes, it was all she could do not to draw her katana with her free hand.

By this point, a space had widened around us. Char and Marcus, even in their current state, took note and came to back me up. I noticed, out of the corner of my eye, the piano player closing the instrument's top and beating a hasty retreat.

"Hands off, scum," Char said. "Last I heard, the Wastrel was a free bar open to any and all."

The man gave a sour smile. "You need to get with the times, old man. The Krakens had to step in and protect this place years ago."

"Things have changed, then, since Raine's time," Marcus said.

The burly man said nothing. Now that it was not just me, but Char, Marcus, and the sailors that had been cheering them on, the Krakens weren't so sure of themselves.

"Maybe we should let her go, Crash," Rummy said.

"You should listen to your hound, Kraken," Marcus said.

Crash's face seethed with anger, but in the end, he let Anna go.

"You'll regret this, all of you!" he spat. "You'll rue the day you crossed the Krakens."

This man was in no way intimidating, and in fact was quite pathetic. He and his cronies backed off, tails between their legs. Several of the sailors clapped and hooted at the gang's hasty retreat.

"Come on," Char said. "I've lost all taste for this place."

"Me, too," Marcus said.

We turned and headed for the door, Anna casting a glance backward to where the Krakens had retreated. They were nowhere in sight. I noticed an open doorway, partitioned with a curtain. The curtain shifted, as if someone had just entered.

I kept my hand on my gun, watching that doorway as we walked toward the exit. It was still crowded, even more so than when we'd entered.

We were halfway across the floor when the first shots came, echoing loudly in the bar's confines.

"Go!" I yelled.

The bar turned into a panicked and screaming mass as men made for the one exit. We were pressed in from all sides. If we fell, we were more likely to be stampeded than shot.

Several men screamed as bullets ripped into them. Bar stools splintered as men tumbled to the ground, and mugs filled with ale shattered on the floor.

The Krakens had cleared half the bar – there were five of them. More must have been in the back room.

"Just get out," Char yelled. "No use risking a fight."

More sailors went down. The exit was so jam-packed that there was no way to get through.

"Alright, we *do* have to fight!" Char said.

Together, the brothers upended a nearby table, facing its top toward the Krakens. Anna and I ducked behind the table, joining Char and Marcus. I pointed my Beretta outward, letting off several bullets. I struck one of the Krakens standing in the corner. He yelped before falling to the floor, a spray of blood bursting from his shoulder.

The three Krakens near the curtained partition retreated into the back room, leaving one last Kraken exposed near the piano. Char and Marcus shot, missing each time because their aim was less than steady. As bullets riddled the tabletop near the Kraken's side, I took careful aim, firing and hitting the gang member in the chest. Red sprouted on his shirt as he fell to his knees, curling on the floor.

The sailors had mostly cleared from the doorway and were out in the streets. It was time to make our own retreat.

"This reminds me of Raider Bluff," Char said.

"Only worse," Marcus said.

"Come on," I said. "Let's slide the table over to the door. And keep your heads down."

We did just that, using the table as our shield. When we reached the exit, we ducked outside into the dull sunlight.

Sailors formed a ring around the bar, and more still were coming to join the throng, asking questions. Fingers pointed at us as we stepped onto the sidewalk. I scanned the crowds, looking for our ride.

Francisco honked from the Recon. It was already pointing in the direction of the freeway.

We hurried, pushing our way through the crowds before any more Krakens showed up for revenge. I imagined they weren't the type to take a slight lightly, especially when it concerned their home turf.

Char sat in the front seat, while Marcus, Anna, and I piled into the back. No sooner had we entered the Recon than Francisco hit the accelerator, the hydrogen tank in the cargo bay emitting a high whine.

Several Krakens stood by the side of the Wastrel, pointing guns in our direction. Several bullets glanced harmlessly off the vehicle's sides, and two were repelled by the windows' bulletproof glass.

"What *happened* in there?" Francisco asked.

"Pissed off the wrong people," Anna said. "What else is new?"

"Remind me to never take you to a crowded bar filled with drunk men," I said.

"Things have changed around here," Marcus said. "Before I headed over to Bluff, you could always count on Port Town for a good time."

"Yeah, that was back in the forties," Char said. "Things are worse, now."

We reached the bridge, passing away from Port Town and merging back onto the freeway.

"Let's try to stay out of trouble for a while, brother," Char said.

Marcus smiled. "True enough. It was good to get into one more bar shootout before the world ended."

Apparently, Char and Marcus considered their outing to Port Town a success. I reached for my radio to update Makara on the fact that we'd found them.

"We're on our way back," I said.

"Good. Listen. We're about to leave for Bunker One. Be sure to tell them everything we've learned so far."

"Wait," Marcus said. "Bunker One? Didn't you kids already go there?"

"Hand me that radio," Char said, suddenly very sober.

I handed it to him, and for the next ten minutes, Char and Makara argued over whether heading to the fallen Bunker was a good idea. I let them have at it; it got me out of explaining everything to everyone, which was a job I was tired of getting stuck with.

With *Perseus* gone, that would leave Anna, Char, Marcus, and me alone in the city. I just hoped to find something to do to pass the time. Sitting aboard *Orion,* waiting for updates from the other team, was going to be torture.

"I want you to stay on that ship and not go anywhere," Makara said, now talking to me.

"Fine," I said. "I won't leave the ship."

"Good," Makara said. "I know sitting around might be boring, but we need to keep you safe."

I'd heard it all before, so I said nothing. In case something went wrong at Bunker One, which was very likely, Anna would fly the ship out there. For now, it had to stay in Los Angeles so Carin could run his tests with the railgun, which wasn't expected to take long.

Char handed me my radio back, and we watched the buildings go by. Soon enough, we were back in the clustered towers of downtown. I took out my radio.

"We're back," I said.

"Meet us by *Orion,*" Makara said. "We're ten minutes or so from liftoff."

Francisco, hearing that order, turned the Recon around the corner, making directly for the U.S. Bank Tower.

Chapter 5

Francisco pulled to a stop at the intersection where *Orion* and *Perseus* were parked, but it wasn't either of the spaceships that caught my attention.

The railgun stood to the left of *Orion,* its long barrel pointing skyward. It was basically a larger than usual halftrack with a giant gun on top, as Carin had said. The barrel was almost rectangular in shape, extending as far up as the third story of a nearby building. The base of the barrel extended from a metallic turret that looked capable of swiveling 360 degrees. The turret itself could also aim the barrel up and down, giving the railgun a wide range.

And, apparently, Carin wanted to test this weapon in the streets of downtown Los Angeles.

All of us stepped out of the Recon. Both of the ships were humming with power – *Perseus,* because it was about to take off for Bunker One, and *Orion,* because it was providing power to the railgun. Thick power cables ran from *Orion's* blast door, under the ship's hull, connecting somewhere under the halftrack. A swarm of Reapers gazed at the gun from the ground, laughing and joking among themselves. Carin stood with them, giving orders.

Makara exited from *Perseus's* boarding ramp and headed toward us. We walked over to meet her. While Anna's, Francisco's, and my gaits were steady, both Char's and Marcus's were tilted.

"Makara..." Char said.

She looked him up and down before shaking her head. She then looked at Anna and me.

"Will you make sure he doesn't get into trouble?"

"Really, Makara," Char said. "There's no need to..."

"Char, no arguing." She looked at me, including Anna in the stare. "Make sure he gets on *Perseus.*" She looked at Marcus. "And his brother, too."

"Are you leaving now?" Anna asked.

Makara nodded. "Yeah. Carin has my go-ahead to test the railgun. He said it shouldn't take long. Unfortunately, I don't have time to watch it personally."

"They're testing it *here?*" I asked.

She looked at me. "The gun moves slowly, and the streets are hard to navigate. It's the best option, as crazy as it sounds."

Carin stood a ways off, directing the movement of the railgun turret. It swiveled, from right to left, making a whirring sound. As the turret spun, the barrel itself moved up and down. The two separate movements, in tandem, could point the barrel at a new target surprisingly fast.

At last, the barrel pointed directly down the street, right at a tall skyscraper perhaps half a mile away.

"Well, at least that part of it works," Anna said.

At that moment, the halftrack's treads dug into the dirt, jerking the vehicle forward in a cloud of dust before coming to a stop. The power cords connecting the railgun to *Orion's* fusion generator extended no further.

"Logistics might be a problem," I said. "That gun can't go far from the spaceship."

"It wouldn't have to be connected all the time," Anna said. "Just when firing."

"Still," I said. "Are we sure this is a good idea?"

The barrel of the railgun lowered, homing in on the distant skyscraper.

"I would say we *aren't* sure," Anna said.

"Fire when ready," Carin said into his radio.

Suddenly, the railgun gave a kick and a *pop* so loud that it was near-deafening. A trail of fire issued from the barrel of the gun. A massive *crack* split the air, like a whip. Before the thunderous, resounding boom even reached my ears, the top half of the skyscraper collapsed in on itself. At the same time, the fire trail dissipated into the air. Everything had happened almost instantaneously.

The building ahead crumbled to the ground, the sound taking a few seconds to reach my pounding ears.

Makara ran over to Carin, whose pale blue eyes danced at the sight of the destruction.

"What the *hell* are you doing?" she yelled. "Did I *say* you could fire yet?"

Carin shrugged. "I don't recall needing to ask your permission."

Makara's face reddened, but she said nothing. Onyx stood by his father, staring sullenly at Makara. After a moment, she shook her head and came over to us.

"They weren't supposed to do that until we were ready..."

There was a great crash in the distance as the building continued its collapse. To the Reapers' credit, they had used a round that wasn't incendiary, so the force destroying the building was purely kinetic. Still, it was an awesome display of power.

"Those dragons won't stand a chance," I said.

Even Makara had to admit that much.

"I've changed my mind about Bunker One," she said.

Both Anna and I looked at her, wondering what she meant.

"I want all of you to come," she said. "Not to go inside, but to stay above. To be ready to come in if we need you."

"We can do that," I said.

It was much better than waiting here in Los Angeles.

"Of course," Makara said. "Char and Marcus won't be going inside, no matter what the situation."

"I guess I should just be grateful that we're being included," Char said.

"You're not," Makara said. "You're to stay aft and sober up, and not get in the way."

"And I suppose we should also think about what we've done?" Char asked.

"Sobering up on a tossing and turning spaceship," Marcus mused. "Good luck with that one."

"You'd rather stay here?" Makara asked.

Marcus got quiet at that, so I knew the answer was no.

"Should we follow you?" Anna asked. "Or should we wait until Carin destroys the rest of the city?"

"Their tests should be done, so just follow when you can," Makara said.

Both Carin and his son were watching us from beside the halftrack. When Onyx saw me looking at him, he gave a yellow smile.

"Anything else?" Anna asked.

Makara shook her head. "No. We should probably get moving."

With that, Makara turned and walked toward the boarding ramp of *Perseus*. The blast door shut behind her, and it wasn't long before its fusion drive thrummed louder.

Everyone backed away as *Perseus's* retrothrusters pointed downward, lifting the ship into the dull red sky. Everyone covered their ears at the thrumming pulse of the fusion drive, only uncovering their ears when the ship's thrusters swiveled and carried the ship behind a skyscraper.

As *Perseus* faded with distance, I turned my attention back to the building the railgun had obliterated. It was now a pile of rubble obscured by a cloud of dust spreading ever outward, darkening the already dull sky.

Apparently satisfied at the way things had gone, Carin ordered his men to disconnect the power cables. As we stood and watched, the Reapers coiled the cable and gathered their things into a nearby Recon. When everything was gathered up, the Reapers, Carin, and Onyx got into the two Recons. The vehicles set off, kicking up clouds of dust. Once the Recons started moving, the halftrack also turned around in a wide arc, barely having the space to maneuver on the four-lane street.

As the lead Recon passed, Carin winked from the passenger seat at Anna and me. The second Recon trailed Carin's.

As they disappeared toward the center of town, Anna nodded toward the ship.

It was time to get moving.

***

I took my place in the copilot's chair, even though I didn't know how to do anything besides control the frequencies. Marcus and Char were in the wardroom, drinking plenty of water in order to sober up. Francisco had dismissed himself a long time ago, so quietly that I hadn't even noticed him leaving.

I put the copilot's headset over my head. I had always wanted to learn how to pilot, but so far had not been granted the opportunity.

"What now?" I asked.

"Your first lesson," Anna said, "is to sit back, strap on your seatbelt, and let me do all the work."

Before I could say anything more, *Orion* lifted off. Anna angled upward, engaging the thrusters to push the ship forward.

"This part looks easy enough," I said.

"Taking off is not so bad," Anna said. "It's the landing you have to worry about. That, and dragons. Let's just hope we're not attacked, because I can't fly like Makara or..."

Anna trailed off, but she didn't have to finish her sentence. Ashton had been the best pilot of us all, and there was no one who could replace him.

Instead, she opened the line to *Perseus*.

"*Perseus*...this is *Orion*. We're in the air and en route to Bunker One, over."

It was a moment before Makara's voice exited the dash.

"Roger that. Wasn't expecting you for another hour or so."

"Well, Carin seemed to be in a hurry to get out of there. He made off pretty fast after blowing that building up."

"Weird. Nothing to report on our end. We're thirty minutes out from Bunker One. Plan's the same – just stay in the air and stand by for further orders."

"Copy that. How long should we wait before following you inside, if we don't hear from you?"

"If you don't hear from us in two hours, by my count, 14:00, consider that confirmation to follow and proceed to lab levels. If you encounter *any* resistance, evacuate immediately. Assume that we have been compromised."

"At least let us *all* come down," I said. "We might need the firepower."

"That's a negative," Makara said. "Four should be enough to go unnoticed. Julian has to stay with the ship. Trust me, we're not going *anywhere* near that Bunker if we detect any threats."

"If you're only scanning for radio waves," Anna said, "they could just be lulling you into a trap. A loud predator doesn't catch its prey."

"This is something we have to do," Samuel said. "We need to know what we're up against, and analyzing the ichor could be the key."

"We'll be in touch when we begin our scans," Makara said.

"We're thirty minutes behind you," Anna said. "Standing by."

With that, Makara cut out. Char walked onto the bridge, appearing completely sober.

"They there yet?"

Anna shook her head. "Not yet. I can't imagine a scenario where something *doesn't* go wrong. They're very determined."

"That Bunker was filled with Blighters the last time we were there," I said.

"They only came when Askala discovered us," Anna said. "Maybe we'll pass unnoticed this time. Maybe Askala is so focused on attacking the Wasteland that she doesn't have anything guarding Bunker One."

"No," Marcus said. I turned to see that he, too, had entered the bridge. His eyes narrowed as he looked out the windshield. "She'll run into something down there. You can count on it."

"Augustus made it all the way to Bunker Six," I said. "He even managed to escape with most of his army."

"Maybe Askala *is* distracted," Anna said. "Still, even Augustus said he lost men doing it. It can't have been an easy task."

Whether dangerous or not, we'd find out soon enough.

***

"Preliminary scans show the area to be clear of threats," Makara said. "We're going in."

"Nice landing job," Julian said.

"You've already landed?" Anna asked.

"No," Makara said. "Julian's talking about the airplane that went over the side of the cliff."

"Oh," I said. "Right."

I'd almost forgotten *that* near-death experience. When coming to Bunker One for the first time, we'd nearly all gone off the cliff with the plane. Only jumping at the last second, once the plane had slowed down enough, had saved our lives.

"No crawlers visible," Makara said. "It's all snow down there."

"Land as close as you can to the door," Samuel said.

"Wind's picking up a lot of that snow," Makara said. "The thrusters should blast most of it away."

We waited a long moment before Makara's voice returned.

"Touched down. Plan's the same. Julian will stay with the ship. Once we reach the labs, we'll connect the line with *Perseus*. You're to stay above the Bunker and connect to Julian's line."

"What if we don't hear from you?" I asked.

"Under no circumstances are you allowed inside the Bunker," Makara said. "Not until 14:00, when you are clear to proceed forward *with caution*. We won't be anywhere except on the path that leads directly to the labs, so *do not,* under any circumstances, expand your search elsewhere. Am I clear on that?"

"Clear," I said.

"Makara," Char said.

"Yeah?"

"Be careful down there."

"We will," she said.

The speakers went silent, leaving only the surrounding hum of the spacecraft, sailing above the clouds.

"We need to get there," I said.

"Still thirty minutes out," Anna said. "If everything goes well, they should be getting in touch in fifteen minutes."

***

We joined Julian's line and waited.

Twenty minutes later, I felt relief at hearing Makara's voice exit the dash.

"We're in."

"Resistance?" Julian asked.

"None. Unless you count the detour we had to take around the collapsed tunnel. We had to come in through the back way."

"I can't believe it's clear," I said.

"They're gone now," Makara said. "There's still plenty of signs, though."

"Signs?" Anna asked. "Like what?"

"Slime, mostly. The bodies are all gone, even the ones we killed in the lab. I guess Askala leaves no man behind."

"How noble," I said.

"Has Samuel started analyzing the sample yet?" Char asked.

"He's still trying to find the right equipment," Makara said. "The bio-lab is pretty big. It's actually where we are now."

"And where's the bio-lab?" I asked.

"Not far from the main lab floor," Makara said. "Trust me, you wouldn't have trouble finding it. Not that you'd need to."

We were still several minutes out from the Bunker. Marcus and Char stood behind us, listening quietly. I could tell that they were both on edge. I didn't blame them; so was I.

"It may take a while," Samuel said. "The system is calibrating the ichor's genetic sequence. At the same time, it's referencing older xenoviral strains so we can see if anything matches the new ones."

"And how long, exactly, will this gobbledygook take?" Anna asked.

"Thirty minutes to an hour," Samuel said. "The Bunker servers are still online, and their computing power is enormous. It was common for the scientists to add new strains to the databanks, but this ichor appears to be chock-full of strains. That'll take some time."

"What else?" I asked.

"That's it," Samuel said. "I'll know more when the calibration is done."

I guessed there was nothing to do but wait.

Chapter 6

We reached the Bunker, landing next to *Perseus* on the runway. There, we waited as forty-five minutes passed without incident. No crawlers. No flyers. And no dragons. It was almost too good to be true.

Samuel's voice exited the speaker.

"The calibration is done. It's loading the results now."

We waited a moment. I heard Makara talking to someone; I realized that it was either Ruth or Michael, who were both down there with them. Samuel's voice went on.

"Alright," he said. "As expected, the strains in the ichor don't match anything on file. However, it looks like the strains were designed to plug into various older xenoviral strains."

"Meaning?" Anna asked.

"Meaning, Quietus was right. We have some new evolutions on our hands. Thankfully, by plugging in the strains, the computer can model what we might be up against in the future."

"What's it showing?" I asked.

"Hold on," Samuel said. "I'm going to plug in the crawler strain. That's one we're all familiar with." Samuel paused. The clacking of keys exited the dash. "Well. There's actually several different crawler strains on file. All of them are outdated, as might be expected. Still, there should be enough similarities to the new strains to show effects." He cleared his throat. "It wants me to name this new strain. Hmm..."

"Is that really important?" Makara asked. "If we have to sit here all day and name everything, we won't get anything done."

"Sorry," Samuel said. "It's just part of the data entry system. I guess I can just name it 'A.'"

Samuel clacked the keys again. A disagreeable buzz emanated from the speakers.

"Damn. 'A' has been taken."

"Let me see that," Makara said. I heard her mash on the keyboard. "There. That should do it."

Samuel grunted disapprovingly. "I...guess that works. Strain *rt3jwot9* has officially been named."

"Very creative," I said.

"Alright," Samuel said. "This thing doesn't even *look* like a crawler anymore..."

Everyone went quiet. I could only imagine what the creature in question looked like.

"Maybe you plugged in the wrong strain," I said.

"No, it's inputted correctly," Samuel said. "Still..."

"Well, then," Makara said. "Can I change the name of this one to 'Giant Bug-Thing from Outer Space with Creepy Eyes'?"

"It has wings," Ruth said. "Does that mean it can fly?"

"I doubt it," Samuel said. "According to this, it would stand sixty feet tall. Which makes me wonder how it could even *stand*."

"With legs?" Makara asked.

"Funny. Except the larger a creature becomes, the more muscle it needs in order to move around. You see, if you even double the size of a creature, it would need four times the muscle mass to move with the same agility as a monster half its size." Samuel paused. "It's basic physics."

"I'm going to have to trust you on that one," Makara said.

"Maybe it's not suited for Earth gravity," I said. "After all, didn't Quietus say these strains came from different worlds?"

"Who knows?" Samuel asked. "This is just one of many things the *Radaskim* might be cooking up. And it might be more lightweight than it appears on the screen. Let's have a look at some of these others."

"Look," Michael said. "Is there a way we can transfer this data to *Perseus?* It'll be risky to stay down here too long."

"It's too much data," Samuel said. "We have to learn what we can and get out."

"How many new manifestations of the virus are there?" I asked.

Samuel paused a moment before answering. "One hundred and six."

"That might take too long to go through," I said. "Especially if you have to log every entry."

"I agree," Samuel said. "At least from this, we know what we might be dealing with."

"What's *that?*" Ruth asked.

The speakers went quiet for a long time.

"It looks like a worm, or something," Makara said.

"Small," Samuel said. "Two millimeters in length. A parasite?"

"Gross," Ruth said.

"Yeah," Makara said. "I don't like the look of that."

It was interesting how we could joke around about a sixty-foot monster, but we were afraid of something so tiny.

"Does this thing already *exist?*" Makara asked.

"Apparently," Samuel said. "It's logged in the databanks. If it's gone unnoticed by us, maybe it's because it's so small."

"Click on its data file," Makara said. "We need to learn more about it."

A moment later, Samuel read aloud.

"Strain M-006," Samuel said. "Strain M-006 forms the xenogenetic sequence of the 'writhe.' About two millimeters in length, writhes serve to supplant the host's decision-making with xenoviral directives."

Samuel paused in reading the description to let the information soak in.

"What does *that* mean?" Makara asked. "Mind control?"

"Because of its exceedingly small size," Samuel went on, "the writhe went undiscovered until 2046 by Dr. Cornelius Ashton."

"Aston *knew* about this thing?" Makara asked. "Why didn't he say anything about it?"

"Maybe it wasn't that important," I said. "The writhe seems to be a bit outdated. After all, the xenovirus alone is capable of taking over a person's mind."

"Not important?" Samuel asked. "Eighty-three of the one hundred and six strains found in this ichor have to do with modifying this little creature. It can hardly be unimportant."

I had no idea what this writhe looked like, but it must have been tiny indeed.

"According to this," Samuel said, "the writhe begins its life in a microscopic state. Over the course of months, it engorges itself on organic matter found in the host's body. Usually the brain. Somehow, it goes undetected as a threat by the host's immune system. They never really discovered why, but it might have something to do with the alien structure of its DNA. The writhe grows freely in the brain, until it reaches a maximum length of two millimeters."

"Help me understand," Makara said. "What does this thing actually *do?*"

"There are two different types of infection, for two different purposes. There's the xenovirus, which makes its host part of the *Radaskim* consciousness. Then there is the writhe, which does something more...subversive."

"Subversive?" Anna asked. "Subversive, how?"

"A person under the influence of the writhe will still keep their cognitive capacity," Samuel said. "But at the same time, they are controlled completely by the Voice. Askala."

That made everyone go quiet. If what Samuel said was true, then I didn't even want to think of the ramifications.

"It doesn't just affect humans," Samuel said. "There seem to be writhes for every *Radaskim*-controlled species on file. It might give Askala a bit more direct control. The writhe's main purpose is serving as a communications medium between Askala and the host's brain."

"That reminds me of Elias," Anna said. "He might have acted weird, but he was otherwise human. He looked like us, spoke like us, but Askala had dominated his mind. Is *that* the influence of the writhe?"

"Perhaps," Samuel said. "Although, he had to have been infected with the xenovirus as well, given his later transformation. Perhaps the writhe held back the effects of the xenovirus – at least, until Elias had died."

"If Ashton knew about this, why wouldn't he have said anything?" I asked.

"About Ashton, I have no idea," Samuel said. "He never mentioned anything about a writhe to me, either."

I wanted to say maybe he *didn't* know about it, but it was credited to him right there in the files.

"Let's focus on the other evolutions," Makara finally said. "We can try to guess all day about Ashton, but it's not going to get us anywhere."

"I agree," Samuel said.

"What are some of the other writhe evolutions?" I said. "You mentioned there were eighty-three."

"Right," Samuel said. "It looks like each writhe targets a different species. Humans are only one. Scanning through the xenoviral strain profiles, it looks like many of these writhes correspond with monster species that have already been documented. Those that *aren't* documented here probably correspond to species that arose after Bunker One fell."

"So, you're saying there's one new writhe species for each species of xenolife?" I asked.

"Yes. Most of the changes that are present in the ichor affect *Radaskim* writhes – that is, eighty-three strains. The remaining twenty-three correspond with plant, fungal, and microbial species already on file."

"So, there's one writhe for each *Radaskim* species," I said. "I want to know exactly what it *does*."

"As I said, the writhe serves as the communications hub between the *Radaskim* Voice and the infected host. It's possible for the *Radaskim* xenovirus to transform a human, or any animal for that matter, into its infected variant given the correct xenoviral strain. A writhe is not needed. Even though the writhe appears to be a more primitive form of mind control, it has its advantages. The writhe could control a person *without* that person's needing to be infected with the xenovirus. And, in the case of Elias, a person can be infected with both the writhe *and* the virus. In his case, the writhe had dominance over the xenovirus, allowing him to retain his thoughts – although, the nature of those thoughts were controlled by Askala. It was only upon his death, and the writhe's death, that the xenovirus was allowed full reign."

From what Samuel was saying, there appeared to be three types of infection: with the xenovirus only, with the writhe only, and with both.

We already knew what happened to people infected with only the xenovirus; after a time, they died and became Howlers.

It was the next one we weren't familiar with, and if I understood Samuel correctly, it meant this: those infected with *only* the writhe appeared normal and human. Except, they were far from that, because their thoughts and behavior were dictated by Askala through the writhe. *Anyone* could have a writhe, and we'd have no way of knowing. We hadn't known about this before, because it was apparently a more primitive form of infection, and Ashton hadn't told us about it for some reason.

The final form of infection was with both the writhe and the xenovirus, which seemed to be the rarest of all. This is what happened to Elias. The writhe controlled his mind, but he could still talk and behave in a humanlike way, even if the writhe made him go insane. The writhe, besides acting as a conduit for Askala's will, also suppressed the physical effects of the *Radaskim* xenovirus. It was only when Elias was killed, and the writhe dead, that the xenovirus had free reign.

This was just one version of the writhe. There were eighty-two others, animal and Blighter variants that probably performed a similar function.

"So," I said. "Someone infected with the writhe, and the writhe *only,* would look like us completely. We would have no way of knowing they were controlled by Askala."

Samuel did not answer me for a long time.

"I....I believe that's what this is saying."

I didn't have to point out the obvious implication: one, or more of us, might be infected with a writhe, and could turn upon the rest at any moment.

***

After a long time, Makara spoke.

"I don't want anyone to speak. No one speaks except Samuel, unless you have an important question to ask. We still don't know enough about this. After he finishes explaining, *then* we can decide what to do."

Her words were met with silence. After a moment, Samuel cleared his throat.

"Well said, Makara. No, we don't know enough yet, and none of us should jump to conclusions about anything."

"Explain, then," I said.

"I'm paraphrasing from Ashton's research now," he said. "According to this, when a writhe affects a human, every conscious action must pass through it for approval. Various autonomic functions, such as breathing, aren't screened."

"How can a tiny little worm control so much?" Makara asked.

"The writhe itself subverts its victim, and acts as a communications hub to the *Radaskim's* xenofungal network," Samuel said; "meaning that on its own, the writhe doesn't have the intelligence to give its host complicated commands. However, such commands can be given by the *Radaskim* consciousness. The writhe conveys *Radaskim* directives to its host, while suppressing anything that goes against that directive. This causes a slight delay in reaction on the part of the infected in some experiments Bunker One conducted, but it's so nominal that it can only be measured by computers. Indeed, the infected have no idea that they *are* infected."

"How does infection occur?" Anna asked.

"Prolonged exposure to various xenolife greatly increases the risk of infection," Samuel said. "The presence of the writhe is fairly ubiquitous in xenoviral flora. Whether a particular form of writhe has to find the right host, or whether all writhes begin the same way and only *change* upon infection, this doesn't say."

"You mentioned experiments," Makara said.

I was reminded of the experiments Bunker 114 performed on Kari, the scientist who'd been infected with the Behemoth strain of the xenovirus. The scientists there, against Samuel's wishes, had experimented on her to ill effect. Kari escaped her cell and laid waste to the entire Bunker.

I could only hope that such experiments here didn't have such a dark history.

"Yeah," Samuel said. "Ashton authored an addendum to the Black Files. It details the research done on the human parasitic writhe."

Makara sighed. "Read it."

"Alright," Samuel said. "It's quite lengthy, so I'll try to paraphrase."

It was some time before Samuel began.

"The research focused mostly on physiological responses people had while under the influence of the writhe," Samuel said. "Some of the research is a bit...disturbing, to put it lightly."

"No wonder Ashton didn't want to talk about it," Anna said.

"What happened?" I asked.

"They didn't purposefully infect subjects with the writhe, thankfully," Samuel said. "The discovery of the writhe occurred when a man was brought to the med bay after assaulting his wife. He was a soldier, who'd made lots of rounds into the Great Blight to the north. Guarding research teams, that sort of thing. They thought it was PTSD, a fairly common diagnosis in those days. Aggressive wildlife was becoming more common."

Everyone was quiet as Samuel continued.

"Back then, the Great Blight only extended as far as northern Colorado. It would still be a while before it posed a threat to Bunker One."

"Did the man go insane because of the writhe?" I asked.

"Yeah," Samuel said. "Once it seemed to be more than PTSD, they did a scan to check for tumors or other abnormalities,. They almost missed the writhe, it was so small. The heavier brain activity in the amygdala tipped the doctors off. Other parts of the brain lit up as well – the hippocampus, along with Broca's area and Wernicke's area."

"And all that means?" Makara asked.

"The hippocampus is related to memory, while the amygdala processes emotion. Broca's area and Wernicke's area have to do with the speaking and understanding of language. For all intents and purposes, even though this man was out like a light, he was having a conversation." Samuel paused. "Upon closer inspection, the scientists *did* find the writhe, and cleared the patient for immediate delivery to Level One."

"Level One," I said. "You mean the bio-lab."

"Correct," Samuel said. "The patient was given into the care of Ashton. There are parasites of Earth origin that are known to cause mental changes in their hosts. Some even cause insanity. Anytime *this* patient was conscious, though, he would attack, as if that were the most important objective in his mind. When he was kept in isolation, however, he seemed practically normal. He wondered where he was, where his family was, expressed sadness at his isolation. He even believed he was being imprisoned. But every time the patient caught sight of another human being – even loved ones – he attacked without reservation."

"How horrible," Anna asked.

"Ashton and his colleagues discovered that the writhe was responsible for the physiological changes in the patient. President Garland himself ordered all residents of Bunker One to be screened for the parasite." Samuel paused. "They were surprised by what they found.

"Twenty-seven people were infected with the very same parasite. They performed another screening, and found an additional five, for a total of thirty-two infected. These people showed no obvious ill-effects on account of the writhe, unlike the soldier, but many of them were soldiers themselves with heavy exposure to the Great Blight."

"So...they tested. And tested. The thirty-two were quarantined and kept in isolation. Because of the one soldier who went rogue, Ashton wasn't willing to let these thirty-two back into the general population.

"Ashton needed to study the parasite to be sure it was of xenoviral origin, but none of the patients agreed to a biopsy. For good reason – such an operation was life-threatening. But even with the promise of a great reward, such as more credits in the Bunker's exchange system – no one budged. Even *if* the operation carried such a risk, Ashton thought it was strange that no one would take him up on his offer.

"Eventually, an opportunity *did* come. The original patient, the soldier, died. He'd somehow found a blade to cut himself. Ashton took the opportunity to extract the writhe and take a sample. By doing so, he confirmed that it was of xenoviral origin."

"What happened after that?" I asked.

"Ashton didn't have a lot to go on," Samuel said. "He knew there was an alien parasite inside the brains of at least thirty-three Bunker One residents. In at least one of those cases, it caused the host to go insane. Then again, he was receiving pressure from the President and the Citizens' Council to either come up with a cure or release the residents back to their families. The other patients had shown no violent tendencies, and pressure was mounting for the patients' release.

"Ashton knew he was far from finding a cure. That wasn't even his expertise. Rather, he was concerned with the danger the patients would pose if released prematurely. But it'd been three months since the screenings. Since there were no adverse effects seen from the parasites, Ashton was forced to release them by executive order, and could only conduct research on a volunteer basis."

"So, they were released back into the Bunker?" Anna asked.

"Yeah. They were released. None of them volunteered for research. This reflected badly on Ashton, and many questioned the ethics of his research. He became a pariah. Some even said that he murdered the original patient in order to extract the writhe."

"It goes into *that* level of detail?" Anna asked.

"This is more of a research journal than an actual scientific paper," Samuel said. "It tells Ashton's story – and the beginning of the fall of Bunker One."

"This was all in 2046, though," I said. "Bunker One didn't fall until 2048."

"Yeah," Samuel said. "But the undoing was a long work in progress. Through the writhes, Askala – then only known as the Voice – was able to discover everything she ever needed to know about toppling the Bunker through the eyes of its own citizens. Askala discovered Bunker One's layout, its weaknesses. She waited until the time was right. Beginning in the mid-2040s, Askala's swarm was forming. Many of her first creatures were turned animals – either infected with the xenovirus, or controlled by their own forms of writhe. And using the genetics stored in the vast memory of the xenofungus itself, she began to form the crawlers in her Warrens at Ragnarok Crater. The *Radaskim* machinery of life, evolved over the eons, is so much more complex than any technology humans have devised. In 2048, the writhes had done their work. Under the influence of Askala, they opened the gates to Bunker One."

Chapter 7

No one spoke for a very long time. The writhes, even when discovered by the authorities of Bunker One, were thought not to have posed enough of a threat to quarantine the infected.

The authorities had turned out to be wrong, and that led to the Bunker's eventual fall. Ashton had probably blamed himself, which would explain why he never mentioned the writhe. Maybe he'd thought all that was behind him.

We knew now, however, that the writhes were still alive, and that Askala might be using them against us.

"There are eighty-three new writhe evolutions," Samuel said. "That number probably corresponds to each species Askala uses in her swarm. We've only seen a few of those so far, admittedly, but that might change soon. The contagion in that pool will not only be giving some of the Blighters an upgrade – it will be changing the writhes as well."

"So, they're going into these pools to evolve?" Makara asked.

"Something like that," Samuel said.

"What about *us*?" Anna asked. "Is it possible that *we* could be infected?"

It was a while before Samuel answered. "It's possible. Maybe even probable."

"What can we do?" I asked.

Samuel sighed before answering. "I don't know. If someone has a writhe, it wouldn't allow the person to reveal that fact. That person probably wouldn't even know they're infected."

"I'm not saying any of us are," Anna said. "But what if? Askala would know everything we're planning. Even where we are."

"We can't discuss this," Makara said. "Not now. I won't have everyone turning on each other."

An uneasy silence followed. Just because writhes existed didn't mean any of us were infected. But just wondering about it was killing me. We *had* to find a way to screen everyone – only I didn't know what that was.

"I think it's time that we left," Makara said. "We can talk about this while we're in the air."

"I'll prepare the ship," Julian said.

***

"It's been thirty minutes," Char said.

Anna had landed next to *Perseus*. She stared at the Bunker exit intensely, as if willing Makara and the others to come out.

Char was right – it had been thirty minutes, and I was starting to get nervous.

"Let's wait a few more minutes before we do anything," I said.

Julian's voice came through the dash. "Still no response."

"They may not be close to the surface," Anna said. "Like they're stuck."

"I'm done waiting," Char said, loading a magazine into his assault rifle. "I'm going in."

"So am I," Marcus said.

I was starting to think along the same lines myself. They should have been back by now.

I looked out the windshield at the Bunker exit connecting to the runway. A path had been forged through the snow by the others earlier, leading right to the Bunker entrance.

Staring at that path, I made the decision.

"Julian," I said. "Lock down *Perseus*. We're going in."

***

The heavy Bunker door opened with a metallic groan, revealing a passageway of darkness.

"Makara?" I called. "Samuel?"

My voice echoed into silence.

"Keep it down," Char growled, clicking on a flashlight.

He strode forward, his brother following silently. As they went ahead, Anna, Julian, and I brought up the rear. I retrieved my own flashlight and clicked it on.

We followed the corridor until it arrived at a set of stairs. Just being here brought back horrible memories. A rotten musk clung to the air. The signs of our flight three months ago were still here, evidenced by traces of purple slime coating the walls, hardened with cold.

When we had reached the runway that night, I'd thought all was lost, even if Ashton had said he'd get us out. I hadn't believed we were safe until we were inside *Gilgamesh*.

Now, that spaceship was gone, along with the man who had piloted it. The very thought of Ashton filled me with a pang of sadness. And with Grudge dead as well, our team had now taken two serious hits.

Anna's voice snapped me back to attention.

"Almost to the stairs."

We began the long descent to Level One. With this Bunker, the floors were numbered more traditionally – Level One was at the bottom, Level Fifty-Two was on top. In Bunker 84, it was the opposite. Level One was at the top while Level Twenty was at the bottom.

However you figured it, the result was the same: fifty-two floors was a long way down.

But we had only descended a few flights before I heard voices.

I held up a hand, bringing everyone to a halt. In the following silence, the voices had ceased.

"Anyone down there?" I asked. "Hello?"

Looking over the railing, I shone my flashlight down. Below, three faces looked up at me – Makara, Samuel, and Michael.

Ruth was lying on her back, eyes closed.

I rushed downstairs, the others following. After four more flights down, we arrived at the landing of Level 38.

"She collapsed at the bottom," Samuel said. "We've had to carry her the entire way."

"What happened?" Anna asked.

"We don't know," Makara said. "She's out cold."

"You weren't attacked?" I asked. "She just...fell?"

"Yeah," Samuel said. "Michael said she doesn't have a medical condition that he knows of."

"We need to hurry it up," Makara said.

I knew she was right. Together, we lifted Ruth from the floor. Every muscle in her body was limp. I had no idea what could have knocked her out like this, but connected to what we had just learned about the writhes, it was more than a little worrisome.

We went up the steps. With all of us lifting, it went fast. Within a few minutes, we had reached the top level, huffing from exertion. We carried Ruth down the dark corridor, toward the door still open to the runway.

"We need to get Ruth to the Xenolith," Samuel said.

"The Xenolith?" Anna asked. "Why?"

"We think she might be infected with a writhe."

***

We put Ruth in the clinic aboard *Perseus*. Her face was pale and her form limp. Her chest rose and fell in shallow breaths.

"You think it's a writhe?" I asked.

"It just seems awfully convenient," Samuel said. "The moment we learn about the writhes, Askala triggered this reaction in Ruth. For all we know, she has swarmers on the way."

If that was the case, then they hadn't reached the Bunker in time.

Samuel continued. "Whether it's a writhe, or something else, we know for a fact that the *Elekai* ichor has healing properties. And if it *is* a writhe, Askal or Quietus might be able to confirm."

"Get to *Orion*," Makara said. "And follow our lead."

***

Both ships touched down by the Xenolith. We exited the ships, entered the Xenolith, and ran down to the *Elekai* pool, toting Ruth with us.

When we arrived at the shoreline, there was no sign of either dragon…until an angular head emerged from the water. The size and shape told me immediately that it was Quietus. As she arose further from the ichor, the liquid streamed down her dark scales, glittering and returning to the pool. Her white eyes radiated light as her neck stretched out, lifting the head far above the pool's surface.

I didn't waste any time.

What do you know about the writhe?

The writhe, human? You ask about something that is ancient indeed. The writhe existed even before the virus. Why do you ask?

How come you didn't tell us about it?

It cannot harm you, Elekim, Quietus said.

It's harmed Ruth, I said. *At least, that's what we think.*

Quietus's eyes turned to Ruth, gazing at her inert body for a moment before turning back to me.

It might be that she has a writhe. Bear her forth to the pool, Elekim, and we can know for certain.

I turned to the others. "We need to bring her to the pool."

After exchanging glances, Samuel, Char, Marcus, and Anna carried Ruth to the pool, laying her face-up in the warm ichor while Makara and Michael watched from the shore. I strode forward, entering the ichor. I pulled Ruth farther away from the shore. Around her form, the liquid frothed and bubbled. It reminded me of when the *Radaskim* dragons entered the pool – the ichor had done the very same thing.

Yes, I can see now that there is darkness within her. The pool alone will avail her not – only by your power might she be freed from the clutches of the Dark Mother. The pool will give you strength, Elekim...but the battle will still be fierce. You must drive it out!

How?

You must sever its connection to Askala. As far as how to do that...I know not.

I looked down at Ruth, having no idea what I was supposed to do. All I knew was that I had to connect with the writhe mentally, as if I was trying to communicate with it. After all, its chief purpose was communication. As Quietus said, I had to cut it off from Askala.

I closed my eyes and reached out to Ruth's mind. When I did so, my vision went black.

***

I didn't know where I was. I didn't feel like I was...*anywhere*. Just a mind, floating in a void.

But someone *else* was there. A dark dread came over me, draining me of hope. I felt cut off from all memory, goodness, and existence. In the darkness I heard my heart beating, the blood flowing through my veins...

Something was out there, watching me from the darkness. I directed my thoughts toward it.

Who's there?

It felt as if I were being enveloped in a dark cloud. A cold breeze blew, tickling my skin. Sharp laughter resounded in the void – I couldn't tell if it was real or imagined.

I see you, Elekim...

The voice came out in a harsh, inhuman whisper.

Who's there? Show yourself.

I don't think you would want that...

A physical heaviness surrounded me, compressed me...

What are you doing to me?

Crushing you.

The heaviness increased, and everything pushed...inward. As the pressure became more unbearable, my panic mounted.

Why are you doing this?

For the same reason the blade cuts, the serpent bites, or pestilence wastes...

The pressure was now sheer agony. I opened my mouth to scream, but no sound came.

I do it...because it is my nature.

You will leave her, writhe, I said.

You do not command me, Elekim. *She is mine.*

You will *leave her.*

The pain and the pressure increased sharply, like I was being swallowed by a black hole. I couldn't bear this a second longer.

Yet, I had to. For her.

Her? I didn't know why I was fighting anymore. I saw little point to this struggle, this resistance.

But didn't people have to fight, even if they didn't know the reason? Sometimes, losing a battle meant to lose oneself. It was important to fight, no matter the darkness, no matter the pain...

Something greater than me rode on this. I was fighting for Ruth, for her freedom.

You will not have her, I said, for a third and final time. *You will leave her.*

The pressure was maintained for a moment, but eased ever so slightly. This was my chance to fight back. And so I pushed back against the darkness with all my will. A terrible scream resonated as the darkness was filled with light, excruciatingly bright. This brightness was maintained for a long while, until it began to dissipate.

I felt my consciousness slip away as I rejoined the waking world.

***

I opened my eyes, seeing the glowing ceiling of the cavern above. I was lying on my back, floating on the surface of the ichor. Anna's face appeared above mine.

"Alex?"

I tried to move, but found that I couldn't. So Anna grabbed me by the shoulders and pulled me to the shore.

Once I was lying on dry ground, I finally found the strength to move. I pulled myself to a sitting position. Everyone stood around me, Ruth included. She was shaking all over.

"You're alright," I said.

She nodded. "Yeah. I think I am."

I thought about the voice I'd heard. At the time, I thought it was the writhe. But could it have been Askala herself?

"I heard her voice in my mind," Ruth said. "That's all I remember. I think...she was trying to get me to hurt you."

At last, it became clear to me. That was Askala who was attacking me, not the writhe. Samuel said the writhe was merely the means by which Askala communicated with the host.

That meant Askala had spoken to me. That meant that I had driven her out of Ruth, somehow, by my will alone.

"It was her, alright," I said. "It couldn't have been anyone else."

"You mean Askala?" Makara asked.

I nodded. "Yeah. No doubt in my mind."

"The writhe is a connection to Askala, according to Ashton's report," Samuel said. "If you connected to it, you must have connected to Askala's consciousness."

Everyone looked at me, as if realizing the gravity of that sentence. *I had connected to Askala's consciousness.* It seemed unreal.

"It was horrible," I said. "I forgot everything about who I was, why I was fighting. I felt like I had no hope." I paused. "I still feel that way, a bit."

"I don't want you to try anything like that again," Anna said. "What if *you* were knocked unconscious, too?"

"What about the writhe itself?" Julian asked. "Is it still...there?"

Ruth shook her head. "Don't even talk about it. Just the thought of that thing, in my head still..."

The writhe probably *was* still in Ruth's brain. Even if it was dead, that was still a horrifying picture. And having that writhe in there could have some ill effects.

"Is there any way to get it out?" Makara asked.

"At this point," Samuel said, "the only thing we can do is allow her immune system to run its course."

"What will that do to me?" Ruth asked.

"Probably nothing," Samuel said. "It's possible you might get a fever, but I'm definitely no expert."

Whatever the situation, we would have to keep an eye on it. For now, though, it seemed as if Ruth was okay.

I stood up, and turned to face the pool, where Quietus stood in the ichor, watching me in silence. I walked to the shoreline and met Quietus's eyes.

You could have warned me about what would happen.

Would that have made a difference? You stand victorious, and you saved the girl's life.

I heard her voice, Quietus, I said.

Ah, yes, Quietus thought. *What you endured for a mere two minutes I've endured for eons. It is a voice that only becomes more hellish with time.*

How did you survive it?

Quietus became silent, as if hesitant to revisit that former darkness.

One cannot endure against her, Quietus said. *Not for long. She will relent for a short time – only to become even more terrible than before. This is how she teaches her truths, and I will not go into any further detail. It is not good to understand darkness. You must defeat her,* Elekim.

What about Ruth? I asked. *Is the writhe still in her brain?*

In her brain, yes, though it is dead. She will be fine, Elekim. *Just see that she gets proper rest.*

I'm worried about the others. Are there any more writhes among us?

Beware if there are, Elekim, Quietus said. *There is nothing you can do but be on your guard. And if there* are *writhes among you…do* not *attempt to free anyone outside the confines of this pool. Without its power to aid you, it would be foolish indeed to attack a writhe. Just because you are* Elekim *doesn't mean you are invincible.*

You don't have to remind me of that, I said.

I resisted the temptation to turn around and look at the others. If any of them were controlled by a writhe, wouldn't they have been knocked unconscious, like Ruth? I had no idea.

I decided to turn my attention to other matters.

Will your dragons be ready for the final battle?

Some of Askal's dragons are still healing from their last battle, but they should be ready to fly soon.

We have to return to Los Angeles, I said. *If the new evolutions are any indication, we need to move quickly.*

Go in haste, then, Quietus said.

I left the pool, returning to the shore. I stood there for a moment, thinking, as everyone watched.

"Quietus says the writhe is dead. All the same, we need to be on our guard."

"Even from each other?" Anna asked.

I didn't want to admit that truth, yet I didn't want my silence to become my answer.

"We have to trust one another," I said. "Ruth was the only one who fell unconscious, so there's no reason to believe another person is infected. It's just time for us to move on to planning the final battle."

"Well said, Alex," Makara said. "Now, we need to get back to Los Angeles. Augustus needs to know what we've learned."

Chapter 8

When we returned to Los Angeles, it was almost fully dark. Makara, Char, and Marcus went to brief Augustus and Carin about what we had learned. She told the rest of us to eat and get some sleep.

We took her up on that, gathering in *Orion's* wardroom and making a meal of the leftover wedding food – pork, rice, and veggies. It seemed strange that the wedding was only three days ago, yet here was the evidence of it on my plate. There was also the ring on my finger that felt like it didn't belong.

Who got married when they knew they were going to die in a few days?

Nothing more happened that evening. We said our goodnights and headed straight for our bunks. Even though the captain's quarters were open, Anna and I still made our way aft to the smaller bunk in one of the crewmen's cabins, more out of habit than anything.

When I awoke around 08:00, I found that Anna was already gone. I took a shower first thing and made a breakfast of fruit and granola. Once done, I washed my plate and walked outside to find Makara standing in the street, gazing in the direction of Reaper HQ. She looked at me as I emerged from the ship and walked down the ramp.

"What's going on?" I asked.

Makara didn't break her focus. "They're mobilizing."

"Already?"

Down the street, there must have been hundreds of men forming up between the buildings. It was hard to believe that it was happening now. Makara must have finalized the plans with Augustus and Carin last night, even while I was sleeping. Seeing those hundreds of men forming their lines had a sense of finality to it. It was like I was seeing the rest of my life laid down like tracks before me.

All I had to do was follow them, until the end.

"They're hoping to get past Last Town by tonight," Makara said, breaking me from my thoughts. "From there, they'll set up camp and begin the push into the Great Blight."

The final battle was getting so close, and we were on the second day before the final evolutions took place.

"Do you think we can win?" I asked.

"We have to win," Makara said. "Those men down there..." She pointed toward the gathering soldiers. "I can't stand that I'm the one sending them to their deaths. They're just bait and they know it. Still, they march."

"They know what will happen if they don't fight."

"True," Makara said. "And who knows? Miracles have been known to happen."

She half-turned, ready to walk away.

"I'm off to *Perseus*. Sam, Michael, and I are going to Bunker 84 to get the nukes online. I have to fly, Sam can take care of the computer stuff, and Michael wants to see his family. We have to decide on targets as well."

"Targets?"

"Well, with nine nukes, that gives us nine potential targets. We need to save some for the battlefield, in case things don't go our way. Which is pretty likely." Makara sighed. "Hopefully we won't have to use them."

"Well, good luck with that. I wouldn't know where to start."

"You, Anna, and Julian can scout ahead of the army. We need to make sure our forces aren't walking into a trap. It's an important task, so don't take it lightly."

"You're leaving now?"

She nodded. "Yeah. Samuel and Michael are already waiting, so all that's left is to head there. The thing is getting back in time to power the railgun. We've picked a plateau to make our stand. It's flat, but with sheer cliffs on every side but the west. If we can take the fight there, we can last a lot longer than we would otherwise."

"And what about attacking the Crater?"

"Tomorrow, if at all possible."

With that, Makara headed down the ramp and toward *Orion*. I stood there in disbelief. She wanted to attack Ragnarok Crater tomorrow. I really didn't have to ask why. If there was some unknown evolution taking place in two days, it made sense to strike before that happened.

All the same, it was too soon. *Any* time would have been too soon.

As *Perseus's* engines fired up, boots clomped down the ramp behind me. I turned to see Julian. He planted a hand on my shoulder.

"You alright?" Julian asked.

Perseus lifted off and circled above the buildings. Julian and I watched the ship's departure.

"Yeah," I said. I shook my head. "No, actually. The attack on the Crater is tomorrow, you know."

"Tomorrow?" Julian asked. "I'll believe it when it happens. Something will crop up before then. You'll see."

"It's better to just get it over with."

"Well, if it does happen tomorrow, these soldiers have to get moving. There's no way you're going near that Crater before the battle starts. The attack on the Crater can't start until the army is fighting, until the *Radaskim* are distracted."

"You don't think the battle will happen tomorrow?"

"No idea," he said. "I'd be surprised if they make it past Last Town today, like Makara hopes." He looked at me. "You've got another few days, man. Go spend time with Anna."

"What do you think is going to happen?"

Julian shrugged. "Don't know. I'm just trying to do my part. I'm not as smart as Samuel. I can't use a blade like Anna. All I've got is my willingness to help. That's all I was given, so that's all I have to give. That's alright, though. I was always meant to play a bit part."

"That's not true."

"I lived a lot of my life as a slave, so I'm used to helping out. Going unnoticed. Not saying much."

"That's not who you are now," I said.

"It was who I was," Julian said. "No getting around that. Back to your question, though…I have no idea when the battle will start."

"I'm not ready for it," I said. "I might have less than a few days to live."

Julian smiled grimly. "That's probably all of us, Alex."

Julian and I both gazed down the city streets, seeing a lone female figure with a blade walking toward us. I headed in that direction. It wasn't long before Anna and I stood facing each other.

"You've heard about what we're supposed to do?" I asked.

"No, what?"

"Makara told us to recon ahead of the army, using *Orion*."

She nodded. "Makes sense. I saw them take off."

We turned back for the ship. I felt directionless, like there was something I was supposed to be doing besides waiting around. It would drive me crazy if it went on for much longer.

When we arrived, Julian had gone off somewhere. Down the street, men still gathered at the base of Reaper HQ. The railgun was with them now.

We stood there, watching, for the next ten minutes, as the army began to march. It was more people than I'd ever seen gathered in my life.

Still, I knew it paled in comparison to what we were up against.

It was a strange mix. Augustus's legionaries were the most numerous, in their dusty leathers and spears and shields. Some carried rifles or handguns, but not many. Carin Black's Reapers, by contrast, were equipped with rifles. They marched at the rear, after Augustus's legionaries. Interspersed with the marching men were the vehicles – Recons, mostly, the lead one containing Augustus and a few of his Praetorians. The Reapers had their own Recons with machine guns mounted on the top. In the center of the Reapers' procession was the halftrack and railgun, rolling slowly and kicking up a cloud of dust. Right behind the railgun, in a Recon painted jet black with skulls and cross-scythes on the door, rode Carin Black and his son, Onyx. Their eyes gleamed at us almost mockingly as the vehicle passed. Julian emerged from the ship and came to watch with us from the ramp.

"I hope the Blighters get him first," Anna said.

"We might need him for a little while longer," I said. "As much as that hurts."

"It's time we got going."

For now, we were leaving Char and Marcus on the ground. They needed to be with their men. I hadn't seen them marching in that teeming mass, but that wasn't surprising. The numbers of Raiders and Exiles was a drop in the ocean compared to everyone else – and the strength of the entire army was just a drop when compared to the *Radaskim*.

"You coming?" Anna asked.

I realized I was still staring at the train of supplies being carried in a seemingly never-ending line of flatbed trucks. Food, ammo, guns, medicine, whole tanks of water...the hundreds of vehicles and personnel outnumbered even the soldiers of the army.

I turned and boarded the ship. The door shut behind as I walked to the bridge. Anna fired up the ship, and a moment later, it lifted from the ground. Most of the men looked up as we rose into the sky.

"Taking off," Anna said, after setting the frequency to Makara's line. "Proceeding with aerial recon. What's your status, *Orion?*"

Makara's voice came through.

"We're a few minutes out from the Bunker. Lauren has things running smoothly, as expected. We'll be touching down in thirty minutes or so."

"Copy that," Anna said. "We'll be here."

Anna then switched to Augustus's line.

"Augustus, we're proceeding with aerial recon. If we notice anything unusual, we'll let you know right away."

"Copy that," he said. "Expand your reach farther than our line of travel. Don't want anything catching us with our pants down."

"Will do. I'll see what I can find."

Now, from well above the buildings, the marching men and slow-moving vehicles below looked like toys. It was hard to believe that this was finally happening.

Anna accelerated the ship over the building tops toward the brown lifeless hills flanking Los Angeles's eastern side. We stayed just below the red cloud layer.

"We'll be there soon," Anna said to me.

"Where?" I asked.

"My home."

She followed the line of the highway, past deserted buildings that stretched beyond the hills. She angled down toward a mountain pass though which the highway traveled.

As we drew closer, buildings appeared on the road. A dilapidated wall surrounded the town and separated it from the rest of the Los Angeles Basin. It was all but abandoned. Dust covered the highway running down its middle, and its wooden buildings stood in shambles.

"There it is," she said. "Home. Or what's left of it."

I touched Anna's hand. "You going to be alright?"

"I think so. Last Town is just a reminder that nothing lasts in this world. We live each day expecting what we have to be there tomorrow. It's funny how we think that, because most of the time, it isn't true. When you expect to lose everything…it makes having anything all the more miraculous."

"You're here now," I said. "That's what matters. Despite everything you went through, you made it."

"I'm still making it. I don't care what either of us has to go through in the coming days. We're going to make it. Somehow."

We were nearly over the town.

"Which was your house?"

Anna smiled. "I can't tell from here. But maybe I can show you."

"How?"

She gave me a quick glance before angling the ship downward.

"By landing."

Chapter 9

We landed in the center of the highway running through town, where the army would be passing through later this afternoon. It was still morning, so we had plenty of time to complete the recon, but all the same, I knew Augustus wouldn't be happy with this hiatus.

We disembarked and found ourselves standing in the center of a town in shambles. Watchtowers on stilts rose from the eastern and western palisades. The wooden buildings were deteriorating into the dust. Most of the squat buildings lined the highway itself, or were even built on top of it. Last Town had arisen after Ragnarok's fall – set in the pass connecting the Wasteland to the city, it was well situated to take advantage of the trade routes that arose out of the Chaos Years. For almost two decades, the town thrived, especially when protected by Raine and the Lost Angels.

However, after the Lost Angels fell, the Reapers had conquered Last Town five years ago. It had then been maintained as an outpost of the Reapers, but at the moment, the entire town was abandoned. Anna and her mother escaped this place five years ago, but her father had died in the fighting.

"This way," she said.

She led Julian and me between two buildings. We climbed over piles of wood and rubble. Most of the buildings looked as if they could collapse at any moment. I began to wonder how Anna knew where she was going.

After I thought about it for a moment, I realized that I could close my eyes and see every angle, intersection, and corridor in Bunker 108. There was something about growing up somewhere that made that place stick with you for the rest of your life, even if you never saw it again.

It was the same for Anna; she knew exactly where she was going, and it wasn't long before we stopped in front of a small wooden house.

"This is it," she said.

Or, at least, what remained of a small wooden house. One of its walls had completely collapsed. Inside, I could see splintered chairs, an upturned table, and two cast-iron pots strewn among the debris.

Anna stepped over the shattered wall and walked on the debris-covered floor. The roof had collapsed some time ago.

"My dad built this place when I was little. He was good with that sort of thing. Putting things together. Making things work." She paused. "Of course, it's different now. I wasn't expecting to find much here. My mom and dad both scavenged. The L.A. ruins, mostly. The Angels made it safe to do that sort of thing, and the town saw some prosperity for a time. There was plenty to eat."

Julian and I listened as Anna walked to one of the corners.

"My bed was here," she said. "We called it a bed, but it was really more of a pallet. And it got cold. We had a chimney, but firewood was hard to come by. A man named Harold would chop some for us."

"Would chop it?" Julian asked.

"Yeah. Pun not intended." She frowned. "I didn't realize it then, but we had a nice community here. You always take what you have for granted until it's no longer there. When you're a kid, you don't think about the future. We are free to enjoy life, each moment, at least until something goes wrong." She paused again. "It was all snatched away in a single night. And everything changed."

Even though I was married to Anna, there was so much I still didn't know about her. So much I wanted to know. When you were running and fighting for your life, it was sometimes hard to find the time to just...talk. Be still. Listen.

"I remember always wanting to have brothers and sisters, growing up." She paused. "But looking back, maybe being alone wasn't such a bad thing."

"I thought the same thing," I said. "After my mom died, my dad never remarried, even though I wanted him to."

"I think...my parents might have tried. But for one reason or another, it never happened. Such things can't be explained. We had no doctors, and few knew how to use medicine. They were precious, always guarded. The property of the Wise." She sighed. "You never realize when you're happy. Until you aren't. I was happy, until the Reapers came. They killed, they raped, they burned. The dream ended, and somehow, my mom and I were spared, but after the next few years of our life, death might have been preferable. We lived through hell, on the edge of starvation and sanity. I was only twelve. Twelve."

There were now tears in her eyes. I went over to her, and held her in my arms.

When she had gained control, she continued.

"Sometimes, I wonder how I made it. There were so many times I should have died. But I never did. Even when mom died. I'd survive, keep feeding myself for another day, and wonder why I was doing it. You ever have that?"

I nodded, saying nothing. Julian was also nodding.

"That house, right there," Anna said, pointing past the crumbled wall. "That's where Jason and Gwen lived. They were family friends. He kept an orchard, on the heights, in an old greenhouse. Gwen was a scavenger, like my parents."

"How many lived here?" Julian asked.

"Two hundred, maybe. Of those two hundred, I don't know how many died. I don't know how many were taken as slaves. And I don't know how many of those are still alive today. There's me, so there's that."

"You made it," I said.

"Yeah. I did. For the longest time, I didn't believe it was worth it. Especially when mom died. Some disease took her life, but in the end, that's not surprising. Finding food was hard, and when we did find it, a lot of the time it wasn't good to eat. We ate it anyway, because we had no choice." She paused. "We would read to each other, at night. It kept the darkness at bay. Books were the only escape. We'd find them everywhere. Of all the items we found, they were the most ignored, except when people needed something to light a fire. We never burned books. It seemed a travesty, to destroy all these words from a better time. A wiser time. And one day, they might all be gone."

"What did you do?" Julian asked. "When she died?"

"What any of us would do. I cried. I cried until nothing came, until every ounce of my soul was emptied and dried on the cold, harsh rocks. And I walked. I ate. I did not smile. I did not remember. By that time, I'd found the blade, and books that showed me some basic forms. I practiced endlessly, moving only when I had to. I...killed my first man, when I was fourteen." She shook her head. "I don't know why I'm saying all these things, things I told myself I'd never relive."

"It's alright," I said.

She looked at me in a way that said she wasn't sure if that was true.

"We are the sum of our experiences," Anna said. "No more, no less. But I'd like to believe there's something more to all of us. That we have the strength to defy our experiences and rise above them, to push back against the world that has treated us so cruelly. To hold out arms and make it a better place to live. Sometimes, all that gets lost in the madness. It all gets overwhelmed. Yet, here we are. Still standing."

Julian and I merely stood, listening.

"There are things we'd all rather forget," Anna went on. "But we can't. The pain becomes a part of us. There were times where that was *all* there was. That's the way the world is. You can see beauty, or you can see ugliness. You can even see both, if you want to. Even without the *Radaskim,* this world would be a dark place. But even in the ruins, a flower can bloom. Even in a land without the sun."

"It will," I said. "It's what we're fighting for."

I followed Anna's gaze, and was struck to see what she was looking at. Her word choice turned out not to be merely metaphorical.

In a crack of the concrete, a green stem rose, studded with thorns; at its end a red bud bloomed. A rose in the ruins. How it existed or even grew here, I had no idea. But there it was.

"Some miracles do exist," she said. "Jason grew roses like these, and even five years later, they're still here." She looked at me. "Life is as fragile as it is resilient. We're built to survive. We're built to endure. No matter what happens, as long we don't quit, we'll find a way. Even if we cry...we don't cry to quit. We cry to go on."

We stayed in the house another few minutes. Anna just stood, looking with reminiscent eyes as if seeing through time. She saw things far beyond what Julian and I could see. Ghosts. Memories. Laughter.

She turned, taking my hand.

"Alright. We've seen enough."

We left the house and made our way back to *Orion.* As we weaved between the buildings and stepped onto the highway, I looked toward the right.

To see a man standing there.

Julian and Anna pulled up beside me, and the three of us faced the man. He wore all black – pants, collared shirt, and a wide-brimmed hat; a black duster jacket, the tails of which blew in the wind. A long, scraggly red beard fell down his chest, and eyes as blue as ice stared at us. He wore a belt, on which a handgun was holstered.

The man didn't move, but I moved my hand to my Beretta.

In the end, the man advanced toward us, slowly.

"Stay there," I called. "And don't move. Put your gun on the ground. Slowly."

The man paused. After a long, watchful moment, he reached for his gun belt, slowly, and removed it. The belt contained not one, but two holsters, one for each side. Next, he shucked his duster, revealing a rifle strapped to his back. He took the strap and the rifle off, laying them on the dirt at his feet.

"Jesus," Julian said.

The man reached into his left boot, and withdrew a long dagger. He set the dagger on the highway before him. Holding out his gloved hands, he advanced forward, one step at a time.

When he was about twenty-five feet away, Anna called out.

"That's far enough."

The man stared at her with those blue eyes. A long moment passed before anyone spoke again.

"Do you recognize this guy?" I asked Anna.

To the side, I saw her shake her head.

"Who are you?" I asked.

The man's gaze focused on me. Even if he had removed every weapon, he was still dangerous. The way he carried himself, the way he looked at me, told me that. It was impossible to live this long alone and not know how to kill.

"My name..." the man said, slowly and drawing it out in a raspy voice, "is not your concern. I'm the Last Man of Last Town. That's all you need to know."

"What do you want from us, Last Man?" Anna asked.

The Last Man stood as still as a statue.

"For you to leave," he said. "No man can walk inside these walls. I drove the Reapers out, and I will drive *you* out."

The man didn't seem to be concerned with the fact that we had a spaceship. That seemed strange in itself. It meant that nothing was important to him but what he said. He wanted us out.

"We're leaving now," Anna said.

The man's eyes focused on Anna.

"I know your face," he said. "But I don't know from where."

Anna looked at him, not letting her guard down. "Did you live here, Last Man?"

The man gave the slightest of nods. "Yes. They all died. I remember it like yesterday. I left this place a village, and returned to find it a graveyard."

"What is your name, Last Man?" Anna said. "I lived here a long time ago, but haven't been back until today."

"Yours first, girl," the man said, in a harsh tone. "I tire of people and their tricks."

"Anna," he said. "My mother was Heather. My father, Ben. We lived at the crossways. The north side."

The man was silent for a long time. His posture relaxed, ever so slightly. But he was by no means less dangerous.

"Yes. You're Ben's girl, alright. You have his eyes. His fierceness. There's no doubting it." He spat at the ground. "Ben's dead, now. I thought you were, too."

"Now tell me who *you* are."

"Victor."

"Victor," Anna said. "I don't know that name."

"Few did," Victor said. "I was a hunter, far away from the town. It doesn't surprise me I escaped your notice. But if ever you ate some wild game in this place...it might have been by my shot that it came to be."

"And you live here, in this place?" Anna asked.

Victor shrugged. "It is better than the west, with the Reapers. And better than the east, with its death. Here, there is a spring, and food in the hills for a man who knows where to look."

"And what do you do, when you're not hunting game?" Anna asked.

"I hunt men. Reapers, mostly. I hunt them where I find them. I think they avoid this place, now. They say it's haunted."

Victor gave the tiniest trace of a smile.

"There will be plenty of Reapers today," I said. "They're coming from Los Angeles."

"Why?"

"They are making a final stand," Anna said. "The Empire. The Angels. The Reapers. If that stand isn't made together, then the monsters will win."

Victor gave a bitter laugh. "Angels. An Angel hasn't walked this town in five years."

"The Angels have reformed," I said. "We're three of them."

"Is that so?" Victor gave us an appraising look, but it was hard to tell whether or not he approved. "No true Angel would work with a Reaper."

"They would," I said. "If the world were ending."

The man gave a bitter laugh. "The world has already ended, boy. The Old World has passed, and if one day no man wakes to see the new, I won't grieve for it. Man, monster, what's the difference?"

I realized we were speaking with a man who saw no good in this world, who saw no reason to fight for it. There was little we could do to change the mind of such a person. He had suffered more than his share of evils, and those evils had broken him.

"There's still hope, Victor," Anna said. "Just as you believed I was dead, in truth, I was alive. Just as you believe that we are all going to die, and that we are deserving of that death, we believe you're wrong. My friends and I worked hard to get everyone to stand together. Many have died to make it happen. This is our last chance to make a difference, and every man's support counts. Even yours."

The man merely stood and watched us. It was hard to guess at his age – he could have been thirty, or sixty. The face was red, wind-chapped, weather-beaten.

After a long while, he nodded.

"So you say."

"The army will be passing through here this afternoon," Anna said. "If you change your mind...ask for Char."

The man looked at Anna for a long time, before giving a slow nod.

She turned to us. "Come on. We should get moving."

We turned back to the ship. As we ascended the boarding ramp, I looked back one last time. He stood there, the wind blowing the tails of his duster. He raised a single hand in farewell. The eyes were sad. Watchful.

We entered the ship and once more took to the air.

***

We flew eastward beyond the mountains, right over the border of the Great Blight. Anna lowered the ship to better survey the xenofungal surface, but the terrain below was empty.

When Anna veered north, Makara's voice came through the dash.

"Alright. Sam and I have connected the ship's drive to the Bunker's grid. We're en route to Level Three."

"Copy that," Anna said,

We continued our recon, scanning the Great Blight in a wide arc. From time to time we'd see evidence of xenolife – crawlers running in small packs, swarms of birds, even a Behemoth or two – but nothing approaching the size of the *Radaskim* horde.

Anna switched frequencies to Augustus's line.

"Not seeing anything, Augustus," Anna said. "Just a few crawlers here and there, about what you'd expect from the Great Blight. I think you guys will be good."

"Copy that. The troops are in eastern L.A. right now. We should make it to the pass this afternoon."

"Great. Listen..."

Augustus waited, but Anna hesitated to speak. I knew she was about to tell him about the man, Victor. In the end, though, she shook her head.

"Just be careful. You're clear all the way past the mountains."

"Thank you, Anna."

Augustus cut out, and we continued with our recon.

Chapter 10

Thirty minutes later, we still hadn't heard from Makara or Samuel.

Anna, Julian, and I watched the Great Blight from an altitude of two thousand feet

"We should have heard from them by now," I said.

"I'll call them again," Anna said.

Once the line was established, nothing answered but silence. I had no idea why they weren't picking up.

I was beginning to wonder if some of those Lords had survived...

"Something's wrong," I said

"Let me call Michael's line," Anna said.

She switched frequencies. "Michael? You have a copy, over?"

Again, silence was the only answer.

"The army won't be here until nightfall," Julian said. "Plenty of time to get there and back."

Anna and I looked at each other. Wasn't this just overreacting? We were supposed to be watching the Great Blight, but there was nothing here. If Makara, Samuel, and Michael weren't answering, something might be wrong.

"We *can* be there in an hour," Anna said, thinking.

"There's no harm in going to check," I said. "*Orion* is fast. We'll be there and back in a couple of hours."

Anna thought for a moment, at last turning the ship and pointing it to the north. She increased the speed to full, and all of us were pushed back into our seats.

"Hopefully, this is nothing," she said. "We'll keep calling as we head north. It'll take forty-five minutes to get there. If they don't answer in that time..."

She left the rest unsaid as we sped over the Great Blight.

***

During the journey, we repeatedly called Samuel, Makara, and Michael. Each time, there was no response, and I became increasingly worried.

As we traveled north, the clouds hung gray and heavy over the mountains. Most of the time, we couldn't see the land below. We kept well above the mountains, only descending once we were close.

By the time we reached the Bunker, the air had cleared, revealing the large mountain 84 was housed in. Anna angled *Perseus* toward the mountainside, where the hangar opened vertically to the air. The entrance tunnel led straight down into darkness.

"Control, this is Anna aboard the *Orion*. Do you have a copy?"

"*Orion?*" a man's voice responded. "What are you doing here?"

"Clear us to land," Anna said. "There's something we want to check on."

"You're cleared," the man said. "You can park next to *Perseus.*"

"Where's the crew's location?"

"You mean Makara and them? They went up a while ago. Why?"

"Up to Level Three?"

"Yeah," the man said. "Is something wrong?"

"We don't know. That's why we're here."

Anna lowered the ship vertically over the hangar opening. As we descended, the darkness was replaced with the dim fluorescence of the hangar below. I looked down to see people watching our approach from the hangar floor. *Perseus* was parked nearby.

"They're here, alright," I said.

Neither Anna nor Julian said anything as *Perseus* landed on the floor. We unstrapped ourselves and headed to the wardroom to exit the ship.

When we entered the hangar bay, Lauren was waiting at the bottom of the ramp, flanked by several civilians.

"What on Earth are you doing here?" she asked, arms crossed. "You're supposed to be with the army."

"Makara, Samuel, and Michael weren't answering their calls," Anna said. "We came to investigate."

Lauren frowned, puzzled. "Aren't you overreacting a bit? They went up to Level Three not an hour ago. What could have possibly happened?"

"I don't know," Anna said. "Probably nothing. But it's unlike any of them to go so long without answering. We decided not to take the chance."

"We shouldn't be long," I said.

By now, a large crowd had gathered around us, asking questions, but we pressed through and headed to the stairs.

"Wait!" Lauren said.

We stopped, and turned around.

"What *aren't* you telling me?"

"Don't worry about it," I said. "We need you to stay here and watch over our people."

She laughed in disbelief. "Alex, you don't tell me what to do."

"All we know is," Anna said, "Makara said she'd call us from the control room first thing." She looked at Lauren pointedly. "That hasn't happened, and it's not like Makara to forget something that important."

"I'm sure something came up, or..."

"That's what we think, too," Anna said. "Still, better safe than sorry."

"If that's what you think, then I'm going, too."

"Lauren," Anna said. "Please. Stay here. We won't be long, and we need someone to watch over these people."

"You think it'll be dangerous?"

I decided to share my earlier thought. "It's possible some of the Lords were left behind. We just don't know what it could be. That's why we're going up."

"We'll be back soon," Julian said.

Before she could protest further, we turned and headed toward the stairs that would lead up to Level Nineteen. Lauren harrumphed behind us. I turned to see her walking away.

As Anna dug out a flashlight to light the way, Julian spoke.

"Do you really think there's a danger?"

I shrugged. "I don't know. There's no reason to think there is. But still, sometimes you just get a feeling about something...if you ignore feelings like that, you'll be sorry."

"I feel the same way," Anna said.

We ran up the steps until we reached Level Ten, where we had to take a corridor to the other side in order to continue our ascent. We were gasping for breath by the time we started climbing the stairs again. Only our flashlights lit the complete darkness until we arrived at Level Three, where the power was on.

"Looks like they're here," I said.

As we headed to the Command Center, the corridors were quiet and cold. My apprehension increased as we walked on. We turned onto the final corridor that led to the Command Center. From there, it was a straight shot to the railing overhanging the control room below.

We ran along the corridor until we reached the railing. There, Michael stood alone behind one of the computers, typing. There was no sign of Makara or Samuel.

"Michael?" I called.

He tensed a moment before turning his head, showing only the left side of his face.

"The silos are almost fully online," he said. "It took it a while to reroute power from *Orion's* drive."

"Where are Makara and Samuel?"

"Down below," he said. "Making sure the power flows smoothly."

There was an edge to his voice that made me stiffen a bit.

"Down below? What do you mean?"

Michael seemed annoyed by our presence, turning back to face the computer.

"Yeah. At the fusion reactor. We couldn't get enough power, but Samuel must have been successful." He paused. "It's working now."

I looked at Anna and Julian. We knew something wasn't right.

"None of you answered our calls," I said.

"They're too far underground to get reception, Alex. And me...well, I left my radio back on the ship." He forced a smile. "Sorry to have caused such a scare."

Something about this wasn't adding up. It was his manner, his tone...it was very unlike Michael. If things were going to take a little longer, Makara would have let us know.

"The Command Center has a direct line to the outside," I said. "Why didn't you establish a connection?"

"I'm busy here, Alex," Michael said.

I just stared at him, shocked. Now, I absolutely *knew* something wasn't right.

"*Michael,*" Julian said.

At Julian's voice, Michael turned. There was a strange look in his brown eyes. It took me a moment to figure out what it was. They say the eyes are windows to the soul. Only I saw no soul, nothing that was Michael. The eyes were dead, emotionless. A chill came over me.

"What happened, Michael?" Julian asked.

There were too many things going wrong, too many things being shrugged off.

Everything clicked at once. I raised my Beretta.

"Step away from the computer, Michael."

Anna's eyes widened. "Alex, what are you doing?"

I didn't know how it happened, but the answer seemed obvious. "He has a writhe."

As if he didn't have a gun pointed at him, Michael merely continued to type, a smile playing on his lips.

"You won't kill me, Alex. If you kill me, you let her win."

Now, both Julian and Anna drew their handguns, pointing them at Michael's back.

"I'm warning you!" I said. "Step away!"

"Michael, please," Julian said. "Step away from the computer. You don't want to do this."

The wall screen flashed on, displaying a map of the United States. Several lines arced from Bunker 84 to Los Angeles.

"You're reprogramming the flight path of the nukes," I said. "What did you do to Makara and Samuel?"

Michael didn't answer. He merely continued to work.

"Michael, step away!" Anna yelled.

"Do you really think I could stop myself, even if I wanted to?" he said. "I can only do what she says. You know that. So why do you threaten me? If you don't want these nukes going off on the army, then pull the goddamn trigger. It's what Michael would want."

There were only two options before us. Let Michael live, and have him destroy the entire army. Or shoot him, right here, right now.

I decided to buy more time. I wasn't going to shoot him unless I absolutely had to.

"What did you do with them, Michael?"

"I did what I had to," he said. "All I needed was Samuel's clearance. After that...*she* showed me the rest."

I felt a sick twisting in my gut such as I had ever known. How long had that writhe been living in his head, unknown even to him, waiting for the right moment to strike? Ruth's going unconscious was, in a way, a red herring. It made us think no one else on the crew could be infected. And now, the writhe had led Michael to where it mattered.

More than that, there were so many times Michael could have ended my life, but Askala and the writhe had waited for *this*. She considered the nukes a greater prize than even *Elekim*. Askala had conquered this Bunker once for the very purpose of gaining the nukes.

Now, she was conquering it again.

"You killed them, didn't you?" Anna asked.

Michael didn't answer. Now, he had stopped using the computer completely. I knew, at some point in the next few seconds, the shooting would start.

Unless I found a way to stop it.

Quietus had warned me not to do this, away from the strength of the ichor. But I saw no other choice. I didn't want to shoot Michael, and I didn't want Askala to use him to fire the nukes.

I closed my eyes and reached out for the writhe.

"Alex!" Anna said. "Alex, don't..."

It was the last thing I heard before I was swallowed by darkness.

I could only hope that Quietus's warning had been enough to prepare me.

***

The darkness was far more oppressive than it was in the Xenolith. There was only coldness and pain, like I was being crushed in the deepest pressures of the sea. There was nothing but the pain, the panic, the realization of my mistake in doing this.

Here, Askala whispered. *Here I shall keep you until the end of time.*

I tried to scream, but there was nothing for me to scream with. I couldn't even form thoughts with which to defend myself.

You've given yourself into my hand, Elekim. *Now, despair, as I crush you.*

The darkness was then pinpricked with thousands of points of light – white, blue, yellow, deep red. The points were different sizes, and it was a moment before I realized they were stars, and that I was in space. A white-hot light brightened in my vision, making it impossible to see. Heat baked my skin, a heat that increased with each passing second. It was a pain beyond imagining.

As I screamed, the heat subsided, ever so slightly. I felt a weakness in Askala's will, a hesitation.

I realized I wasn't alone.

Now, Alex. Attack!

The voice was Anna's. I didn't know how she was here, but I used this chance to focus on the writhe. At last, I found it, forming a connection with my mind. The will of the writhe wavered, but did not break. I attacked it with all my conscious energy, knowing that this was my one chance to defeat it.

But I didn't have the strength. I held firm, not letting the writhe push back against me, but I could only hold this for so long. Suddenly, I became aware of Anna joining her will to mine.

Together, she said.

We pushed against the writhe. A burst of light, brighter than any star, ignited in the darkness. The writhe let out a long scream, alien and terrible. The surrounding stars burst into novae, blinding in their mutual radiance.

We waited in the following silence for a long time, until the light faded, until the stars were gone and a great, warm emptiness had been left behind.

And then, there was only darkness.

***

When I awoke, it was not on the Command Center floor. It was in a bed. I still saw the stars floating in an endless black. My mouth was dry, and every muscle was stiff.

With effort, I opened my eyes to find my vision blurred. A face swam before me. I couldn't tell who it was; the room was dark, and my eyes couldn't seem to focus.

A hand closed around mine, its warmth entering my skin.

My voice came out raspy. "Anna?"

"Who do you think?"

And like that, she held me, her hair pressed against my cheek.

"Where am I?" I asked.

"You're on *Perseus*. It's 01:34."

01:34. I'd been out ten hours, give or take. Trying to remember anything was a great effort.

"How did I get here?"

"You fought the writhe, remember?" Anna asked. "It controlled Michael's mind."

I wanted to ask more, but it was too hard to even think. I settled back on my pillow, closing my eyes once more.

"The army must be at the Great Blight now," I said. "Did they make it past Last Town?"

"Yeah," Anna said. "An entire day has passed. You slept through the night, through today, up until now."

So, I had been out not for ten hours. It was more like thirty-plus.

"And I just *now* woke up?"

Before Anna could answer, everything returned to me. Anna had been there with me, in the darkness. Without her, I would have lost the fight with the writhe.

"You helped me," I said.

Anna nodded. "Yeah. I don't know how it happened, but I just sort of...reached out. I found you there, fighting the writhe."

"How did you do it?" I asked.

"I have no idea. It all just sort of...happened. Like I had no control over it."

There were so many things we didn't understand, but one thing was for sure: without Anna, I probably would have never woken up.

"Whatever you did, you saved me," I said. "As far as *how* it happened...we'll have to ask Quietus the next time we see her."

"I was knocked out, too, but I woke up this morning. I guess you had it a lot worse."

"What about Makara and Samuel?"

"They're both alright. Pretty beat up, but alright. Michael overpowered them both, disarmed them...I can only speculate why he left it at that. Makara thinks the writhe somehow made him stronger. He waited just long enough for Samuel to put in his password before knocking them both out cold. He slammed their heads against the wall, one with each hand." Anna shook her head. "Neither saw it coming. It almost seems...unreal. He dragged them into one of the dorms."

"And they're alright? After all of *that?*"

"We should count ourselves lucky. Askala wasn't worried about killing them, so much as getting Michael to the computer. He had just started programming the nukes to hit Los Angeles, when we came along. Julian said you, I, and Michael just went down on the floor. There was really nothing he could do, but he watched until we all had gone sort of...still. He found Makara and Samuel in the adjoining dorm, and was about to go down for help, only Samuel and Makara came to. Long story short, Samuel was able to clear the nukes' flight path."

It was hard to believe all this had happened.

"And Michael's still out?"

Anna nodded. "Yeah. Makara and the rest have been working with the troops on the plateau, setting up the lines. It seems Askala has noticed. A huge swarm is coming to the plateau." Anna paused.

"They should be there by tomorrow."

"Is that where we're headed?"

"Yeah. We should be there soon."

***

We approached the plateau from the air. It commanded a high view of all the surrounding terrain, so when the swarm attacked, they would have to climb sheer cliffs on all but its western side. *Orion* was parked right next to the railgun, power cables stretching from the ship to the gun. The entire area was covered with xenofungus, lit and glowing in the night. Just a month ago it would have been nothing but rock and dust.

We landed next to *Orion*. When we disembarked, the ground squished beneath our boots as we went to *Orion,* where we found Makara standing in front of the ship. A deep bruise discolored her forehead. Both she and Samuel were lucky not to have any serious damage, but the wound looked nasty.

"We're going to meet on *Perseus,*" she said.

Samuel, Julian, and Ruth exited *Orion,* coming to stand by Makara. Lauren was the last one out – if Michael was in the clinic on that ship, then it made sense that Lauren would be here, too.

Everyone headed for *Perseus,* going to the conference hold once inside.

Everyone took up their seats, and we waited for a long, drawn-out moment. Lauren was the first to speak.

"What are we going to do?" Lauren asked. "Michael is showing no signs of improving. We're going to run out of IV fluid, and he *can't* keep living in this state." She sighed. "Maybe now that Alex is awake, we can take him to the *Elekai.*"

"Going to the Xenolith would be a good idea," I said. "Not just for Michael. There is something I should have done the first time we were there." Everyone looked at me, wondering what I was going to say. "I need to screen everyone for writhes."

"You can do that?" Makara asked.

"I think I can," I said. "I only wish I had thought of it earlier. If I try to reach out to someone's mind, and there's no connection...then I'll know that person doesn't have one."

"Alex, this could be dangerous," Anna said. "You were out for over twenty-four hours."

"I'll have the ichor to draw on. It won't be *as* dangerous." I paused. "Besides, this is something we have to do. I don't *think* anyone else is infected, but we have to be absolutely sure."

Everyone exchanged looks.

"You won't be able to read our thoughts, or anything like that?" Lauren asked.

I shook my head. "No. That's not really how it works. I can only do that sort of thing with the *Elekai,* and even then they have to allow me to see it."

"I think it's a good idea," Makara said. "I mean, if it's possible."

"I think it is," I said.

I looked at Anna, whose green eyes looked at me worriedly. I wanted to tell her that I wasn't afraid, because she would be with me – not just physically there, but with me in case things went bad. I still didn't understand how she had been able to follow me into that darkness, but it was comforting to know that she could. I didn't want to mention that to everyone else; not unless Anna herself wanted me to say it. But Anna looked away, appearing troubled.

"We should sleep," Makara said. "Tomorrow morning, we'll head for the Xenolith."

"What time?" Samuel asked.

"Let's try to head out at 0:800. It's a little late, but we'll need the sleep. We have a full day tomorrow."

Full day didn't even begin to describe it. Besides our seeing if the *Elekai* could heal Michael, and my screening everyone for writhes, the *Radaskim* would arrive at the plateau at some point tomorrow. And even more, we would probably fly to the Crater when that happened. Another thing I had to do at the Xenolith was talk to Askal and Quietus both, finalizing plans for their part in the battle.

In short, this would probably be my last normal night of sleep for a long time.

"Are we going in *Perseus?*" Lauren asked.

"Yeah. *Orion* stays here to power the railgun." She faced everyone else. "That's it. Try to get some rest. We've come a long way, and we need to go a little further still."

"Once we're done at the Xenolith, what then?" Ruth asked. "Are we actually fighting in the battle, or…"

"The plan is to stay as far from the battle as possible," Makara said. "Not because we're trying to avoid it, but because our mission is at Ragnarok Crater. Char and Marcus will be commanding the New Angels. That frees me to go to the Crater with everyone else."

"When the battle joins," Samuel said. "Then we leave."

"Any more questions?" Makara asked.

No one said anything – either because they had no questions, or because they were tired.

"Get some shuteye," Makara said. "I'll see you on board at 0:800."

Chapter 11

At 0:800 we converged on *Perseus*. We left the plateau behind, and I watched *Orion* and the neighboring railgun drop away with distance. The xenofungus was a blazing spread on the plateau's flat surface, and Reapers milled around the gun's position, setting up sharp, wooden stakes that were to form a perimeter.

As we rose higher and higher, I could see the eastern fringe of the plateau, where Augustus's men were setting up additional defenses. Machine gun nests were being constructed on the higher portions of the plateau; they would have a commanding view of the steep slope that led down into the western valley, where xenofungus and xenotrees expanded in an orangey shimmer.

That valley was where the majority of the battle was to take place; as the crawlers and other monsters tried to ascend to the heights of the plateau, they would be held in check by Augustus's legionaries, who would use their shield walls to batter back the monsters and jab them with their spears. From the machine gun nests, gunners would rain a hail of bullets on the charging horde.

Dragons, as always, would be the main concern, and they would be here by the hundreds. That was what the railgun was for. Mach 10 rounds would be fired from the center of the plateau, disintegrating any dragon that showed itself in the open air. The railgun would cover the machine gunners. Being in the center of the plateau gave the railgun the widest range possible – the turret and barrel could be turned in any direction needed.

The railgun's main weakness was that it would be far away from the main bulk of the army, exposed in the center of the plateau where it could be overwhelmed on all sides, either from the ground or the air. To mitigate this, the Reapers were driving sharpened stakes, about twelve feet long, deep into the xenofungus, which proved to be a pliable surface. Together with the stakes, a force of two hundred Reapers would be guarding the gun at all times from both ground and air incursions. If the railgun itself were ever attacked from the air, the turret could be turned to meet that threat.

The stakes, the constant guard of men and Recons, and the railgun itself would hopefully be enough to protect the railgun from a determined attack. Since the eastern side of the plateau would be the most heavily defended, that meant the railgun could only be attacked from the north, the south, or west. The *Radaskim* would have to wrap around the western side of the plateau, giving the railgun's defenders enough time to prepare for the attack. Hopefully.

Carin, Augustus, Char, and Marcus had been responsible for most of the battle plan. It seemed like a good plan, but we were counting on Askala throwing the full weight of her force at the eastern line. The *Radaskim* seemed to rely on overwhelming numbers more than anything else. We weren't sure how many there were going to be, but we expected there to be far more *Radaskim* than we had ever seen. This battle would be impossible to win, in the long run; even without the slightest strategy on the part of the *Radaskim*, their numbers, their big monsters such as the Behemoths, and their dragons would wear us down eventually.

I'd consider it a success if our side managed to last three days.

The only purpose of the army, and this battle, was to buy us enough time to reach Ragnarok Crater and deal the death blow to Askala. I had no idea if we could do that in two to three days. It *seemed* like it should be a good enough time.

It was scary to think about how much of our plan was based on assumptions – but assumptions were all we had.

***

We arrived at the Xenolith before midmorning, landing on the padded surface of the fungus not far from the entrance of tangled roots. I looked up at the massive Xenolith; even after seeing it more than a few times, it never ceased to amaze me. It stood hundreds of feet tall, and gave off a silvery aura in the midmorning light. Its entire gnarled trunk was composed of countless vines, each one as thick as a tree, and its spread at the top fell down in countless fronds that provided shade to the entire area surrounding it.

This part of the Great Blight was comparatively bare – endless xenofungal plains stretched in every direction, except for the few odd hills that rose above the horizon. Even though this Xenolith was plain for all to see, somehow the *Elekai* had managed to keep it hidden from Askala. Or, I thought, maybe it *wasn't* hidden; after all, a battle had been fought here just days ago. Maybe Askala was so focused on the army in the west that this place wasn't a priority. Sooner or later, she would attack it.

We approached the large roots, Samuel and Lauren pulling Michael on the gurney. It wheeled surprisingly well on the xenofungus. Michael's eyes were closed, and he lay on his back and was kept in place only by Ruth and Makara holding him and making sure he didn't fall.

I focused my attention on the twisted roots that were the door into the Xenolith. At my touch, they unraveled and revealed the glowing spiral tunnel within.

We followed it down in silence, the gurney's wheels squeaking. It was a few minutes before we reached the massive entry cavern, glowing and glittering. The ichor lake spread before us, its surface as smooth as glass.

This was Lauren's first time here. She stepped away from her husband toward the lake, staring at it with wide-eyed wonder. Even though I'd seen it quite a few times, it *still* had the ability to awe me.

Neither Askal nor Quietus was here to greet us. I watched the lake, expecting one of them to emerge from the surface. But it was eerily silent.

We stood there for a moment, waiting. It was hard not to be solemn in this place.

Lauren was the first to speak, turning to me.

"What now?"

We were here for three reasons – to screen everyone for writhes, to heal Michael, and to finalize plans with the *Elekai*, getting them to the battlefield as quickly as possible. I thought about which of these was the most important.

"I guess we can screen everyone first," I said. "That will probably be easiest."

It would be easiest, supposing no one was infected. I didn't think anyone else was – surely, Askala would have used them against the rest of us by now – but it paid to be careful.

"How's this going to work, Alex?" Makara asked.

"First, we need to enter the pool, one at a time. I think that's the easiest way to do this. After everyone's been screened, we can put Michael in the ichor."

"Are you sure it will heal him?" Lauren asked.

I didn't want to tell her that I wasn't one hundred percent sure.

"It healed Anna," I said. "Hopefully, it will do the same for Michael."

Lauren didn't like that answer, but there was nothing I could do about that.

"What *is* this stuff, exactly?" Lauren asked.

"The ichor is like life for the *Elekai*," I said. "It heals. It nurtures. It transmits thoughts and intent, and probably does a hundred other things that I don't know about. Somehow, it gives me power, too, which is why we're here in the first place."

It was a hard question to answer, because even *I* didn't know enough, and I was *Elekim*.

I strode forward and entered the warm liquid, walking until I was waist deep. As the ichor soaked through my clothes and made contact with my skin, I felt my eyes warm. I knew then that they had whitened. This was something I could control, but I allowed my eyes to change this time.

I turned to face the shore. Everyone's eyes widened a bit – no matter how often they saw me with white eyes, some part of them would always be shocked by it.

"Alright," I said. "Who's first?"

Unsurprisingly, no one took me up on it. After a moment, Anna stepped forward.

"I'll do it."

As she entered the ichor, I was actually glad she was first. I would have been extremely surprised if she was infected, because at Bunker 84 she would have sided with Michael.

She held my hands, and I looked into her green eyes. Unlike the others, she didn't seem nervous to look at me. She had accepted it.

"Alright," I said. "This shouldn't take long."

I closed my eyes, focusing on Anna's mind.

To my surprise, there was a connection. I felt a surge of fear, but nothing bad happened. I still stood in the ichor, holding Anna's hands. I opened my eyes, looking at her. I felt surprise and fear clouding her thoughts.

And in a moment, I realized the truth.

You're Elekai...

She looked at me. From the widening of her eyes, I could see she had read my thought.

That's how I was able to find you, she said, in realization. *It all makes sense, now.*

You didn't know?

She shook her head. I imagined how our conversation must have looked from the shoreline – the others would just see Anna and me staring at each other.

"You guys alright?" Makara asked.

"Yeah," I said. "Just a second."

I've been Elekai *all this time,* she said. *How could it have happened?*

You were infected with the Elekai *xenovirus, somehow...*

Nothing was different about me, until you attacked that writhe. Something inside me snapped, made me reach out to you. I didn't understand what it was. Maybe I've always been infected...it just took that crisis to awaken my abilities.

I turned back to the shore. Everyone was looking toward us questioningly.

"Should I tell them, or should you?" I asked.

"Okay," Makara said. "You *really* have to tell us what's going on. You're making me nervous."

"Alright," Anna said, gathering herself. "When Alex attacked the writhe infecting Michael, he would have died. I haven't told this to anyone, yet, because I didn't think it was that important. Somehow, I was able to help him fight it. That probably saved his life. I didn't know what made me able to do that...but now, I do." She looked at everyone on the shoreline for a moment before continuing. "I don't know how, or why, but I am *Elekai*...just like Alex."

Everyone looked at her in shock. Whatever they had expected her to say, it wasn't *this*.

"You're *Elekai?*" Makara asked. "How..."

"I was infected with it, somehow, at some point. I didn't realize it. Not until now. But when I saw Alex fall to the floor, after fighting the writhe..." Anna shook her head. "Something inside me must have snapped. I was able to go to that dark place with him. All

I wanted was to save him from Askala." She paused. "Now, I know why I was able to do that. I'm *Elekai*."

"It makes sense, actually," Samuel said. Everyone looked at him for further explanation. "They are husband and wife. It might have happened that way."

"Or maybe it was when Anna was healed," Ruth said. "Her rib was fixed by that ichor. Maybe it made her *Elekai* in the process."

That was something I hadn't thought about. No one else, besides Anna, had ever been healed by the ichor. Maybe part of that process involved becoming *Elekai*. The closest equivalent was the Wanderer and Ashton being put into the ichor – it was a way for them to join the collective consciousness of the *Elekai*. Maybe it also imparted the *Elekai* into whomever it healed.

"Maybe that's it," Anna said. "For some reason, that seems more correct."

That was what I thought, too. I looked at Anna again, unbelieving that we had this connection. All along, it was there – there just had to be something to bring it to the fore. For Anna, that was seeing me battle the writhe. Her being *Elekai* meant we could speak to each other with just our thoughts. It meant she could speak with the dragons, and understand everything they said.

It meant that I didn't have to be so alone.

I had so many questions. Would her eyes turn white when she was communicating through her thoughts? So far, it seemed like the answer to that was "no." Her eyes were as green as they ever were.

"This is all interesting," Samuel said, "but we should probably move on."

I knew Samuel was right. All these questions would have to be answered later.

Anna stayed with me in the ichor. I knew, without her even speaking it, that she wanted to help me. In case anyone else had a writhe, she would be that extra layer of protection. I didn't know *how* I knew this was her intent – either I intuited it, or I read it in her thoughts.

"I'll go," Lauren said.

She stepped into the ichor, a bit stiffly, as if afraid it might attack her. She walked until she was standing in front of us.

"Let's just get this over with."

"Shouldn't take long," I said.

I connected my thoughts with Anna's. *You ready?*

Her response was nearly instant. *Yes.*

I was nervous. I knew Lauren probably wasn't infected with a writhe, but the possibility of it was still unsettling. Hesitation would be my worst enemy. So, I reached out, feeling Anna's presence with the action. Somehow, she had managed to join her intent with mine.

Together, we sought a connection inside Lauren's mind, but there was nothing there. After a moment, I let go of the power, when I was sure there was nothing there.

Clear, Anna said.

"Nothing," I said.

Lauren's eyes filled with relief.

"Did you feel anything?" I asked.

She shook her head. "No. Nothing. Was I supposed to?"

"No," Anna said. "If you felt something, that would mean there was something in your mind to connect with. It's a good sign that there was nothing."

"I'm good to go, then?"

I nodded. "Yeah. You're good."

As Lauren headed back to the shore, Anna and I remained in the ichor. We worked our way through everyone else – Samuel volunteered next, followed by Ruth and Julian. Makara, to my surprise, was the very last to volunteer.

As she stood before Anna and me, she seemed very nervous.

"Let's just get this over with."

So, we did. Makara was also clean, and she looked extremely relieved to be going back to the shoreline.

"That's everyone," Anna said.

It *was* everyone – everyone except Char and Marcus, or even Augustus or Carin for that matter. Testing everyone who could be host to a writhe would take far more time than we had. We had tested every person that would be going with me to Ragnarok Crater, and that was what mattered.

I saw everyone's gaze shift past me, so I turned to see Askal entering the chamber from one of the back caverns. It was strange to see a dragon swimming. The massive creature pretty much floated in the ichor, relying on the currents to push him toward us. From time to time, he would give a flap with his large wings to reorient himself in our direction. A moment later, he was before us, floating twenty or so feet away in the lake.

Did you know Anna was Elekai? I asked.

I felt surprise from Askal. *No,* Elekim. *When did you convert her?*

I didn't, I said. *Wait...convert?*

Yes, Askal said. *The* Elekim *has the ability to allow anyone to join the* Elekai, *given that person is willing.*

That was certainly how it had worked with the *Radaskim* dragons, but I couldn't remember converting Anna like that.

Somehow, it happened to Anna differently, I said. *I never did all that.*

Then the Wanderer must have.

The Wanderer? Would he have been able to make Anna Elekai *without her knowing?*

It must have happened during healing, Askal said. *I never realized it, but it makes sense: to have access to the ichor and its healing powers, one must first be* Elekai. *The Wanderer must have converted her, first; only Anna must have been willing to be converted to accept the healing.*

So she had to have known, I said.

I didn't, Anna said, adding her thought. *I know for a fact I didn't. I must have forgotten, for some reason. I don't know why. Maybe...the Wanderer wanted to hide it from me, for some reason. Could he have done that?*

It's...possible, Askal said. *Perhaps Anna accepted only for the purpose of being healed. Perhaps the Wanderer did keep that knowledge, that self-awareness, from her. But that lack of knowing did not change the fact that Anna was* Elekai. *Yet the potential was always within, to be unlocked, should she remember and embrace it in full.*

So she knew about it, and she didn't *know about it? And now she knows again?*

Something like amusement came from the dragon. *It's confusing, I know. But that's the best I can explain it. Even* I *never sensed that she was* Elekai. *For me to have done that, Anna herself would have had to be aware of it.*

It was very confusing, but I guessed that now Anna was aware of the fact that she was *Elekai*, she could embrace its powers and abilities.

Now that I think about it, Anna said, directing her thought to both Askal and me, *I heard the Wanderer's voice while I was being healed. I must have accepted then, but I don't know why I would forget something like that.*

There are many mysteries, Anna, Askal said. *Some even the* Elekai *do not understand. Whatever the case, you are welcome here. Your brothers and sisters will be anxious to meet you.*

Is that why you came here? I asked.

Yes, that is part of what drew me, Askal said. *The other part was to bring you to our council. The dragons are meeting by the Glittering Pool with Quietus and me. We were deliberating how best to divide our forces – whether to aid the army in the east, or to help you in the north. We are much divided on this question, and need your guidance.*

I'll do what I can, I said. *So, the* Elekai *are healed from the previous battle.*

Yes, Elekim...and we are ready to fly at your command.

We still have a problem here...with Michael. He was infected with a writhe.

I then told Askal the entire story, directing my thoughts into his consciousness. Anna, from time to time, would fill in a pertinent detail. Such a telling did not take long – images and feelings communicated far more efficiently than words.

The writhe is a powerful evil indeed, Askal thought. *Anything imbued with the Dark Voice of Askala is powerful. It is clear that Michael needs the cleansing of the ichor, but I would not be surprised if your other friend needed it as well.*

You mean Ruth?

Yes, Elekim. The power of the Elekai *protected you and Anna from the worst of the exposure, but* Radaskim *thought has a poisonous quality. My guess is that Michael was possessed for far longer than Ruth – however, it is necessary that both of them be cleansed in full.*

Askal paused a moment, looking toward the shoreline from where everyone was watching. I looked to see Michael still there on the gurney.

Bring them both to the pool.

I turned to face the shore. "He says that both Michael and Ruth need to come to the pool."

Ruth's face blanched. "Wait. He wants *me* there, too?"

I nodded. "He said you might have traces of the writhe's damage. It's just to be safe."

I felt bad for Ruth; she'd thought that this was over, but I knew Askal was right. It was better to be safe than sorry.

"It shouldn't be that bad," I said.

Ruth said nothing, walking toward the pool. While she entered the ichor, the others helped with carrying Michael off his gurney. It was hard to look at him, completely helpless like that. In fact, as

Samuel and Julian worked together to drag him to the pool, he looked all but dead. No wonder Lauren had tears in her eyes as she watched. She came into the pool, toward where Samuel and Julian were dragging Michael.

Ruth stood next to Anna; Michael now floated on his back next to us. With tears in her eyes, Lauren held her husband's head above the ichor. Samuel and Julian backed away, stepping out of the pool and standing on the shoreline with Makara.

"Let's give them some space," I said.

Lauren looked at me. "His head will go under."

"I know," I said. "Both of them will. It will be scary. I had to watch it happen to Anna. But I promise: he *will* be okay." I turned to Ruth. "You *both* will. I know you're probably scared, but there's nothing to be afraid of."

It was easy for me to say that, because I didn't have to go through it. It was the only way, though, for them to heal.

I turned to face Askal.

What now?

Command the ichor, Elekim, Askal said. *All that the Wanderer could do,* you *can do. You must reach within yourself and find it.*

Find what?

Your power. Your authority. Your ability to heal.

At first, I didn't know what Askal was getting at. The closest I had gotten to doing something like this was converting the *Radaskim*. But if what Askal said was true, then no one could be healed by the ichor until they became *Elekai*.

That meant Michael and Ruth had to become *Elekai*. It made sense. At least, as much sense as it could. The Eternal Song of the *Elekai* had been the key to making the *Radaskim* convert. Would it convert Michael and Ruth as well?

There was nothing to do but try.

Chapter 12

Everyone but Michael, Ruth, and I now stood and watched on the shore. Ruth and I held Michael above the surface, waiting until I was ready to begin the conversion.

"Hold him up," I said to Ruth, who nodded nervously. "There's no reason to be afraid."

"What will happen to me?"

"I really don't know," I said. "Just close your eyes and listen."

"Listen for what?"

"You should hear a song, soon," I said. "After that..."

Ruth looked at me, waiting for me to continue.

"Just close your eyes and listen."

After Ruth had done so, I closed my own eyes and expanded my awareness to seek the Eternal Song, becoming conscious of all life in the cavern – the ichor and its countless life forms, the dragons in the cavern, and even the million upon millions of alien plants sprouting from the fungus. Even the air teemed with life, alien microbes singing in harmony with the consciousness of the *Elekai*.

It was hard to believe that I was *Elekim,* supposedly the leader of all this. The same power the Wanderer possessed was now mine.

When every *Elekai* was in tune with my consciousness, my thoughts turned upward, the direction from which the Eternal Song streamed. At first I heard nothing, but as time drew on, I could hear the harmonized singing flowing from hundreds of stars. I wondered at the sources of this Song – how could there be any singing when the *Elekai* were all but destroyed on every world the

Radaskim had conquered? Apparently, a remnant of these *Elekai* had been left behind...*something* out there was singing.

I remembered that the Wanderer himself had asked if I was willing to become *Elekai,* and that it wasn't realized until I had agreed.

That meant I had to ask both Michael and Ruth that very same question. I turned my attention back to them. Ruth's eyes were still closed, and she still held Michael's head above the surface. I felt as if I were in a dream, and I could feel the power of the Song flowing through me.

Ruth?

Her eyes seemed to focus, if only a little.

Ruth. Can you hear me?

Slowly, she nodded. A connection had been made.

In order to be fully healed, you have to become Elekai. *Being* Elekai *will drive the last vestiges of the writhe from your mind. Do you want to become* Elekai?

Yes.

Every muscle in her body slackened, and she slipped below the surface of the ichor. Everyone on the shore cried out in surprise, but I held up my hand. This had happened to Anna, when she had become *Elekai.* After a moment, Ruth broke the surface, coughing. She opened her eyes and looked at me.

After she'd caught her breath, she spoke to me.

"I heard you speaking in my mind."

"You're *Elekai,* now. You can pull the same stunt on me, if you want."

Her eyes widened. "Seriously? That sounds weird, so maybe I'll hold off on that for now."

I turned my attention to Michael, still full of the power of the Song. I could hear the notes in my mind, voices in a language I couldn't understand. I had no idea if my voice would reach Michael, but surely the song would.

Michael. It's Alex. Can you hear me?

I felt Michael's consciousness stir at my words. He was much less responsive than Ruth. I could *feel* how much damage the writhe had done to his mind, as if whole parts of it had been killed off to protect the rest from its poison. I could only hope that any brokenness could be healed by the ichor.

Alex?

There was a connection. Now, the question has to be asked.

You're in the ichor lake of the Xenolith. I don't know what the writhe, or Askala, did to you. I don't know how much you remember about it. Everyone's okay, though. Makara, Samuel...they're both okay. Lauren is waiting for you. She's here right now. I can bring you back, but you have to become Elekai *before the ichor can heal you. They're worth coming back for, aren't they?*

There was a short pause before Michael answered.

I have one question about becoming Elekai.

What's that? I asked.

Does it mean I get superpowers?

That question was nothing I expected.

I guess...

You guess, or you know? This is very important.

Well, you'll be telepathic with other Elekai, *including the dragons, and it will make you immune to writhes and the* Radaskim *xenovirus.*

Sounds pretty sweet, he said. *Yeah. Make me* Elekai.

And with that decision, he was pulled into the ichor. The surrounding liquid frothed and bubbled, becoming murky. I heard Lauren cry out from the shore, but she was restrained by Samuel from going in. Michael *was* under there a lot longer than Ruth had been, but the extent of his infection was deeper. It would take longer for him to cleanse.

At last, he broke the surface, sucking in a deep breath. Lauren ran into the ichor and threw herself on him. Michael barely had time to react. They both fell into the ichor before pulling themselves up.

"Easy there," Michael said.

"Are you alright?"

"Yeah, fine." He frowned. "Only, there's a blank space starting from when we got to the control room, up until here. What the hell happened?"

"I'll explain it all later," Lauren said. "I'm just glad you're alright."

They parted, and Michael faced the rest of us, a wide smile splitting his face. He looked right at me.

"Where are my superpowers?"

"Try them out," I said.

"How?" he asked.

"It works like thinking," I said. "Just *think* at someone, and it should work. You can try it on me, or even Anna or Ruth, if you prefer."

He frowned. "I thought *all* of us were *Elekai*."

"I'm next in line," Julian said. *"Elekai* me, Alex."

Actually, making everyone *Elekai* would be a good idea. We'd all have immunity to the *Radaskim* xenovirus, which would be useful if we were going to Ragnarok Crater. We would also be able to communicate without speaking a word. And talking with and riding dragons would be useful skills as well.

Michael narrowed his eyes at Ruth, focusing intensely.

"Did you get that?" he asked.

She rolled her eyes. "Unfortunately, yeah."

"What did he say?" I asked.

"That he *really* had to pee."

"Seriously?" Lauren asked.

"Don't profane the pool," I said. "This is a holy place."

Michael raised an eyebrow. "Well, I'll profane somewhere else, then."

"Seriously, though," Makara said, taking up Julian's idea, "we should *all* become *Elekai*. If we're all going to Ragnarok Crater, we'll need the protection. It just takes the right strain of the xenovirus to infect us, and yes, the telepathy thing would be very useful." She looked at me. "Make us all *Elekai*, Alex. I mean...if everyone else is willing."

"I know I am," Samuel said. "The advantages are too useful to ignore."

"I think I'll take a pass," Lauren said. "I definitely won't be going to Ragnarok Crater. I can see why you guys would want it...but it's just not for me."

So we had Julian, Makara, and Samuel. Together, they entered the ichor. I closed my eyes, tuning my consciousness to the Eternal Song above. Now, filled with its power, I directed that energy not just at one of them, but all three of them.

And one by one, I felt acceptance from each of them.

They sank below the surface, and were only there a moment before resurfacing.

It was time to see if it had worked. I directed my thoughts toward all three of them.

Can you all hear me?

Yeah, Makara thought. She frowned. *This is weird.*

Having regrets? Julian asked.

No. It'll take some getting used to.

I think the telepathy only works when you're touching someone, I said. *Sometimes, it works without it, under great need.*

Whatever the case, Samuel said, *things will be very different now.*

"You guys care to speak?" Lauren asked. "You know, for the non-*Elekai* around here."

"Sorry," I said. "Michael's awake, so the only thing left is to go to the dragons' council."

"The what?" Makara asked.

"The dragons are meeting in the back to coordinate battle plans," I said. "They need our input."

I turned to face Askal. This entire time, he had been waiting patiently for us to follow him.

Welcome to the Elekai, he said to everyone. *Are you ready to follow?*

Yeah, I said. *Lead the way.*

With that, Askal fluttered his wings, reoriented his large frame in the direction of the back caverns. The current pushed him away from the shore, and the rest of us followed in his wake.

***

Askal led us to the final cavern, which was the largest of all. All the dragons were gathered on the far shoreline, which formed a sort of lagoon surrounding the ichor. Within that lagoon, the ichor seemed to glow a little more brightly. I remembered what Askal had called it: the Glittering Pool.

There were a few dozen dragons waiting. The *Elekai* and former *Radaskim* were mixed; they were all equals among each other. Quietus was the easiest to pick out, mostly due to her size. The pink shimmer of the pool reflected off her dark scales, and her white eyes glowed brightly as they watched our approach. Another dragon sat next to her with gray scales – I remembered her name was Mordium.

As we left the ichor of the Glittering Pool and walked on the shore, the dragons watched us with silent eyes. Askal plodded past us on all fours, joining the line of *Elekai* dragons, and turning to face outward, taking care to make sure his tail didn't hit any of the other dragons.

Not so much as a sound came from the line, all fifty or so of them. They were waiting for me to speak.

When I did, I made sure to include everyone else in the interaction.

We have some new Elekai, I said.

The dragons stirred at that announcement, several fluttering their massive wings, snorting, or stomping their feet on the padded fungal surface. None of them spoke, which was probably for the best since fifty dragons trying to communicate with us at the same time might have been a bit overwhelming.

When the commotion ebbed, Quietus got right to the point.

When do we fly, Elekim?

As soon as we can, I said. *The battle will draw most of the* Radaskim *to the plateau. Once that happens, that's when we'll attack.*

We dragons were deliberating on what would be best, Quietus said, *only we could not come to an agreement. You would have us all attack the plateau?*

Is that a bad decision?

Perhaps, Quietus said. *Perhaps not. It is my belief that you are overly optimistic about how much Askala will empty Ragnarok Crater.*

I frowned. *You think she'll leave a lot of defenders there?*

Most assuredly, Elekim. *Yet sending a large force of dragons to fight is too brazen. Such openness will arouse Askala's suspicions.*

So, if I send dragons there, she'll be overly cautious. If I do nothing, then there will still be enough Radaskim *there to make it difficult to get inside the Crater.* I shook my head. *What am I supposed to do?*

She stared at me for a long while before answering. *There is a third option. I will go to Ragnarok Crater alone,* Elekim. *I can make sure Askala empties the Crater of her army, and distract her when you draw close. She will believe me. I can convince her that I am on her side, and in so doing, she will let me in.*

That sounds dangerous. You're too valuable to risk like that.

But Quietus saw right through my trepidation.

I care not for that, Elekim. *Allow me to go, and Askala will let me deep into her counsel. I can convince her to commit her entire force to the plateau and leave not a fraction behind. I can convince her of your power, how your great weapons and your soldiers can destroy the paltry force Askala will commit.*

Paltry?

A lie. The force she is sending is by no means paltry – it will surely destroy your army in mere days, if not faster. Even so, I can play on Askala's fears. She has always been overly cautious, and I will remind her of this. I can convince her to empty the Crater. Quietus paused, staring at me with her white eyes. *You will never reach her,* Elekim...*you will never reach her, unless you allow this.*

It seems risky, I said. *Wouldn't Askala expect you to betray her? Won't she sense that you are* Elekai?

Perhaps, but I believe I can keep my nature hidden. Besides...it is a necessary risk. I know how she thinks.

I still felt that it was too dangerous, but Quietus had a point. She had been close to Askala, and the Dark Xenomind might welcome Quietus's return. I was worried, though, about another option: would returning to Askala lead Quietus to betray us? She could give up our entire plan to Askala in a heartbeat.

I kept this thought hidden. To doubt Quietus's loyalty was to doubt the power of the Eternal Song she had listened to, to doubt the power of the *Elekai* consciousness. Quietus *had* to be fully *Elekai* – the *Elekai* xenovirus was dominant over the *Radaskim*.

All the same, I couldn't help but worry.

I can hide my true allegiance, Quietus said, *and Askala would never know. The Dark Mother is cunning, but so am I.*

And what if she *convinces* you, *Quietus?* I asked. *What will we do then?*

Quietus was silent for a long moment. It was a question that she, apparently, had not considered.

I understand your hesitation, but my loyalty is true. You must decide, in your wisdom, what the best course is. I have been deep in Askala's counsel on many worlds before this. I know what words will persuade her. And with Chaos gone, there will be no one to challenge me. Let me fly, Elekim!

I knew it was a risk. On one hand, having Quietus on the inside would be invaluable. If she could even do *half* of what she said, getting into Ragnarok Crater would be far easier. In fact, telling her "no" might even be the greater risk.

What can you tell us about the Warrens? I asked. *How do we actually* find *Askala?*

Everyone listened intently; this was something we all needed to know.

The Warrens are a great rending in the earth, Quietus said. *Its center point is a fiery abyss, and many tunnels open into the earth. Monsters haunt the twisting, descending passages, guarding the way to Askala's sanctum at the junction of the Two Seas – called the Point of Origin. It is the meeting of the two worlds – the physical world, and the world of the* Radaskim *consciousness. It is here you must go.*

The picture Quietus painted was bleak. It was hard to see how we'd *ever* reach Askala. Not only did we have to survive the journey there, we had to survive the descent.

Magma and monsters, Anna said. *Two of my favorite things.*

Are you sure you can empty the tunnels, Quietus? Makara asked. *Is that even possible?*

I will do what I can, Makara, Quietus said. *I dare not push too much, lest Askala suspect me. With the right words, she might be cajoled to part with a great portion of her host, especially if the humans fight valiantly. Then, it will be easier to persuade her to commit more of the* Radaskim.

I realized then that we had no choice but to trust Quietus. If she truly *wasn't* on our side, then this mission to save humanity would fail. But if I didn't allow her to go to the Crater, we'd probably fail as well.

Quietus was too useful to deny. Only she had the ability to empty the Warrens.

Alright, I thought. *What you've said makes sense. Do what you need to do.*

Quietus gave a slow nod of ascent. In that moment, I realized that Quietus was risking her very self. There was a chance that she would suffer, or even die, for doing this. I felt a pang of guilt; I suspected her of betrayal, but at the same time, if she was on our side, there was a chance she would die trying to do this.

Thank you, I said.

Quietus looked at me for a moment, her white eyes haunted.

Think nothing of it, Elekim. *We all must play our part if this story is to have a happy ending. What is the life of one dragon, in the end, especially one that has brought so much pain and suffering?*

You're healed, now, I said. *You're on our side.*

Yes, Quietus said, *but there are many wrongs that must be atoned for. This is the best way I know,* Elekim, *and that is why I must go. Even if it means my life, then I will not hesitate to sacrifice it. And who knows...perhaps I will find a way to make it through and help you when you arrive.*

I hoped that was the case.

Whatever happens, I said, *thank you for doing this. And please...be cautious.*

I will be cunning, and she will never know my intent, Quietus said. *But now, there is no time to lose. The flight is far, and it will be a long journey – I expect not to reach the Crater until I see the gray of dawn. I will leave now, if* Elekim *permits it.*

Of course. Please be careful.

Quietus stepped away from the surrounding dragons, who looked at her and beat their wings in farewell. I didn't know the significance of that gesture, but it seemed like a sign of respect. Quietus paused just a moment before spreading her wings and pushing from the ground with her powerful legs. A couple of flaps, and she was airborne, flying across the surface of the Glimmering Pool.

As I turned to watch her go, I gave her some final words.

Remember the Song, I said.

I could never forget it, Elekim. *Farewell.*

Quietus had now soared to the glowing ceiling. She paused, hovering in the air. A moment later, a sliver of light appeared above, revealing red sky. She flew through the Dragons' Way before it closed, shutting out the sky.

Now that she was gone, I had no idea if I'd made the right call. Either way, the die was cast, and there was no going back.

What about the rest of the dragons? Anna asked. *Where do they go?*

We are ready to fly to battle, Askal said. *Although it will be some time before we can arrive...many hours. We will leave as soon as we are finished here.*

I nodded. It seemed like we had our plan.

With everyone in agreement, I turned back to Makara.

"That battle will be starting soon," I said. "We should head back."

After saying our farewells to the dragons, we entered the Glimmering Pool and swam back for the entry cavern.

***

We exited the Xenolith and were halfway to the ship when a blur swooped overhead.

A dragon.

"Down!" Makara said.

After everyone had dropped, I looked up at the red, clouded sky. First one, then two, *Radaskim* dragons streaked above us. I knew it couldn't have been Quietus or any of the others. Too many of them were *Radaskim,* and they passed above one after the other, by the dozens, far more than there were on our side.

Well over a hundred dragons had flown overhead by the time the line ended. In the western sky, the first of the dragons that had passed were now small blots in the sky.

"They completely ignored us," Anna said.

Michael grunted. "Your feelings hurt?"

"I wonder why they didn't attack," Makara said.

"They're on one program, and one program only," Samuel said, standing up and looking to the west.

Everyone stood, looking to Samuel for further explanation.

"They're going to the battle, aren't they?" I asked.

Samuel nodded. "Yeah. Let's just hope these guys are the first line, and not just the reinforcements."

We headed for *Perseus* at a run. I gave one last look at the diminishing trail of dragons before boarding the ship.

Once inside, we ran to the bridge. Makara and Anna took up their places, readying the ship to take off.

"Four missed calls from *Orion,*" Makara said.

As Makara fired up the drive, Anna connected to *Orion's* frequency.

"Orion, you copy?" Anna asked.

Jonas's panicked voice responded. "Where the hell have you been? There's *hundreds* of them."

Two thunderous sounds emitted from the speakers.

Crack. Crack.

"What is going on there?" Makara asked.

Jonas yammered on, unintelligible among the loud blasts. Makara nodded at Anna.

"You handle this."

Makara lifted the ship from the ground, spinning it to face west. Out the windshield, I could still see the trail of dragons in the distance.

"Jonas," Anna said. "Calmly explain what's going on. You're breaking up pretty badly.

Crack.

"I'm *not* breaking up," Jonas said. "That's the railgun. The damn thing's louder than..."

Crack. Crack.

"Jonas. *Explain.*"

"They started attacking thirty minutes ago. We need you *here.*"

"We're on our way," Makara said.

"Not until we drop my wife off," Michael said. "I'll be fighting, but I'll be damned if she is."

"That'll add two hours to our travel time," Makara said. "We can't allow that."

"This is non-negotiable," Michael said. "We have a daughter, Makara. If both of us die in the battle...one of us will need to stay at 84."

Before Makara could respond, I cut in.

"Maybe we can make this work," I said. "Anna and I can take Lauren to 84. We can drop everyone else off."

Makara paused, considering that. "I don't like us getting split up."

"Taking Lauren to 84 is necessary, anyway," I said. "We need someone to pull the trigger on the nukes if it comes to that."

"Alright, I see you have a point," Makara said. "But I don't want those nukes going off until every option has been exhausted."

"I'll be there to do it, if we have to," Lauren said.

"Quietus said it will be a while before she reaches Ragnarok Crater," Makara said. "That means we can't attack it until she's done her work. We have to last at least a day in the battle before we can head there. Until then, everyone helps with the fighting."

We entered the clouds. As we raced across the sky, I knew only time would tell what the battlefield would be like.

Chapter 13

"Descending," Makara said. "Stand by. This might get a little rough."

I looked out the windshield from my spot in the jump seat. Red clouds completely obscured the sky. Makara dipped *Perseus's* nose down, and when we broke through, it was into a vision of Hell.

The entire ground was a single, teeming mass of movement. It seemed to...*slither*...from east to west in an unending tide, breaking against the steep eastern slope of the plateau, an island in a roiling sea. The tens of thousands of monsters on the ground seemed to move as a single entity. And above, swirling by the *hundreds,* were the xenodragons. More yet joined the fray from the east. This swarm was at least five times bigger than the one we'd seen in Los Angeles, and perhaps even larger, especially as more monsters reinforced from the east.

The plateau, by contrast, was bare. A thick line of soldiers manned its eastern flank, defending it from the coming storm. I couldn't even imagine what was going through those soldiers' minds.

Situated in the center of the plateau was the railgun, pointing to the east. A streak of fire shot from its long barrel, almost instantly connecting with an unsuspecting dragon. The force of the projectile pushed the dragon upward, sending a purple spray of blood out the dragon's back. It spiraled to the ground below, just as a thunderous crack and boom resounded, audible even inside the bridge. The ship's hull vibrated.

"Damn," Julian said.

"We can't come in from the east," Makara said. "It's too thick."

The railgun shot again, blasting another dragon from the sky.

"Go around," Anna said. "Come in from the west."

"Yeah, on it."

Makara changed the ship's trajectory, sticking to the periphery of the battle.

Jonas's voice left the speakers.

"Makara, that railgun will tear you to shreds. It's completely automated and might mistake you for a dragon."

"We're moving," Makara said. "We'll be on the ground soon. From the west side."

"We need everybody down here. The men could use your encouragement."

"Where's the Emperor?"

"On the frontlines, with his men," Jonas said. "Same as Carin."

"I didn't ask about that scumbag. Just tell Augustus we'll be there soon."

Before Jonas could even confirm that order, Makara switched the channel off.

We descended toward the plateau's western side. The mood on board became tense. I could see the railgun firing another shot, not too far away. Yet another a stream of fire belched from its barrel.

At last, *Perseus* touched down next to *Orion*. Everyone made for the armory, where Samuel doled out its stock of rifles, handguns, grenades, and hundreds of rounds of ammunition, all of which everyone stuffed into their packs. Fully loaded magazines clicked into place. Once everyone was armed to the teeth, he shut the armory door.

When we had all gathered in the wardroom. Samuel faced us all. Anna joined me.

"Whatever happens out there," Samuel said. "We *will* make it through, believe me. I know what we saw out there might seem impossible to deal with. We just have to hold on, for as long as we can. Let's give them hell."

Makara walked to the door. "Alright. Let's go kill some crawlers."

She pressed the exit button, opening the door to the plateau. Anna and I watched as everyone walked out.

Michael was the last to go. He held Lauren, kissing her on the lips.

"Don't die," Lauren said, after they had parted.

"I won't. Tell Callie I love her."

"Don't talk like that," Lauren said. "I thought you were coming back."

"I am," Michael said. "Still...tell Callie I love her. That I always will."

"Go, Michael," Lauren said, tears in her eyes.

Michael adjusted his rifle strap, looking at Lauren a moment longer before walking off the boarding ramp. He didn't look back as the door shut behind him.

Lauren turned to us, wiping the tears from her eyes. "Let's get moving. We can't hang around here any longer."

We returned to the bridge, Anna taking up the controls. The engine had merely idled while we waited. With a pull of the control stick, Anna lifted *Perseus* into the air.

In front of the ship, I could see my friends running to the frontlines – Makara, Samuel, Michael, Ruth, and Julian.

I could only hope they were still standing by the time I got back.

***

We were making good speed north when the first dragon attacked. A whoosh of wind, followed by a piercing wail, shook the frame of the ship.

Anna angled the ship into a dive. "It's to starboard."

"Two more aft," I said, looking at the LCD. "Make that three chasing us."

Anna increased the thrust, pushing me back into my seat. Lauren gritted her teeth against all the twists and turns.

A dragon appeared from the sky above, dead ahead. It went into a dive.

Anna mashed the control stick and two missiles streaked outward, hissing in the air. Anna swerved to port just as the explosion crackled and boomed, shaking the bridge in a fiery explosion of light.

Ahead, no dragons threatened us from outside the windshield, and the safety of the clouds was near.

"Those dragons are still riding our ass," Anna said.

"They're so *fast*," Lauren said.

"Yeah," Anna said. "They *do* seem faster."

"It's the evolution," I said. "They're stronger."

The entire ship jerked from back to front, the motion sending the ship into a slight spin. Anna steadied the ship's course, giving it more thrust. The ship pitched again, violently, pointing the nose downward at the xenofungal plain below. Lauren screamed as we fell forward in our seats, restrained only by our seatbelts.

"Let me try something," Anna said. "Hold on."

She angled the ship even *further* down, at almost a forty-five degree angle. Lauren continued to scream as butterflies flew in my stomach. It was astounding how quickly the ground rose to meet us. The ground was close enough for me to see individual xenotrees and crawlers.

There were but a few seconds until we crashed.

"*Anna!*"

At last, she pulled the control stick back. The ship's hull gave a great groan, as if it would rend in two. The ground was so near we must have been no more than thirty feet above it. Several of the crawlers were even trying to *jump* at us.

By the time we leveled out, I glanced at the LCD. The two dragons exited their dive, wings outspread. They had no problem keeping up with us, despite Anna's gymnastics.

"Shit…" Anna said.

"Do something!" Lauren screamed.

"I'm trying! And *you're* not helping."

Anna swerved to the right, still skirting the ground. Hills, boulders, and dips in the terrain changed so quickly that it seemed impossible that Anna could react in time. I closed my eyes, knowing death was a possibility with every passing second. We zoomed over a hill filled with xenotrees, dipping over it as quickly as we'd gone above it. The LCD showed the trees ripping to shreds in our wake.

The dash read 168 mph.

"Anna…" I managed. "You have to end this."

Gritting her teeth, she lifted us from the ground. The two dragons followed as if they were on leashes.

"I can't lose them," she said. "Anytime I pick up some speed, they cut me off and slow me down."

Ahead, a flock of dragons swarmed toward the frontlines. Three of these dragons peeled off and headed in our direction.

"They're herding us over there," Anna said.

She turned to starboard, only to see two dragons blocking the way out. She angled upward, back for the clouds. Again, a dragon bashed the ship's stern, making the ship lurch. In the crimson sky above, yet two more dragons went into a dive.

"We're through," Lauren said.

Jonas's voice escaped from the dash.

"Anna. To port!"

"That'll throw me right into the dragons!"

"If you want to get out alive, you better do as I say. Now *do it!*"

After a slight hesitation, Anna swerved left, directly toward a massive dragon gunning right for us.

"Time to play chicken," she said.

"You can't play chicken with something that doesn't care if it dies," Lauren said.

"Jonas!"

"Hang in there....any second now."

All we *had* were seconds. The dragon neared, neck outstretched and jaw agape. It let out an unholy roar. I closed my eyes and screamed.

When I opened them, a massive geyser of purple blood gushed from the dragon's side. It shrieked as it spiraled to the ground. Anna lifted the ship just enough to pass over its falling form. The air crackled with the energy of the projectile that had obliterated the monster.

In the LCD, *more* dragons erupted in bursts of organic matter and chips of bone, misting the air with purple blood. Another dragon's head simply disappeared, its neck writhing like a worm as it plummeted to the ground. Several more *cracks* resounded in the air.

The railgun had opened an escape path, and Anna veered the ship upward, at last gaining the speed necessary to outfly the dragons. As we ascended, several trailing dragons were shot down. Ripping sounds emanated long after the projectiles had hit. Realizing we were going to escape, the remaining dragons turned to rejoin the main host assaulting the plateau.

We sailed upward, none of us speaking. Anna didn't slow down, even as we raced above the clouds.

We had escaped with our lives, and we had Carin and his railgun to thank.

***

The rest of the journey was made mostly in silence, and it wasn't long before we began our descent. Anna alerted control of our arrival, and soon enough, we were descending through the open hangar door and settling on the floor. Word of our arrival had spread quickly – people stood on the periphery of the hangar, staring up at us.

As we walked Lauren to the blast door, we made our farewells.

"Please be safe," Lauren said, pressing the exit button. "Don't do anything stupid. Make sure Michael doesn't do anything stupid, either. We've come too far for anyone to die now."

"We'll be careful," I said.

When Lauren left, we returned to the bridge and immediately lifted off. We had to return to the battlefield as soon as possible.

During the flight south, Anna and I were quiet. I stared out the windshield, thinking mostly about Quietus. It had been about four hours since we left the Xenolith, and it would be quite a few hours more before Quietus even arrived at Ragnarok Crater. Considering how long she would have to speak to Askala to convince her, the clock was running against us.

And these dragons definitely seemed to be flying faster. What changes had the new strains made to the crawlers, or the Behemoths, or even other forms of xenolife that were surely attacking us? I thought of the three-headed Hydra we fought in Bunker One, and that strange, creepy monster we found in the *Elekai* forest underneath the Xenolith – the one that had attacked the Wanderer.

We would only find out what we were up against in due time.

***

We landed on the other side of *Orion,* near the railgun, within the circle of stakes the Reapers had built. No dragons had intercepted us during our descent, seeming to be concentrating mostly on attacking the front lines.

Anna called Makara's channel. At first, there appeared to be an answer, but the only thing that exited the speakers were terrible sounds – screams, inhuman wails, high shrieks, and gunshots. Outside the ship, the railgun gave a deafening crack, followed by a deep boom.

"We have to go after them," I said. "I'm not waiting here while Makara and the rest are in danger."

"Let's go, then."

We headed for the armory. We slid the door open and filled our packs with ammo. I grabbed some 9 mm rounds for my Beretta, and 5.56 mm rounds for my AR-15. I hastily loaded the magazines for each weapon, throwing the rest of the ammo boxes in my pack. Meanwhile, Anna armed herself with her own assault rifle – she preferred to use her katana, but firing at long range would be a necessity out there. With just the two of us, we needed all the firepower we could carry.

We entered the wardroom and stood before the blast door. Anna looked at me.

"Ready?"

Before we stepped out, I kissed her on the lips. She seemed surprised by the move.

"Let's kill as many of these freaks as we can."

Locked and loaded, we stepped outside to face whatever was to come.

Chapter 14

When I hit the ground, the stench of blood, rot, and God knows what else assaulted my nostrils. The plateau appeared empty beyond the stakes implanted in the xenofungus – empty to the frontlines, perhaps half a mile away.

On our right, the railgun fired again, deafeningly loud, the sound like a colossal whip. The wind blew from the east, carrying with it the reek of thousands upon thousands of monsters.

Men stood at the railgun's perimeter, their rifles pointed outward. We'd have to run across the empty expanse of the plateau to reach the frontlines, where Makara and the others had gone.

Anna and I weaved between two of the stakes and looked across the plateau. Nothing moved in any direction, so we set out at a quick run, toward a small rise a few hundred feet away. The shorter the amount of time we were exposed on the open terrain, the better.

We reached the rise, not slowing our pace as we raced to the top. I felt my heart beat wildly, but I only had to push myself long enough to reach the battle. Once we crested the top, we saw two crawlers engorging themselves on the flesh of a fallen soldier. These things were covered in thick chitin, from their angular heads to the tips of their scorpion tails, and were far more armored than any crawler we'd ever encountered. Three glowing eyes shone through their armored shells, one on each side of their heads, and one in the center.

Upon seeing them, Anna and I dropped to the ground, working ourselves back so the hill would obscure us. Unfortunately, both creatures caught wind of us, somehow. Their heads turned in our direction, and they let out shrill shrieks as they charged up the hill.

Adrenaline coursed through my veins as I jumped up, raising my rifle to my shoulder with surprising alacrity. I fired several bursts into the lead crawler, and was soon joined by Anna. Our bullets ricocheted off their chitin, sending showers of sparks to the xenofungal surface. Both crawlers approached at a scuttling run, and our bullets merely glanced off their shells. They would do zero damage unless they hit the right spot.

We could do nothing but back away and take careful aim for their heads and eyes – which was nearly impossible to do considering their speed. The crawlers were now dashing up the hill, and by some stroke of luck, I got a few key hits on the left crawler, in the lower neck. It stopped in its tracks to shake its head, temporarily immobilized. The crawler on the right surged ahead. As it neared, Anna lowered her gun, letting it hang by the strap as she unsheathed her katana.

"Cover me."

The lead crawler's tail arced in the air. The spike jutting from the tip of its tail swirled, rising high over its body. The tail struck back and forth like a scorpion's.

"Back!" I said.

The crawler screamed, charging right for Anna. I fired at the creature, somehow hitting its tiny head. The crawler hissed and changed trajectory, scuttling right for me. Its spike arched back, readying to strike.

Anna intercepted the monster, blade flashing.

I ran forward to hold Anna back, but she only charged for the crawler, closing the distance. The creature drew itself to its full height, at least twenty feet tall – a fair bit larger than the crawlers we'd fought before. The tail swiped around its body, overshooting

Anna by inches, who now stood frighteningly close to the monster. There was nothing I could do but take careful aim above Anna's head and fire into the creature's exposed underbelly.

When my shots connected, the crawler shrieked, but still focused on stabbing Anna with its tail. She lifted her blade, slashing the creature's belly from top to bottom. The crawler screamed as it toppled forward. Anna thrust her katana deep into the creature's gut, withdrawing a blade coated with purple blood. Blackened entrails spewed from the fissure, covering Anna from head to toe in sickening filth. As the creature fell, Anna backed away. The crawler's tail convulsed, wrapping Anna in a viselike grip, constricting. Her arms were lifted above her body, her right hand still wielding her katana. She allowed the katana's blade to rotate downward, grabbing the hilt with both hands.

I ran forward as the tail continued to constrict her, but Anna stabbed into the tail, twisting the blade. A surge of purple ooze gushed upward, splattering her face. The tail's grip loosened slightly, allowing Anna to suck in several deep breaths.

I reached the crawler's tail, withdrawing my Beretta and unloading the entire magazine of fifteen rounds into the open wound. By the seventh bullet, the tail had fully loosened, allowing Anna to crawl free. She was covered head to toe in purple slime. All the same, she screamed as she went back for the attack, stepping past the tail and slashing again and again at the crawler's exposed underbelly. With each strike, the creature convulsed in pain, until it was lying on its side, spindly legs quivering.

With a final scream, Anna brought the blade down on the crawler's thin neck, hacking again and again until the head snapped off. She dodged as the creature slumped onto the ground, finally dead.

She panted as she tried to catch her breath. No part of her body was untouched by the purple slime except the white of her eyes and the blazing green of her irises. She flicked the blade, though it did little to rid it of the slime.

That was when the second creature, the one I'd shot earlier, came charging around the first crawler's quivering form. The crawler's mouth hung agape, flashing rows of sharp yellow teeth. Anna stood between me and the creature, so I couldn't open fire.

"Anna, get..."

But with a primal scream, she turned and extended her blade. It found the crawler's exposed neck, and in one sweep, the head flew right off. An eruption of purple blood issued from its severed neck, slamming into Anna's abdomen, forcing her onto her back. The second crawler twitched and settled into death.

I ran forward, not believing what I'd just seen.

She turned to me, still catching her breath. "I *really* need a shower."

"Really? You can joke at a time like *this?*"

She shook her head. "We can't get caught out in the open like this. We have to get to the frontlines."

We ran for the eastern end of the plateau. The railgun continued to fire at the dragons flying in the east, ripping them from the sky.

Panting, we reached the outer fringes of the battlefront. We came across a group of legionaries; they stared wide-eyed at Anna, who was an alien-gore fest. One of the men reached into his pack, pulling out a towel. He tossed it to Anna, and she gratefully wiped herself down. There was no way she could get it all, but at least she could get a good deal of it off.

She tossed the towel on the ground. There was no chance the soldier would want it back.

"Where's Makara?" I asked one of the men.

He pointed in the direction of the ridge. "Somewhere over there."

"Let's go," Anna said.

We rushed along the rim of the plateau, past legionaries who were sheltered behind sandbags and wooden stakes driven deep into the oozing fungus. We approached the fortifications lining the eastern rim of the plateau. On the flatlands below the plateau, thousands of crawlers worked their way up the steep slope, and thousands more waited in the wings. That slope would have been nearly impossible for a human to climb, but the xenofungus provided an ideal hold for the crawlers' sharp, pointed limbs.

The air was filled with the screams of man and monster, and it took a lot of bullets to bring down even one of the creatures. Still, crawlers would eventually fall under a barrage of concentrated fire. Carin and Augustus must have had a lot of ammunition stocked up, but even mountains of it would exhaust rather quickly under these conditions. I noticed trucks parked up and down the line, with men running back and forth to resupply the beleaguered troops. Machine gun nests on high points swerved their barrels back and forth, painting the slope with a salvo of bullets. The Reapers' artillery fired from behind the lines, the glowing streaks of mortars whistling after they passed. They ignited in plumes of fire on the plain far below. The crawlers that made it past Carin's gunmen were met with Augustus's legions and their spear wall. The line was spread far too thinly, but it was the only way to cover the entire plateau.

From our height, I glimpsed the southern and northern parts of the plateau, each of which was sparsely manned. If the crawlers concentrated their attack there, they could break through easily, but for now, they hadn't figured that out. Their numbers were so high that no matter where they attacked, they would probably win. It was a question of time more than anything else.

"We need to go up the line," I said, pointing to the north.

Anna nodded her agreement, and we ran along the battle line, keeping our eye to the east. Just fifteen feet to our right stood the back ranks of Augustus's legions, spears pointed outward. As the crawlers pushed against them, the legionaries' spears stabbed mercilessly. Piles of twitching monsters piled in front of the soldiers, forcing other crawlers to focus their attacks elsewhere. Meanwhile, Carin's men fired from the high points into the swarming mass.

We were about halfway across the plateau when a *Radaskim* dragon screamed, diving low. I grabbed Anna and fell to the ground as the creature swooped overhead. It passed, raking its claws on a machine gun nest. The Reapers manning the gun ducked behind the stakes, but the gun itself sailed into the air and over the legionaries, crashing onto the slope below. The dragon was wheeling back around for another attack, when a fountain of purple blood shot from the dragon's side. A second later, a *crack* sounded in the air above. The dragon fell in a haphazard dive, crashing right into the legionaries. The soldiers broke to avoid the crash, but the falling dragon crushed many with its impact.

The dragon's fall created an opening, which the crawlers began to assault. As more legionaries broke, centurions barked orders in Spanish to rally the troops.

"We have to do something," I said. "That line won't hold."

First a few, then dozens, began a rout. Crawlers surged into the hole created by the fleeing soldiers. If the line broke here, it would break everywhere.

I ran forward, in the opposite direction of the wide-eyed, panicked soldiers, whose leathers and spears were bloodied purple and red.

"Turn back!" I yelled. "Turn back!"

Anna joined me in trying to rally the troops. Even if they didn't understand our words, they understood our meaning. Maybe the sight of two teenagers running toward the battle would shame them into doing the same. Thankfully, at least a few men began turning back, forming a line with shields raised, as they had been trained. Most of those in the rout were young – the seasoned campaigners were still in the thick of it.

The veterans yelled at the younger men, urging them to stay and fight.

A centurion with a purple plume in his helmet withdrew a handgun, firing at the ground near several in the rout. Now, the men began to turn back, taking up their spears and shields to join the rest of the ranks. The crawlers pushed against the line, throwing everything they had against it. But the discipline of Augustus's troops had managed to close the breach, pushing back the tide of monsters.

Just then, two more dragons swooped down. I aimed my rifle upward, looking through the scope for a decent shot. As I was about to fire, the railgun ripped the beast from the air in a shower of purple blood. I switched my focus to the other dragon. It had gone into a dive, its talons ripping into the ranks of legionaries. Men's screams filled the air as the dragon slashed them with its talons. The dragon passed overhead, letting out a baleful roar, which revealed the inside of its fetid mouth.

I let out a breath, keeping the scope homed in on that opening. Then, I fired at full automatic, doing my best to eat the rifle's kick.

Some of those bullets must have connected, because the dragon suddenly went limp, its muscles slackening as it plummeted past the battle lines. It crashed between two machine gun nests about fifty feet away.

Seeing that dragon fall inspired the men to keep fighting, to keep pushing back against the crawlers, bashing with their shields and stabbing with their spears. The machine gunners in the nests swept the eastern slope with a storm of bullets. The crawlers fought back viciously, stabbing with their long tails, but their opportunity had mostly passed. By now, the line stood strong and held back the monsters.

Anna and I ran to the leftmost machine gun nest to get a better view. The crawlers seemed to be pulling back.

"They're withdrawing," Anna said.

Some of the men cheered, but I knew this was no victory. Perhaps a thousand crawlers lay dead on the slope, twitching and dead, but thousands more still waited on the plain, regrouping. Dragons wheeled in the sky above like carrion birds. Maybe this was a temporary respite, but at some point, the attack would begin anew.

"They're planning a new attack," I said. "I'm sure of it."

"What kind of attack?"

"I have no idea."

The railgun continued to fire, taking aim at the retreating dragons. Range didn't seem to matter; no matter how far these dragons were, its targeting computer could attain a perfect shot nearly every time. The longer we held out, the better things would go for us. Our only limitation was running out of rounds.

"We could really use the *Elekai* right now," Anna said.

"It'll still be a while before they get here. Even then...it'll be dozens against hundreds."

The dragons descended from the sky into the eastern valley, out of range of the railgun. For the first time since we landed, no more cracks echoed on the plateau, leaving a wake filled only with the shouts of men, the screams of the wounded, and the odd bullet being fired.

Anna raised her radio. "Makara? Makara, you there? Please answer."

I heard Anna's voice echo behind us. I spun around, to see Makara standing, purple blood splattered over her entire body.

"You too, huh?" she said, addressing Anna.

"Makara!" I said. "Where's everyone else?"

"I don't know about Michael. Julian, Samuel, and I...we fought with the rest of them. Char, Marcus, and Ruth were there with us. Michael got separated somewhere in the fighting..."

"We need to find him."

"That's what I was doing," Makara said. "I guess he's not to the south?"

I shook my head. "No. Unless we missed him."

She sighed. "We weren't fighting in that direction, anyway. We were where it was thickest."

She stared off to the east, over the slope and at the xenofungal plain.

"Let's get everyone together, first," Anna said. "Then we can search."

Makara looked at us both. "We need to meet up with Augustus and Black to plan our next move. Maybe I can send one person to search. But first things first. We need to head to the Command Post."

There was no arguing, so we followed Makara up the plateau, passing wounded men and dead crawlers. We came upon a wounded legionary, who had a gaping hole in his chest about the size of a fist. It had likely come from a crawler tail. The wound bled profusely, and there was no hope for him. His pallor was deathly, and the pain must have been horrible.

"*Matame...matame...por favor...*"

"What's he want?" I asked.

Anna paused a moment before answering. She withdrew her blade.

"I don't have to understand Spanish to know that."

With that, she sliced his head off.

Chapter 15

Further up the plateau, we found the rest of the crew, minus Michael, walking toward us. Their faces were dirtied, their ragged camo speckled with red and purple blood. Amazingly, all of them were still on their feet, though their features were strained with exhaustion.

"We need to find Augustus and Carin," Makara said.

"And Michael?" Samuel asked.

Makara shook her head. "Alex and Anna haven't seen him."

"I can go look," Anna said.

Makara pointed in the direction of a small rise, upon which several Recons were parked. "That's Command. Whether you find him, or not...be there in thirty."

Anna nodded and ran off, checking first to the north.

As Makara walked toward Command, the rest of us followed. It wasn't long before we reached it, finding Augustus resplendent in his battle armor and purple cape, barking orders to several of his chief centurions. Carin, meanwhile, stood a ways off, ordering some of his men into a waiting Recon. They climbed in and the Recon screamed off, its serrated tires churning flecks of pink growth beneath its wheels. The vehicle headed in the direction of the railgun, where I could see that several crawlers had skewered themselves on the fortifying stakes.

Carin walked toward us while Augustus gave his final orders to his officers.

"Go," Augustus said. "I want one thousand more men on the northern flank."

The centurions nodded, and left to do as they were told.

Augustus turned to us. "Michael and Anna?"

"Anna's looking for Michael," Makara said. "We were separated during the fighting."

"We're not going to last much longer out here," Char said. "When those things attack again...we're dead."

Augustus raised a quizzical eyebrow. "You don't think I know that?"

"We've blown through half our rounds for the railgun," Carin said. "It'll last until the evening, depending on when they attack again."

"How many rounds are left?" Samuel asked.

"One hundred forty-eight. Considering we shoot them off at about two a minute, give or take, we have enough rounds for about two and a half hours."

"Will it work as effectively at night?" Makara asked.

"No doubt," Carin said. "It can read in infrared."

"They nearly punched through the lines, right in the center," I said.

Augustus's face was unreadable. His eyes focused, as if he were deep in thought.

"I'm expecting them to hit us from every side next time," he said. "The first attack was a test of our strength. Now that they see we won't be easily broken, they'll look for new alternatives. Under a constant assault from all sides, we won't last long."

"Which is why we need to stop it at the source," I said. "After we find Michael, we have to find Askala."

"How long will that take?" Carin asked. "The way it's looking, we won't even last the night."

"The *Elekai* will be here to reinforce, probably by evening," I said. "That should help out a bit."

"There's one of those dragons for every ten they have," Carin said. "A momentary distraction."

"As a last resort," Samuel said, "Lauren is standing by in Bunker 84, ready to launch the nukes."

Carin shook his head. "God help us if it comes to that. Which it probably will."

"Alex is right," Makara said. "Killing Askala is the only long-term solution to this. You guys will have to find a way to hold on until we can do that. Quietus is on her way there, working to empty the Crater and make it easier for us to get inside. Hopefully, by the time we get there, she'll be done. Failing that...we might have to use a nuke or two there as well."

"When are you leaving?" Augustus asked. "Who will command your men?"

"Char and Marcus will stay behind to command the New Angels. I have to see Alex through, to the very end."

"So you all go off while we stay here and die," Carin said. "That's rich."

"Where we're going, we're *guaranteed* to die," Samuel said. "At least you have a chance."

Carin didn't respond to that. He frowned in thought.

"I give us twelve hours, before we're completely broken," he said. "What happens, supposing you win at the Crater?"

"The *Radaskim* are stopped," I said. "I suppose they'll become *Elekai*."

"Nice. So we trade one set of aliens for the other."

"You left out the important part," Makara said. "The second kind don't want to kill you." She turned to Augustus before Carin could respond. "As soon as Anna finds Michael, we're leaving."

I looked in the direction Anna had gone. She was nowhere in sight.

"Might be that you have two people to look for, now," Carin said, smiling. "You better get on it."

At that moment, klaxons began to blare, high, whirring up and down, from the direction of the railgun.

"They're coming at us again," Carin said.

The railgun's turret swiveled toward the north, where a line of ten or so dragons appeared from below the distant ridge. The railgun fired, a hellish whipping crackling the air, a fire trail blazing from its barrel. The central dragon, the forerunner, took the shot right in the chest, sending a spray of purple blood shooting behind.

I realized then what they were doing.

"They're going for the gun!"

"Don't you think I see that?" Carin said, face angry. "I'll be damned if they get anywhere near it." Carin turned to his Reapers. "All Recons by the gun, now! Get every gunner you can from the western line. Give those things hell."

The Reapers kicked into gear. While some scrambled into Recons, others ran west for reinforcements. Still, the dragons flew from the north. If they destroyed the railgun, the army was as good as lost.

Carin turned to Makara. "Get *Perseus* in the air. I'll have my men drop you off."

"We need to find Michael," Makara said.

"Michael isn't worth a bucket of piss right now! We have *dragons,* and they'll kill us all if you don't get moving. They might not just be going for the railgun." He cracked a yellow smile. "If your ship isn't in the air, they might attack it, too. Wouldn't want that, would we?"

Judging by the reddening of her face, Makara saw Carin's point immediately. She glared at him for a moment, but in the end, turned to me. "Go find Anna. The rest of you...come with me."

They headed for one the Reapers' Recons while I ran to the north, in the direction Anna had gone. The dragons had flown halfway across the plateau, and it seemed impossible that they could be fended off in time. Gunmen fired at them from both the ground and Recons. One of the dragons fell, crashing into the xenofungal bed. The railgun cracked again, disintegrating the neck of one of the dragons.

As I neared the western side of the plateau, the roar of the swarm grew louder. The smell of blood and rot permeated the air, turning my stomach. I entered the battle lines, watching the legionaries reform their ranks, spears out. Most of the machine gun nests had been emptied, on orders from Carin to defend the railgun. However, the lack of gunners made the western lines perilously weak. I wondered: was *that* part of Askala's plan? Whether we defended the railgun or the western line, we would be spread too thinly on one of these fronts.

I raced up the line, the piercing wails of Blighters filling the air. I searched all the faces I passed.

"Anna! *Anna!*"

I wasn't far from the northern flank. I ascended a small rise containing an empty machine gun nest. Grim-faced legionaries were lined up along the rim of the plateau, facing the second surge of Blighters. The sea of crawlers pushed up the hill in an endless tide. It was hard to distinguish the crawlers from the ground – their colors melded dizzyingly. Other shapes appeared within the swarm – giant Behemoths, Hydras with reptilian faces and serpentine necks.

Then, a great rumbling shook the earth, knocking me off my feet. As the quaking abated, the entire xenofungal surface of the valley below shook with colossal force.

The Blighters stilled, as if in anticipation. I looked out at the plain, seeing a huge portion of it bulging upward, the fungal surface glowing with an angry, fiery light. A great groaning shook the air, vibrated my bones in a deep, booming bass.

A colossal snap jolted the entire plateau, so loud that the railgun was quiet by comparison. That was when a great worm writhed from the fungus, larger than the largest building I'd ever seen. The crawlers, and even the giant Behemoths, scampered away from this terrible monster. The worm slithered onto the ground, its colossal weight bearing it against the earth, the fungus itself pushing it along. Hundreds of white eyes filled its wide face, and it opened a mouth that could have swallowed an entire building. An unearthly bellow shook the air, deafeningly loud, forcing me to cover my ears. The creature continued to writhe and turn, forcing itself from the ground. Its hundreds, and perhaps even thousands, of legs scuttled madly to move its mass.

As if waking, the host of Blighters came alive, charging again up the hill.

"Alex!"

I turned to see Anna at the base of hill, and a body lying next to her.

Michael.

I ran down the hill as the worm roared again. Crawlers screamed as they crashed against the western line behind me. I remembered Quietus telling me that Askala had worse minions than the *Radaskim* dragons. Now, I knew what she meant. I wondered how such a giant creature could travel all this distance. Perhaps the fungus was layered deep, and there were huge tunnels below the surface.

I reached the bottom of the hill. Michael was completely inert, his eyes closed, and a giant bruise covered his forehead.

"He's breathing," Anna said. "I dragged him all the way here from the northern flank."

"Makara and the rest went to get *Perseus* in the air. We're heading for the Crater."

Anna nodded. "We need to get on that ship."

It would take ages to drag Michael to *Perseus*. By then, the dragons might have destroyed the railgun or even *Orion*.

There had to be another way.

"The medics will have stretchers," I said. "We can use one to carry him to the ship."

We dragged Michael down the line, searching for either a stretcher or a medic. Even in the chaos, the screams, and the roaring of the monstrous worm, we finally came upon two medics, running in the opposite direction.

Anna grabbed one of the men by the arm, bringing them both to a halt.

"You. Put him on."

One of the men answered. "This is for Centurion Ramos."

"No," Anna said, pulling the stretcher to the ground. "I have orders from Augustus himself. Michael gets on the stretcher. *Now.*"

The men looked at each other, but acquiesced. They knew we were close to the Emperor, and didn't want to risk disobeying him; Centurion Ramos would have to wait, and hopefully it wasn't too serious. Together, we lifted Michael on.

"We're heading for the gun," I said. "Let's move."

The four of us each grabbed a handle of the stretcher and ran west across the plateau. Dragons circled above the railgun, but many had broken off to give chase to *Perseus*. Gunners in Recons put up a brave fight, firing on any dragon who got too close to the gun.

But it was not enough. Three dragons in tandem dove for the gun. The railgun shot one of them down, and it crashed to the plateau. Another fell to the concentrated fire of several of the roving Recons.

That left one, and there was no way the gun could dodge this attack.

Dread overtook me as the dragon's talons slammed into the gun barrel, bending it just slightly. But even that much doomed the railgun to never be used again.

"Come on," I said, sensing that we had slowed down. "We have to get there."

The dragon wheeled into the sky above, out of range of the gunners below. The dragons retreated, their mission accomplished. *Perseus* swarmed around them, firing and bringing down one of the trailing dragons.

But it was all too late. The railgun was gone, and without it, this army's time was drawing to a close.

***

We panted as we ran across the plateau, my heart racing at the effort. Even with four people, running and carrying Michael over this distance was a huge strain.

Just when we had closed half the distance to the railgun, several crawlers appeared from the south, somehow having slipped by the southern lines. We couldn't get caught out here in the open.

The crawlers increased their speed, coming right at us.

"*Go!*" I shouted.

Somehow, we made ourselves run even *faster,* and it felt as if my heart would beat out of my chest. As the wooden stakes surrounding the gun neared, the crawlers continued their mad sprint, far faster than we were. The Reapers guarding the gun weren't far, but they were so focused on the dragons that they hadn't seen the crawlers coming toward us.

"*Hey!*"

One of the men turned at my voice, almost miraculously hearing me with the dragons screaming and the guns firing. The man tapped his partner, and pointed in our direction.

I held the handle of the stretcher in one hand, using the other to point to the crawlers in the south. Instead of two crawlers, there were now three, surging ahead across the plateau's flat expanse.

They raised their rifles and opened fire. With luck, those bullets would buy us some time.

We were nearly there. Just thirty more seconds of pain. Thirty more seconds to outpace the crawlers.

Just seconds away, I turned to see the crawlers, about a hundred feet away. They were so *fast*. They'd close that distance in mere seconds. But at last, we wriggled between the stakes and to relative safety. I was the last one through.

We set down the stretcher, after which I turned and raised my rifle. The crawlers stopped at the stakes, far too large to work themselves in between. They screamed in frustration.

As the Reapers continued to fire, Anna once again grabbed the stretcher.

"Leave them," she said. "We need to board *Orion*."

"What about us?" one of the medics said.

"Thank you," Anna said. "We can take it from here."

Anna and I took up the stretcher, much heavier without the medics' assistance. *Orion* sat parked next to the broken railgun. Close up, it was easier to see the damage. The barrel was bent at its end. Several men stared up at it helplessly.

But the railgun's being broken meant we were free to use *Orion*. On its boarding ramp was a flurry of activity, several Reapers carrying the cable that had connected the railgun to *Orion's* fusion drive.

"Let's go," Anna said.

We ran inside the ship, positioning Michael and his stretcher on the bridge. We set him down on the deck, then took up our seats. The priority was getting *Orion* into the air safely as soon as possible.

The ship was already powered on, so all there was to do was lift off.

I set the frequency to *Perseus's* channel.

"*Perseus,* this is *Orion,*" I said. "We have Michael."

"Good," Makara said. "Get in the air, now."

"Copy that, on the ascent." Anna said.

At that moment, the ship elevated from the ground.

"We've got dragons heading that way," Makara said. "Get moving, quick."

"On it," Anna said.

Anna accelerated the ship to avoid being blindsided by dragons, pointing it in the direction of *Perseus*. The dragons themselves swirled around *Perseus* in a cloud.

"Makara!" I said.

"I know," Makara said. "I need you to bail me out here."

"On our way."

Orion took on more speed, closing in on the swarm of dragons tailing *Perseus*.

"Aiming for the stragglers first," Anna said.

Before Makara could respond, a missile streaked out from beneath *Orion*'s hull. A trail of vapor colored the air as the missile homed in on a lagging dragon. The dragon ignited in a giant plume of flame. Several of the dragons scattered from the blast, so only a few were now pursuing *Perseus*.

"Get to the clouds," Anna said. "I'll take care of the rest."

As *Orion* changed trajectory, Anna readied another missile strike.

"How many of those we have left?" I asked

"Four," Anna said.

With that, another missile shot off for the central dragon, obliterating it in an orangey ball of fire. The two remaining dragons fanned out, spreading their wings and wheeling toward us.

Anna swerved to port. As she aimed for the sky, following *Perseus*'s trail, it wasn't long before we had broken the clouds.

"Makara...I think we need to call Lauren," Anna said.

"There was a giant worm," I added, "the size of a skyscraper."

"I know, we saw it from the air," Makara said. "You're right, Anna. It's time we called Lauren. If we do nothing, the entire army will be overwhelmed." Makara paused a moment. "Lauren?"

"Makara?" Lauren asked. "How is everyone? Is Michael...?

"Michael's alright," Makara said. "I need you to do this, quickly. You know why I'm calling."

"What's happened?"

"Use the coordinates we programmed. We'll be overrun otherwise. In the meantime, I'll tell Augustus to pull back."

Next, Augustus's voice broke through the dash.

"Makara..."

"I've already called it," Makara said. "Withdraw your men to the center."

"You've...called it?"

"Yeah. Lauren's working on it."

Augustus didn't argue. He didn't say *anything*, not for a long time. Finally, he gave a sigh, long and tired.

"How long do we have?"

"I can be at the Command Center in ten minutes," Lauren said.

"Make it five," Makara said.

"We have to do what we have to do," Augustus said. "What's important is that all of you got out alive. Now, please...hurry to the Crater. We won't last another day under these conditions."

Anna looked at me. I'm not really sure what her expression conveyed – whether sadness, fear, or a combination of both.

"Augustus..." I said. "Thanks. For everything"

"Take care, Alex. I wish you all the luck in the world."

"I'll need it."

"We all do," Augustus said. "We all do."

I felt a chill at those words.

"Augustus..." Makara said. "Hold on, for as long as you can. I'll...I'll see you on the other side. Wherever that is."

"We'll stay here to the last man. Carin has some ideas to draw this out as long as possible. That's all this was about anyway, right? We'll hold them off for as long as we draw breath. The legions of Nova Roma have never lost a war, and I do not mean to lose one now."

"Good luck, Augustus."

"Likewise, Makara."

"I'll advise you when the nukes are out."

The radio was silent for a long time. The two ships joined above the clouds, far out of sight of the killing below. We headed east toward the darkening sky.

At last, Makara spoke.

"*Orion.*"

"Yeah," Anna said, voice thin. "Go ahead."

The following pause was heavy, almost painful. I knew the words to be spoken before they ever came.

"Set course for Ragnarok Crater."

Anna trembled a bit at the words. "Following your lead, *Perseus.*"

I realized, once we were going full speed, that I could now measure the rest of my life in hours rather than days.

Chapter 16

We'd been traveling ten minutes when Lauren's voice returned.

"Alright," Lauren said. "I'm here."

"Are you in front of the screen?" Samuel asked.

"Yes."

"Password is 'Raine'. With an 'E' at the end."

"Alright," Lauren said, a moment later. "I'm in."

"Head to Nuclear Development. Everything is already programmed. You only have to initiate the launch sequence."

"How?" Lauren asked. "How many are we launching here?"

"Just one," Samuel said. "Silo Six. It's programmed to fire. Just click on 'launch'."

"Samuel..."

"We have to do this, Lauren," Makara said. "Men are dying."

Lauren sighed. "Alright. Initiating."

We waited for what seemed a very long time, when in reality it was probably more like thirty seconds.

"Lauren?" Samuel asked.

"It's not working," she said.

"Go through all the steps," Samuel said.

"I did exactly as you said," Lauren said. "It's showing the silo to be online, but it's still armed. Isn't it supposed to give some indication that it launched? Wouldn't I have heard it?"

"It's old," I said. "It might not be operational."

"Alright," Lauren said. "It's saying system malfunction."

"What is the nature of the malfunction?" Samuel asked.

"I don't know!"

"There should be a dialog box of details."

"It's...indecipherable. 'Process could not be executed, vector error.'"

"Vector error?" Makara asked.

"Something's off about the flight path," Samuel said. "I must have programmed it wrong, so my inputs have conflicted with the desired target."

"Meaning?" Makara asked.

"Lauren can reprogram it to where the system can find its own flight path," Samuel said. "Automatically."

"Why didn't we do that the first time?" I asked.

"I was afraid the system could fail, after so many years and with satellites in a questionable state of functionality. So, yes. I programmed it myself. Apparently, it didn't work out."

"If there's a chance the missile could miss, maybe we shouldn't take the chance," Makara said.

"I agree," I said.

"What do you propose instead?" Samuel asked. "Without some heavy damage to the *Radaskim*, that army won't last much longer. Besides, Augustus has already told his men to pull back." Samuel paused, letting that sink in. "We can't just reset."

Makara sighed. "I don't know. Augustus expects that nuke to fall where it's supposed to. What if it doesn't?"

"If it hits the wrong spot, it hits the wrong spot. We can't do anything about that. The army will be dead either way."

A long pause followed, everyone thinking.

"So, what are we doing?" Lauren asked.

Makara paused a breath. "Do it."

"Alright," Samuel said. "Click on Silo Six's program. Clear the flight path. Then hit auto-program."

"Just a second..."

We waited while Lauren worked. Anna clenched her fist on the control stick, keeping pace with *Orion* nearby.

"Got it," Lauren said. "Launch?"

"Yes," Makara said.

"It just went off," Lauren said. "I heard it."

"I'll let Augustus know," Makara said.

"Lauren," Samuel said. "Good work."

"I guess we'll see about that soon, huh?" She paused. "Michael? Is he there, on the bridge? Put him on."

Anna and I looked at each other. Michael was still knocked out on the floor.

"Uh...he's fine," Anna said. "He just...took a hit to the head."

There was a long, cold silence following that statement.

"I'm sorry...*what? You're only telling me now?*"

"He'll be fine," Anna said. "It doesn't look too severe."

"And how long has he been like this?"

"Not long," Anna said. "Look...we're waiting for him to come around. He's breathing, he's comfortable, and he'll be fine. Alright?"

"No," Lauren said. "Not alright. If you're going to the Crater, Michael needs to be at his full capacity, otherwise..." Lauren paused. "What if he's still knocked out by the time you reach the Crater? I want him here. *Now.*"

"There's no time, Lauren," Makara said. "We have so much riding on this and we can't spare the extra two hours. By then, it might be too late."

"That's my *husband!*" Lauren said. "*I* launched that nuke for you, and now you're just going to send Michael to die?"

And that was when Michael coughed.

Anna and I turned around, seeing him try to lift himself off the floor.

"Whoa, stay there, buddy," I said. "Don't move too quickly. You took a nasty hit to the head."

Michael looked up at me. "Yeah. I might not be Einstein, but I know that."

"Michael?" Lauren said.

"Lauren, he's awake," I said, then asked him, "How you feeling?"

"Like shit, but yeah. I'm here."

"Michael..." Lauren said. "Baby, you alright?"

"Fine, honey. Right as rain."

"No, you're not. I can hear it in your voice."

Michael didn't answer for a moment. "Okay. I *will* be fine. Got a splitting headache, though."

He pointed toward my canteen. I passed it to him, and he took several giant pulls.

"Something knocked you out," Anna said. "I just found you lying there."

Michael lowered the canteen. "I lost sight of the group, somehow. Next thing I know...everything's dark. I think a Behemoth might have gotten me." He paused a moment. "Yeah, I remember now. Big one, too."

"Michael..." Lauren said. "Are you going to be okay to fight? I mean...what if you have a concussion, and after that writhe...maybe going to the Crater isn't the best idea. You have me and Callie here."

"I can't miss this fight," Michael said. "The whole world's depending on us. That's how I'm going to protect you."

"You need to be *here,*" Lauren said.

"I can't back down now," Michael said. "I'll make it back."

"No, you won't! You'll *die* if you go there! Anyone with half a brain knows that, which *you* probably do after that knock to the head."

Michael said nothing.

"Sorry," Lauren said. "I didn't mean that."

Michael looked at me. "Where are we, anyway?"

"We're on our way to Ragnarok Crater. And a nuke is on its way to the battlefield."

"That bad, huh?"

"Michael," Lauren said. "Are you okay? *Really?*"

"Yeah. Just fine."

She sighed. "You're not just saying that to make me feel better?"

"If I could have it any other way, I would," Michael said. "If we fail...no one's getting out of this alive. Honestly, Lauren...I might die. We have to accept that. That's what's going to happen to everyone if we can't do this. I would never forgive myself if I sat by doing nothing when I had the chance to help."

Lauren was quiet, knowing she had lost the battle. It was a long moment before she spoke again.

"I'm just sitting here, watching the screen, waiting for the missile to hit. It's halfway over California, now. You're far enough away, aren't you?"

"Far enough," Michael said. "We're fifty miles out by now."

"Michael...I'm not ready for this. I *can't* let you go. I..."

"I know," Michael said. "We're the only ones standing between Askala and the end of the world." Michael paused. "I don't know why, but I believe we're going to win. I believe we'll be coming back. We've gone through so much...it's not impossible, is it?"

Lauren became quiet. The two ships continued their steady course northeast.

Finally, Lauren gave a long, heavy sigh. "Two minutes, now."

"We're over Nevada," Makara said. "Keep trucking." A moment later, she was speaking to Augustus. "Augustus? Two minutes."

When Augustus answered, it was amidst the screams of dragons and crawlers.

"They're acting strangely," Augustus said. "Like they know it's coming."

"Are your men pulled back?"

"Such as we can," he said. "We're bracing for the impact. Carin says we can hold here. Where are you?"

"Over Nevada."

"If we're still here after, Makara, we'll let you know."

"One minute," Lauren said.

"Take care, Augustus. Thank you...for everything."

"Even if we die," Augustus said, "you must not. Promise me that you'll make it. Promise me we fought this for a reason."

"It wasn't for nothing, Augustus. It was for everything. We'll make it to Ragnarok Crater if it's the last damn thing on Earth I do. I promise you that."

Augustus didn't respond

"Ten seconds," Lauren said.

"You better go," Makara said.

"Goodbye, Makara."

The next moment seemed to stretch for an eternity. At last, on the LCD, a bright light colored the distant clouds, visible even forty miles way. There was no sound – just that light. In time, the colors ebbed, and there was nothing but silence on both bridges as we flew east.

It was ten minutes before the speakers once again crackled with Augustus's voice.

"It hit," he said.

"Are you okay?" Makara asked.

"That...remains to be seen. I can tell you that it was too close. Many of my men were burned. All the same...it killed many of the crawlers. That giant...*thing*...is gone."

Above the clouds, we were so far removed from the carnage. The most we had seen was a miasmic burst on the trailing horizon, coloring the crimson clouds with a brief brilliance. Of the untold destruction the nuke had unleashed, we could know nothing.

Augustus, however, could. It was *all* he could see.

"Can you hold?" Makara asked.

"I'm standing on the edge of the plateau. The xenofungal plain stretches on for miles. The slope is incinerated; flames cover the expanse. A few crawlers are all that remain. In the distance, beyond the impact site, more of the *Radaskim* are replacing the ones the blast killed. We stand here now, to hold the western ridge for when they attack. They *will* come again."

Makara paused, considering her question. "How much longer?"

Augustus hesitated. When he answered, his voice was thick.

"I don't know, Makara. An hour. Maybe two. This is all we have left to give, Carin and I. I haven't even seen Char and Marcus."

At that statement, everyone was struck silent.

"We'll be at the Crater in two hours," Makara said. "You have Lauren's frequency. She knows what to do."

"We've given everything for this," Augustus said. "I will die on this plateau. I see that now. They're coming again. The men stand, but they, too, know they will die."

"Augustus..." Makara said. "Don't give up."

"We won't, Makara. We won't. That's not an option. All we can do is stand until we can't stand anymore." He gave a short, bitter laugh. "That's all anyone can do. Even an Emperor."

"It's not over, yet," Makara said. "Hold on."

Despite Makara's words, it felt as if a curtain was being drawn over the world. We were running from the curtain, but no matter how fast we ran, we couldn't escape the gravity bearing it down.

"Strange," Augustus said.

"What?" I asked.

"The eastern sky is darkening," he said, "but I can see your friends have come."

"The *Elekai?*"

"Yes," Augustus said. "The men will take courage, even if they are only a few."

"It may be what we need," Makara said. "Even if they give you a few more minutes more, that might be enough."

According to the LCD, we were now halfway over Nevada. Every passing minute brought us closer to death.

"Augustus?" Makara asked.

"Yes?"

"Thank you."

Without another word, Augustus cut out.

***

An hour passed. While we were on cruise, Anna took the chance to clean up. Since my condition wasn't half so bad, I remained on the bridge to keep an eye on things.

She didn't take long, returning with clean shirt, jacket, and camo pants.

"Updates?"

"Nothing," I said.

Anna resumed control. We were making better time than expected, but it was hard to be thrilled about that. We were over the northwestern corner of Colorado, deep in Askala's turf. We hadn't heard anything from Augustus. We were completely on our own, and when we dropped through the clouds, there was no telling what would happen.

Then, the fateful words came.

"Prepare for descent," Makara said.

"Copy that," Anna said.

"On my mark," Makara said. "Cut off communications. I have no idea if she can hear us, but they speak using radio waves. Better to be careful."

"Roger that."

Anna, Michael, and I watched out the windshield. The sun was halfway obscured behind the top layer of clouds, coloring it like molten metal. As we ducked below, I watched the reddened sun. I wanted to remember it, because where I was going, there would be no sun.

At last, we entered the thick cloud layer, turbulence shaking the ship. Anna said nothing, though everything about her was tense. I stared out the clouded windshield, unable to see anything through the glass.

"What's the plan?" I asked. "Just...land by the Crater?"

"I'm following Makara," Anna said. "After that...I don't know. I guess it's time to do some walking."

We continued to descend at a steady pace. At long last, the clouds ebbed, revealing the glowing, xenofungal surface below. I peered into the distance, but even with the light from the ground, I couldn't see anything. We were still thirty miles from Ragnarok Crater, much too far to see it clearly, even from up here, although the eastern horizon was red and luminescent. That light had to be coming from the Crater.

Nothing stirred in the air or on the ground. To the south and east spread a thick xenoforest of tangled and interlocking trees, silvery and purple in the dusk. Several Xenoliths rose from their dense depths at regular intervals.

For two minutes we flew in a straight line, not changing our course or speed. I expected dragons to attack at any moment. But the skies remained empty, dark, almost...placid.

But that changed in an instant. A streak of fire zoomed down from the sky, followed by others, in supersonic, crackling trails, igniting on the ground below.

"Get to the surface!" Makara said.

Instantly, we dipped, hurrying to land as quickly as possible. Whether we went to the ground or stayed in the air, it didn't matter. Those meteors would kill us all the same.

It was only a matter of time until...

A jet of fire exploded right on *Perseus's* starboard wing, sending the ship careening. I was paralyzed with horror.

"Makara!" Anna screamed.

The ship spiraled as if it were a toy, a fire consuming *Perseus's* starboard hull. Makara did not answer Anna's call. There was no doubt; *Perseus* was going to crash.

All the same, the spinning stopped, but *Perseus* had slipped into an uncontrolled dive, leaving behind a thick trail of smoke.

"No..." Anna said.

A moment later, something shot from *Perseus's* side. At first, I thought it was a piece of debris. But its flight path was too ordered.

"The escape pod," Michael said. "They made it out."

"Let's hope so," Anna said. "We have to follow it."

Another fiery flash streaked downward, right in front of our windshield. Anna slowed the ship as we sailed through a blinding firestorm. Miraculously, we came out the other end.

As Anna turned the ship toward the burning ground, the escape pod had been lost. There was no sign of a parachute having opened, though a parachute might be hard to pick out in the darkness. As the meteors continued to fall, Anna went into a dive. The fiery surface rushed up to meet us as the falling rocks exploded on the ground.

Anna pulled up at the last second, the G-forces practically crushing. At the same moment, Anna engaged the retrothrusters, slowing us to a near stop in a matter of seconds. We now hovered over an empty spot of fungus that wasn't consumed by flame. I realized that Anna meant to land here.

We descended to the ground, the fires burning brightly outside the windshield. Above, the sky seemed to be clear of further bombardments. Whether these had come from space, or had been shot like artillery from the Crater itself, I had no idea. We had to find *Perseus's* escape pod, but it was hard to imagine it *not* landing somewhere in the flames.

We unstrapped ourselves and ran off the ship, taking the time to refill our canteens, grab some food, and load up on ammo.

I pressed the exit button, and when the door slid open, a wave of heat rushed inside, carrying with it the reek of charred fungal growth. I had to shield my eyes against the brightness of the flames. The sky above was dark, brooding, apocalyptic. We ran down the boarding ramp.

"I think it went down over there," Anna said, pointing to our left.

The three of us ran away from the ship, carrying with us our weapons and packs.

From the sky came one final streak of fire.

"Down!" I yelled.

As we dropped to the ground, the meteor coursed downward, frighteningly fast...

...crashing right into *Orion*.

The outward explosion threw us forward, a wave of heat licking my back. A thunderous boom echoed over the smoldering fires. I lay there a long moment before I even dared to move. I looked at the sky, fearing more stray meteors. But the air was velvet-black and empty.

I then turned to the look at what was left of *Orion*.

Its hull was a smoking ruin, consumed by flame. Whether targeted, or just through horrible luck, *Orion* was gone, along with *Perseus,* which must have crashed somewhere nearby.

It was Michael, Anna, and me, alone in the Great Blight, thirty miles from Ragnarok Crater.

Chapter 17

We climbed a hill not far from the wreckage of *Perseus*. The ship lay in a smoking ruin in the center of the flames. If anyone had been left on the ship, there was no way they had survived.

But there was still the escape pod, although from our vantage point, I couldn't see it. We had to find it, which was easier said than done. The glare of the fires made it difficult to see anywhere beyond our immediate surroundings, and worse, standing on this hill made us targets for any of the *Radaskim* to see.

Finding our friends was more important than that issue, though. We had seen that pod fall, which meant there was a good chance they were out there now, looking for us.

"See anything?" I asked.

Anna pointed toward *Perseus*. "We should start by the ship."

I hesitated. Just because the ship was over there didn't mean the escape pod was, too. Walking over there would put us right in the center of the flames, and fires had a tendency to be unpredictable.

"They could be anywhere," I said. "Even outside the fires."

"They might have seen us land," Michael said. "They could be walking to *Orion* right now, hoping to find us."

Anna and I turned in *Orion's* direction. The ship, red-glowing, was still being consumed by the flames, perhaps half a mile away. I strained my eyes, trying to see anything moving down there. I saw nothing but the dancing fires.

If they had landed in there, their priority would be to escape the flames, not search for us within them. Survival came first, as it had for us.

"If they made it, they would've gone outside the fires," I said. "They don't know that we saw the escape pod. For all they know, we're heading for the Crater right now."

Michael grunted. "Makes sense."

"We could go back to those fires," I said. "But I think if they're anywhere, it's not there."

Anna hesitated. "No. Probably not. But if they think *you're* in there..."

"I guess you have a point."

"Try the radio again," Michael said.

I raised the one radio we had between us. It was already on the group channel.

"Makara? Samuel? Anyone?"

As expected, there was no response.

"Maybe you're right," Anna said. "If we waste more time here, crawlers will swarm us. We need to head east, find somewhere to lie low..." She sighed. "It looks like we'll have to go the rest of the way on foot."

"Won't the crawlers be able to see us while we're walking?" Michael asked. "Detect us, somehow?"

"I don't see how we have a choice in that," I said. "We just have to hope for the best."

"If they're around, this crash will draw them like flies," Anna said. "We should get moving."

"Lead on, then," Michael said. "Both of you take point. I'll keep an eye out behind."

I made one last scan of the fires, making sure no one was walking down there. I saw nothing but the flames crackling in the night, burning more intensely than before. I became convinced, more than ever, that they weren't here.

With that conviction, we started down the hill, heading due east.

***

The air cooled as we descended the hill and entered the glowing fields. In the distance, a molten radiance lit the horizon. It was hard to believe that beneath the surface there, Askala was watching. Waiting.

Full night had come, and the sky was a dark mass above. The light of the fires had been left behind, and the way was lit only by the luminescence of the fungus. We had thirty miles to go.

I stared out at the wide, glowing plain pockmarked with stands of alien trees. Besides those trees, the land was empty, and the only movement came from the warm, humid wind.

"We're going too slow," I said. "With the distance we have to go...we should be running."

Both Michael and Anna looked at me. After a moment, each of them nodded.

So, we ran, our steps padding on the fungus. We kept a steady pace for about an hour, running between two hills, each one covered by thick forest. I felt we were exposed out in the open, that thousands of watchful eyes gazed at us from the cover of the trees.

After that hour passed, we began to walk again. I drank deeply from my canteen until it was only half full. As we caught our breath, I realized that this long distance on foot was only the beginning. Once we got to the Crater, we'd have to climb into the earth, through tunnels and caverns filled with monsters and magma. Assuming we passed that, then we had to deal with Askala. I still had no idea what to do when I got there.

The farther we moved from the crash site, the more hopeless it seemed. If the others were alive, surely they were moving in the same direction by now. But there would be no stopping until we reached our goal – it was either that or dying from exhaustion.

Fifteen minutes later, we increased our speed to a steady jog, moving more slowly than in our first stint. We'd gone anywhere from six to eight miles – not even a third of the distance to the Crater. It was already past 21:00, and assuming this same pace and no major obstacles, we'd be at Ragnarok Crater by 04:00 or so.

"It's quiet," Anna said.

"We can't get this close just to let our guard down now," I said.

Right after I'd said that, a gunshot sounded in the distance. It was impossible to tell where it had come from.

Anna drew her katana as Michael and I drew our handguns. We paused to listen. Several more gunshots were fired. The echoes reverberated between the hills and forest.

"It's coming from the east," Anna said.

We ran forward, toward the edge of a forest blocking our path. North, south, and east were all covered by the thick xenotrees, completely halting our advance. If we wanted to keep going east toward the gunshots, we'd have to go through these trees. I had a horrible feeling about it, but there was nothing else to be done. They were on the other side, and in trouble, and trying to go around the forest would take hours of backtracking.

I knew we didn't have hours.

"Let's get through quickly," I said.

We entered the trees, weaving through the tangled undergrowth. The thin trunks and limbs glowed pink and purple, lighting our way. At first, we were able to just push through, but as we advanced, the forest thickened so much that it was almost impossible to proceed. It seemed incredible that the others had gone through this. In fact, they *couldn't* have. They had to have gotten there another way.

Before I could mention this to Anna and Michael, several more gunshots sounded, followed by a high scream. It was *definitely* coming from the east, beyond the forest. Anna raised her blade high and brought it down on the encroaching undergrowth. Vines snapped with her precise cuts, spewing pink fluid.

The trees were close and ominous, as if trying to bar our path. Gunshots sounded from ahead, followed by the high shrieks of crawlers, just on the other side of the trees.

But our progress had come to a standstill. Anna hacked at the vegetation, one mighty swipe after another, until she could no longer even lift her blade.

Now, I was sure that the trees were closing in, their branches blocking every path of escape.

"*Back,*" I said. "We can't get through."

We turned, but the path Anna had cut was all but gone. About thirty feet of thick, tangled growth stood between us and the clearing we had left.

Then, I heard the sound of voices – not from the east, but back to the west. A female voice was shouting, muffled through the trees.

"That *has* to be Makara," Anna said.

"She was just on the other side!" Michael said. "We *heard* them."

"Maybe she went back," I said. "There must be a path we missed."

However, the vegetation was not going to let us through so easily. I took my Beretta, aiming it at a nearby tree trunk. When I fired, the trunk shuddered and bled pink goo. The tree gave just enough of an opening for us to push through a few more feet. Michael took my example and fired on another tree, right on its roots, while Anna slashed with her katana. Now awakened, the forest fought back with a vengeance. Trees closed in chokingly, pressing from every side, wrapping our arms with writhing vines.

From outside the trees, I heard voices. I realized they were trying to get to us. More gunshots came from that direction.

We pushed through, until at last we broke free. I tumbled to the fungus, scrambling up to see Makara, Samuel, and Ruth covered with scratches and dirt.

Anna and Michael came out from behind, all of us ending up on the ground and gasping for air by the light of the xenofungus.

"Why the *hell* did you go into those trees?" Makara asked.

"We heard you on the other side," Anna said. "Gunshots."

Samuel and Makara shared a glance.

"That wasn't us," Samuel said.

I looked around. Makara. Samuel. Ruth.

Julian was missing.

"Where..."

No one answered my question, and that was answer enough.

"He...didn't make it," Samuel said. "We got in the pod, and the door closed. He was on the wrong side."

Makara and Ruth were quiet, saying nothing. Makara just stared at the ground.

"We could have waited," Makara said. "We could have waited ten more seconds..."

"The door closed," Samuel said. "It must have been automatic. None of us did it. The door closed, and we shot off. There was *nothing* we could have done."

"I should have been the last one on. I..." Makara turned her face away, her eyes filling with tears. "It was so pointless. He didn't even have a chance to fight."

"It won't be long until we all go to join him," Michael said. "I guarantee you that. We need to keep it together for a few more hours at least. We need to find a way past this forest. We have a mission to finish."

At last, Makara nodded. "I know that. We just need to keep going."

"Keep going," I said. "How is it you guys got to the other side of the forest, then back here so quickly?"

"We were never on the other side," Samuel said.

"We heard you," I said. "That's why we went in."

"Something was over there," Anna said. "We all heard it."

"It must have been a trap," Ruth said.

Everyone looked at each other.

"How did they make...whatever it was...*sound* like you? Make gunshot sounds?"

"I don't know," Makara said. "But we're wasting time. We need to go."

"Do we backtrack?" Ruth asked.

"We have to," I said. "We can't go into those trees. We'll have to find another route east."

We stood for a moment in silence. My thoughts returned to Julian. I couldn't believe he'd died. I kept trying to think of a way he might have survived, but there was nothing. If he was on that ship, he was gone. There was no way around that.

"Makara..." I said. "I'm sorry."

She paused a moment before answering. "Let's just go. I don't want to talk about it."

With that answer, we started walking.

***

As we backtracked, the trees on either side of us seemed unending. I didn't remember it taking this long to get here, but then we had been running. I didn't even suggest that we run now. Everyone looked so haggard that I knew such a pace couldn't be kept up for long.

I came to a stop. Everyone else stopped, looking at me.

"We have a long way to go," I said. "Might as well eat something."

"Eat?" Makara asked. "At a time like *this?*"

"This is not for fun," I said. "It's necessary. We have at least thirty miles to go, and maybe even more. We need energy to move on."

Makara, at last, nodded. "I have some meat in my pack. And a fair amount of bread, still."

"I have some fruit," Anna said. "Together, they should make enough for a meal."

"We'll eat on the trail," Samuel said. "There'll be no more stopping. And be sure to conserve your water. I doubt we'll have a chance to refill."

As we walked, Anna and Makara dug into their packs for the food. Anna handed me two red apples and six dates; she had come prepared. I started on the apples since they had more moisture. I ate them, cores and all, before starting on the dates. Already, I felt some of my energy returning.

By the time I was done with the fruit, we had exited the valley and left the alien, webbed trees behind. To both the north and the south, the land rose, but to the north, the rise was gentler, so it seemed the better way to go.

Once we started up the hill, I took some bread and meat from Makara. Both were dry, and I needed water to swallow them easily, but I couldn't have cared less.

We made it to the top of the hill after a few minutes of climbing. We looked east, toward the tree-filled valley. A narrow corridor ran between two large hills, each filled with xenotrees. Those forests joined about two miles away, at the end of the corridor. I realized that was where we had come from.

That forest extended north to south, separating us from the Crater like a wall. It stretched to either horizon, completely blocking us from passing.

"There's no way through," Makara said.

We just stood there, staring, as if some secret path might open. There was no way we could push through twenty miles of forest – we had barely fought through twenty feet. Even if the forest *didn't* fight us every step of the way, trying to hack and slash our way through it would be nearly impossible.

We could try to get around, from the north or the south, to perhaps see if there was another way in.

"We could *really* use a ship," Makara said. "Either that or grow a set of wings."

"Quietus..." I said.

"Can you call her?" Makara asked.

"I could try," I said. "Only, she was supposed to go to the Crater. She might not have even arrived yet."

"We've got nothing else," Samuel said. "Try it."

I knew Samuel was right. There was no way we were getting through that forest.

I sat down, closed my eyes, and sought the inner quiet necessary for reaching a long distance. Doing that was easier said than done, and didn't guarantee a result. Deep down, I felt my panic, my uneasiness, but I had to ignore that. Finding Quietus was more important.

A long time passed. I didn't want to call Quietus until I was sure my message would carry far. I let my thoughts and feeling pass, kept my breaths even.

Quietus.

There was no answer in the stillness. As the silence stretched, I slipped even deeper into meditation. There was nothing but the void, my thoughts floating in a vast, black ocean – this was the realm where *Elekai* thoughts connected. If she wasn't here, then she wouldn't be anywhere.

So, I extended the scope of my thoughts further, expanding north, south, west, and especially east, toward the Crater itself. It felt risky, allowing my mind to go that far, but I wasn't going to miss any opportunity to find Quietus. She was our key to getting to Ragnarok Crater.

Then, a voice answered me. I knew from the moment I heard it that it wasn't Quietus, but someone else entirely.

***

This isn't your place, Elekim...

The thought disturbed my peace, like a pebble entering a lake. The voice was featureless; I couldn't identify whose it was. This wasn't Quietus, and yet it didn't feel like Askala, Dark Voice of the Radaskim.

Just as I was about to respond, the voice seemed to sense it.

Do not speak. Think nothing. Listen, for what I am about to tell you is of paramount importance.

I decided to do as the voice said, waiting for it to go on.

Good, the voice said. *It's best not to betray ourselves, even with our thoughts. Remember what I said about silence,* Elekim. *Already, I have overstayed in your consciousness and should depart. But I know what you seek. You wish to enter the Crater and treat with Askala. And if not treat with her, destroy her. Both notions are equally foolish, but I know that this will not dissuade you.*

I wanted to ask who he was, but I remembered what he said about keeping silent.

I am the Nameless One, the voice said. *And that is all you must know. I dare not speak like this, over such distance. Travel north, and you will find me in the hollow of the three hills. Come, before the sun rises. Some secrets can only be whispered in the dark.*

And like that, the voice dissipated from my mind, leaving me reeling. *Whoever* the voice had belonged to, he couldn't be *Radaskim*. But neither was he *Elekai*. If that was true, then what exactly *was* he? Sometimes, those with no allegiance were more dangerous than your enemies. But he had told me to meet him in the hollow of the three hills, that he had what I was looking for.

Troubled, I opened my eyes, to find my friends sitting on the ground, staring into the distance.

Anna was the first to notice me awake.

"He's out of it."

I had no idea who this Nameless One was, but the only way I could find out was by heading north, to the hollow in the three hills...wherever that was.

I rose off the ground, prompting everyone else to do the same.

"We need to head north."

"What's north?" Samuel asked.

I shook my head. "I have no idea, to be honest. A voice came to me. Not Askal. Not Quietus. Not even Askala. It was someone else, who called himself the Nameless One. He said he had an answer, that I should come north. He said it was in a hollow, and there were three hills."

Everyone looked at each other, sensing a trap. If it was a trap, though, we had to walk into it willingly. We had nothing else to go on, and no other option had been given.

"We walk, then," Samuel said.

Everyone looked at me, waiting for me to make the first move.

"He said to come before sunrise."

"Sunrise is four hours away," Makara said.

That meant I had been in my trance for a good two to three hours. We would have to hurry.

Chapter 18

We ran due north, leaving the hills and the forest far behind. A flat plain spread before us in every direction, the pink, milky glow of the fungus stretching for miles. There was no change in elevation, and no sign of any of the three hills. I was beginning to wonder if it was all a trick to lead us out into the middle of nowhere, which was highly possible. If crawlers appeared on this plain, there would be no outrunning them. We were completely exposed, and our only option was to continue to run.

But there came a point where we just couldn't go anymore. I was the first to crash, and the others weren't far behind. As I lay there, catching my breath, my legs felt like fire.

Michael was the first to stand, looking into the distance.

"There's nothing up here. Nothing. We must have gone ten miles by now."

Makara was the next to stand. "We have to keep moving."

She was right, if only because we had no other choice. If we gave up now and turned back, we'd be in the same situation as before, only worse.

Ruth looked to the south. There was nothing down there, either; nothing but featureless xenofungal plain.

Our only shot was to keep moving. We *had* to be believe it was there. We had nothing else.

Everyone now on their feet, we set off north again, this time at a walk. Every step was torture. My mouth was dry and pasty, and my breaths came out in shallow rasps. I was hesitant to drink from my diminishing water reserves. Somehow, even my *arms* were tired, although I hadn't been using them.

"Remember what's at stake," I said, surprised at the rasp in my voice. "I know we can't see those hills. That's not under our control. There is one thing we can always control: putting one foot in front of the other."

Maybe some of my words connected, because everyone seemed to pick up their pace

It was something, at least.

***

Another hour passed. Another hour with no results. Another hour closer to dawn.

Just when I was about to completely despair, a strange, bright light illuminated the horizon. At first, I thought it was the night ending, that we were too late. However, after two minutes of that light's brightening, I knew that *had* to be it. It could be nothing else.

"There it is," Samuel said, as if he didn't believe it.

Our only response was to increase our speed. To the east, the sky was graying. Dawn would not be long in coming, and if we were to make it in time, we needed to run.

"It's just a few more miles," I said. "We can do it."

So, we ran. As the minutes passed, the bright spot grew steadily brighter. After thirty minutes, I could make out the shape of two of the hills. If there was a third, it must have been hidden behind the others.

I didn't know how I was still going. Sometimes, the only reason people keep going is because they had no choice. Stopping meant dying.

That was what would happen to us if we didn't run.

By now we must have traveled fifteen, maybe even twenty miles total. I thought about all those men who had fought and died on the plateau. For all I knew, they were still fighting now. If I gave up, their sacrifice would be for nothing.

My throat rasped as I sucked in breath after breath. All we could do was take the next step – and the next, and the next.

It was 05:30 by the time the elevation started to change. We came to a stop at the foot of the first hill. The voice had said to find the hollow of the three hills. That probably meant the center.

I forced myself onward. The hill was steep, but manageable. The fungus made the terrain even and smooth. After ten minutes of climbing, we were halfway up the hill, and halfway across. To my surprise, the xenofungus thinned and then disappeared completely, replaced by hard rock and dirt. Even more surprising, there were some tufts of green grass, growing in the cracks of the rocks.

From our height, I could see the back hill, now, the largest of all three. These hills were oddly out of place, rising from the surrounding plain. The one we stood on was the lowest, while the second hill to the northeast was only slightly higher. The third hill, toward the north, was the tallest. In the center of the three hills was a valley. Or, I supposed, the hollow, and the sight of it was the most shocking of all.

Green forest filled it thickly, the trees earthly rather than alien. At the northern edge of the forest, at the foot of the northern hill, was a small lake, its surface dark and still in the predawn. A slight, silvery sheen cast the treetops with a subtle glow.

We hurried down the hill, making a direct line for the trees. As we neared, a sweet and foreign aroma filled the air, tickling at my nose. I didn't know how to describe it, but I realized it was the smell of nature, of growing plants. It was something I hadn't experienced all that often. I had no idea why these trees and plants would be here in the center of the Great Blight.

I stepped inside the first of the silvery trees. Even if I didn't know much about trees, I could recognize some of these. Pines. Firs. Cedars. Most were evergreens, but there were others that flowered and bore fruit. And still, every plant emitted a strange, silver glow. That glow suggested this place wasn't as earthly as it appeared.

We came upon a stand of short trees with thin fronds branching upward, their deep green leaves casting a silvery aura. Small, purple-blue fruits grew among the leaves, and many had fallen to the forest floor. I had no idea what they were, but all the same, I reached out and plucked one.

"Alex..." Makara said.

"It's a plum," I said. "Why are plums growing in the middle of the Great Blight?"

"That should be enough reason not to touch them."

"I think they're fine," I said.

To prove my point, I took a bite.

"Alex...that was very stupid," Makara said.

"It tastes good," I said. "Actually...*very* good."

Even though we had already eaten, it hadn't nearly been enough. Around us was an entire forest filled with fresh fruit. The stupid thing seemed to be ignoring that fact and going without when we needed the energy.

Anna pointed toward another stand of trees, bearing white blossoms and large, red fruit.

"There's apples, over there," she said.

I left the plums behind and went to the closest apple tree. One of the apples was at eye-height, red with yellow spots. I pulled it off its stem, and took a giant bite. This time, Makara did not protest. The apple was sweeter and more delicious than I imagined, better than any apple I'd ever had. By the time I started my second one, everyone else had joined in, Makara included.

There weren't just apples and plums. There were cherries, peaches, pears, apricots, oranges, and others beside. I had no idea how these trees were all growing here, but that wasn't important right now. We were starving for calories, and they surrounded us in infinite supply. I feasted until I felt my stomach would burst.

After I couldn't eat another bite, all I wanted was to sleep it off. It was hard to resist that temptation, but we had to continue on.

We made our way past the fruit trees and into a stand of evergreens. The forest floor was loamy and rich, covered in leaves, pine needles, and a thin dew that magnified the silver glow of the trees. The cool humidity collected on my brow and face.

Despite the calming atmosphere, I knew we couldn't let our guard down. Maybe Makara was right, and eating from the trees was a bad call. I felt fine, but maybe that wouldn't be the case later.

We went north through the trees. There was plenty of space to walk between them. Unlike the xenoforest, this place was airy and free rather than claustrophobic.

Through the trees in the distance, I could see the shining silver of the small lake. We made our way there, leaving the trees behind and finding ourselves standing on the water's white shoreline. The pond was nearly circular in shape, as smooth as glass, a thin veil of fog clinging to its surface. The trees, also shrouded in mist, stretched around it. It was hard to decide whether it was a small lake or a large pond.

Whatever it was, I felt like we were wherever we were supposed to be. I reached out with my mind, trying to find the Nameless One.

I'm here, I thought. *Now, answer me. How do we reach the Crater?*

Nothing moved in the early morning light. It didn't seem as if anyone had heard me. I stepped closer to the pool, inspecting it closely. The water was pure, clear, and toward the center of the pond, it went deep.

I knelt at the bank. The water was so still – if it were day, it would perfectly reflect the sky above. As I leaned over, I saw my face. Intense, brown eyes stared back at me, my hair shaggy. A bit of stubble covered my jawline. Where had *that* come from? The face was hardened, almost unrecognizable.

I touched the cold water, ripples spreading out from the point of contact. The ripples raced across the pond, dissipating somewhere in the center.

"Nothing," I said.

Maybe I needed to actually *step* in the water.

I stood and began taking off my right boot.

"What are you doing?" Anna asked.

When both boots were off, I set them beside some moss-covered rocks.

"Going for a swim."

I also took off my belt, which held my gun and knife. I set them beside my boots, along with my canteen and pack. I decided to keep the rest of my clothes on.

I was nervous, but knew that hesitation was the real enemy. When you're scared to do something, it's best to just jump in before doubt has a chance to grow. Many of the things we feel are dangerous are actually innocuous. It's the unknown that we fear, more than anything else.

Only now, this really *could* be dangerous, but that feeling was the same.

Before I could even think about it, I stepped forward, letting my right foot slide into the still, cold water, followed by my left foot. The water was numbing, but I couldn't think about that. I continued to walk into the pond, the bottom dropping steeply. It wasn't long until it was up to my torso. I suppressed the desire to shudder, not allowing the uncomfortable feeling of cold to overcome my control.

I turned back, where everyone stood, watching me.

"Stay there," I said. "I just want to see if there's anything underwater."

I paused long enough to take a deep breath, and plunged beneath the surface.

As I dove, I opened my eyes. The water was pure and clear; the only thing that made it difficult to see was the lack of light from the surface.

But deep down, another light shone. In an instant, I knew this was what I was looking for.

I returned to the surface, taking a breath and facing the shoreline.

"There's something down there," I called. "A light."

"What is it?" Makara asked.

"I don't know. Whatever it is...I feel like it's what we're looking for."

"How far down?" Anna asked.

"Not far," I said.

It wasn't easy to judge distance in water, especially when it was dark. It was thirty, maybe even forty feet below the surface. That was a long way to dive. The pool at Bunker 108 had only been twenty feet deep, and I'd only dove down that far a few times – it was always cold, high-pressure, and dark. This would be even more so.

"Alex," Makara said. "Be careful."

I nodded. Before they could say anything more, I took a deep breath and dove.

The light shone from the same place as before. This time, though, I would reach it. I swam downward, feeling the cold and pressure increase as I descended. Even as the thin light from the surface dimmed, the light at the bottom grew brighter, urging me onward.

About halfway, I knew I was far beyond twenty feet. I'd never been this deep before in my life. My lungs burned for air, but I couldn't give up; not when I was so close. The deeper I went, the more effort it took to move. The light was tantalizingly close, and was much farther than I'd first estimated. From the size of the lake, I would have never guessed it went this deep. I'd been down here almost a minute.

I knew, if I didn't turn back now, I would drown. If I kept going down, I'd be too far down to ever make it back to the surface. If I continued, I had to believe there was something there at the end, waiting for me. With that realization came the panic.

Where are you?

No answer came. If there was an answer, it had to come from myself. Did I turn back, or keep going?

I truly believed the answer was there, with that light. I couldn't give up. Not now.

I wasn't turning back. The only way out was reaching the bottom.

At last, my hand touched the sandy bottom. Confusingly, the light seemed to still shine from below. I realized then that it was coming from a tunnel right next to me, leading directly down from the lake bottom. I had to enter that tunnel and swim straight down.

I didn't have time to think about it. There was no longer any chance of my turning back; I'd never make it. So, I pushed myself down the tunnel, hemmed in from every side. I couldn't have turned around even if I wanted to. I panicked, swimming faster, feeling my consciousness fade and blackness cloud my vision…

The light grew incredibly bright, like I was swimming into a star. I could no longer keep my eyes open. The water warmed. The burning was no longer merely in my lungs. It was on my skin. I didn't know if this was the water getting warmer, or my losing all sense of reality.

It no longer even felt like I was in my body, but like I was floating into a dream. Suddenly, I was sucked down, as if into a vortex.

I couldn't hold out any longer. I sucked warm water into my lungs, and it brought no relief to my oxygen-starved body. As the current pulled me along, I blacked out.

Chapter 19

A long time passed. I knew I shouldn't even be alive, but somehow, I was still here. I could feel that the ground beneath me was rock. My clothes were still damp, but had dried somewhat from the warm air surrounding me. Though my eyes were closed, light found its way through the lids. I was wherever the brightness had been.

I stirred, every muscle sore. I put my hands on the rock below, pushing myself to a standing position. I closed my eyes tightly to shut out the brightness radiating from the surrounding rocks. From behind, I could hear the sound of water lapping against a shoreline.

I walked forward, holding my hands out. I'd only made it a few steps when a deep, booming voice spoke.

"Stop."

The voice seemed to come from ahead, in the light. Its quality was ethereal, supernatural, and definitely not of this world.

"Where am I?" I asked.

"This place," the voice said, "is the final preservation of Earth. Even should Askala dominate the entirety of this world – as she surely will – I will keep this place for my own sake."

"Are you *Radaskim?*"

"No," the voice said. *"Radaskim, Elekai*...I am neither of these entities. I am the Nameless One, and my allegiance is to none."

"You said you could help me," I said. "That you had answers."

"Sometimes, the answers are simple, but the questions are complex. And sometimes, the questions are complex, but the answers are simple."

I frowned at that. Whether *Elekai, Radaskim,* or something else entirely, these Xenominds all had one thing in common – being unnecessarily confusing.

The Nameless One continued. "Answers have a tendency to lead to more questions. A desire for simplicity is natural in a world filled with chaos. On a thousand stars and a thousand worlds, countless eyes stared upward at the sky, seeking answers but finding only their reflections, as surely as if they were staring into a mirror. All races begin by seeking the answers on the outside, before realizing that they can only be found on the inside. Hide the secret of life in the stars, in matter, in numbers, and science will one day unveil it. But hide it in the heart, and you could search for infinite eternities and never find it. As we unlock the secrets of the universe, as we seek a final theorem, in the end we only discover ourselves, looking in the mirror, realizing that we are mere children pretending to be gods."

The Nameless One paused for a long while.

"It is...haunting, to consider these questions," he went on, "to seek the answers. Answers have a way of revealing far more than the asker asked. The quest for knowledge drives some to insanity, and the only freedom from that quest is to kill the curiosity within oneself, to become blind to all views, save one. Your own."

"What are you talking about?" I asked.

"The truth. Ah, but what is it? The irony of seeking the ultimate truth is lost on the seeker – because it takes a special kind of faith to *believe* a final truth exists. The *Radaskim* believe in their own form of truth, believing it is the truth for all. This will lead them to destroy the universe and everything in it. They desire this simple answer from asking a complex question: why are we here? What are we doing? When it all ends, how can we stop it? The *Radaskim* seek to control the very entity from which they were formed: the Secrets of Creation, hidden within the heart of the *Elekai,* the very ones they are sworn to destroy." The Nameless One paused. "It is terribly ironic, no?"

Even if I understood very little of what the Nameless One was talking about, he was right about the *Radaskim*. They feared the death of the universe and they wanted to stop it. It was a goal beyond all imagination or possibility. And it was what I was supposed to stop.

"How does that relate to what I have to do? I need a way to get to the Crater, but the forest stands in the way."

The Nameless One considered. "It relates to everything. Who you are. What you believe. Those two things will determine the fate of the world. Askala will give you a choice, in the end. It will be up to you whether or not to accept it."

"What choice? She won't convince me. Not for anything."

"Then you do not fear her?"

That gave me pause. I'd always imagined fighting Askala would be a gigantic, physical struggle – that somehow, I would have to physically defeat her. Instead, from the way the Nameless One was speaking, it would be a battle of the mind.

"What is she capable of?" I asked. "What will she try to do?"

"She will show you her vision, not just for this world, but for *every* world. Remember: she sees herself as the savior. In a way, she *is* a savior. The savior of this universe, this existence. The *Elekai* are the bringers of death. They would watch the universe disintegrate into nothing. Askala offers immortality. The *Elekai* offer a temporary dream."

"But, destroying the universe to get that?" I shook my head. "I understand her perspective, but I don't agree with it. No one wants to die, but we need to accept that. Even if given the choice to live forever, I wouldn't do it. Something just seems wrong about it."

"But the *Elekai's* impassivity will destroy everyone, as surely as the *Radaskim* will," the Nameless One said. "Is that not why the Eternal War is being fought?"

"There's a difference between willfully destroying and just having things run their course."

"True enough."

"And whose side are *you* on?"

"I've already told you, *Elekim*. I am on no one's side. My role is to stand for nothing, yet to understand everything. I watch. That is my role, *Elekai* – merely to offer every view and to leave no stone unturned. I give my help to all, should it suit my purposes."

"What are you, exactly? You say you're nameless, but that doesn't tell me anything." I paused. "Actually, that tells me absolutely nothing, as if you're not even a person or a consciousness, or…" I shook my head. "I don't know."

"I am a composite of every thought, belief, creed, and memory that the Xenominds think and dream, *Radaskim* or *Elekai*. I know you, just as I have known every *Elekim* before. Yes, even the one you called Wanderer. And yes, even Askala herself, and those who came before her. I manifest wherever there are Xenominds. I cannot be escaped; I am a shadow cast by giants. As the giants rise and fall, so do I. My voice follows and records all the great deeds of Xenominds in the cosmos. My wisdom is free for anyone willing to listen."

"Even for Askala?"

"Yes," the Nameless One said. "Even for her. But my counsels with her are secret, just as ours are secret. And even the sum of all knowledge and wisdom cannot predict future events."

"You are like a recording device," I said. "A storyteller. Recording the history of…everything."

"Ah," the Nameless One said, clearly pleased. "A very human thing, stories. All races have a love for them, but none have been as enraptured by them as yours. Tell a good story and a human will believe you, contrary to all reason and evidence. Very few can escape that trap. Indeed, you see *everything* in terms of stories, so much so that without them, you are soulless. Stories are more necessary to humanity than air, than water, than gravity. Do not think we didn't watch your stories – we watched with great enjoyment. We knew you better than you even knew yourselves. We came as gardeners;

we came as conquerors. There are those who sow, and those who reap. *Elekai. Radaskim.* They are merely opposite thoughts expressed by the same mind."

"And you are that mind?"

"Am *I* the mind? No, *Elekim*...I am not. I am merely an expression of that mind...a small part indeed of the vast panorama of consciousness."

I wasn't going to get anywhere by asking this Nameless One questions; that much was clear. Every question I asked led to a thousand more, as he had so helpfully pointed out earlier. What I knew for sure was that this Nameless One had access to both the *Radaskim* Xenominds and the *Elekai* ones, and if he didn't drive me completely crazy with his philosophy, he might even tell me how to get to Ragnarok Crater.

"How do I reach Askala?" I asked. "How do I defeat her?"

"Your Wanderer was right, *Elekim*. It requires the greatest sacrifice, by the releasing of your power, to defeat Askala. A most curious choice of words, though. To defeat her. Because you wouldn't in fact be defeating Askala. You would be replacing her. In a sense, you would *become* her."

I wasn't sure I'd heard the Nameless One correctly.

"I'm sorry. *Become* her?"

"A Xenomind cannot be destroyed, but it can be converted. Her consciousness would only join yours. This would require your physical death, of course. And that immortality that you said you'd never take? That would be your fate. That is the price, *Elekim*. You will die and lose your humanity. Suddenly, the war of the *Radaskim* makes much more sense. Askala's goal is self-preservation. She cares not for the life of the universe. Those who dwell merely in the physical realm have it easy. They merely die and are no more. But Askala...she must endure, for all of eternity. Only pain, until the end of time, until the end of all existence..."

The Nameless One ceased speaking, at least for the moment. My mind was reeling from what he'd told me. I wouldn't merely be dying, as I thought. I'd be doomed to live for the rest of time, until the end of the universe. How could *anyone* bear that? Suddenly, I saw the Nameless One's point. It might be better for us *all* to die...

My sacrifice had become all the more difficult to fathom. Who could have imagined, or guessed, that my sacrifice would be accepting *immortality*? I had no idea what that even meant, or even looked like. Askala's consciousness would be absorbed by mine, making all xenolife on Earth *Elekai*. Humanity would live on, only I wouldn't get to live among them. I'd have to watch, from a distance, unable to reclaim my former self.

"You know of what I speak," the Nameless One said. "I can now sense your hesitation; it is a difficult question to ponder. Indeed, no champion has lived so far as to even answer it. Though a thousand worlds shall fall, one will remain. A prophecy I revealed to your Wanderer. There is one thing you should note: the prophecy says nothing about the nature of the world that remains. You have the freedom to choose, and you may find that the war has much less to do with Askala, and more with yourself. With such untold power, what will you do, *Elekim*? What will you decide, deep in the heart of darkness of Ragnarok? What is to be the world's fate?"

"I'll stop the *Radaskim*," I said. "No matter what happens. No matter how hopeless. I will never quit, and I will never back down."

Despite the brightness, I opened my eyes and peered into the light. Somewhere in there, the Nameless One stood, masked in a coronal wreath of luminescence. I walked forward, but impeded by some invisible wall, as if the light itself was holding me back.

"You would fight," the Nameless One said, his voice fading as I forced myself forward. "You would fight, knowing what you must become?"

"I have to do this," I said. "I've come too far to give up now. I need to get to Ragnarok Crater, and I need your help to do it."

The Nameless One seemed disappointed. Maybe he thought my choice was foolish.

"So be it, *Elekim*," the Nameless One said. "Walk forward, into the light. Your answer waits above."

I walked forward, the light no longer restraining me. I half-expected to see the Nameless One standing there, in human form. But there was nothing – nothing but the light that began to dim as I walked forward. Soon, it was dim enough to open my eyes fully. I looked behind to see a ball of light floating in the air like a miniature sun.

"Go, *Elekim*," the Nameless One said. "You haven't a moment to waste. And think about what I've told you. There is still time to reconsider."

"That won't be happening."

"I am merely the voice of wisdom. Do with my words as you will."

I entered a tunnel that sloped upward. I began to ascend, the tunnel curving into the darkness. The light faded behind, so I felt my way along the wall. After another few minutes of darkness, the tunnel ceased its curving, and daylight shone at the end. I increased my speed.

I reached the exit, finding myself a good way up the northernmost hill. The lake spread out below, a clear blue-green in the early morning light. Samuel, Makara, Ruth, and Michael stood on the lake's shoreline. I noticed Anna was missing, but her head resurfaced in the center of the pond.

"*Hey!*"

My voice echoed off the surrounding hills and forest. All of them began looking around, not able to pinpoint the source of my voice. As I walked downhill, I waved my arms. Makara was the first to spot me, pointing me out to the others.

When the slope evened out, I increased my speed to a jog. The others were running to the other side of the lake in order to meet me at the foot of the hill. Anna swam toward the shoreline, emerging from the water soaked and shivering.

Finally, I made it to the bottom. Anna ran forward and wrapped her arms around me, her body wet and cold.

"What *happened?*"

"I found him," I said. "We...talked for a while."

"He was underwater?" Anna asked.

"Yeah. Something like that."

"What did he say?" Makara asked.

"Well," I said. "We talked about philosophy, death, and resurrection."

"Seriously?"

"Actually, yeah." I remembered everything he had told me, about having to not only die, but take Askala's place and live forever. "I don't really want to go any deeper than that."

Anna could see that I was troubled, but we couldn't focus on how I was feeling at the moment.

"He said the answer would be out here, somewhere..."

"You mean over there?" Ruth asked, pointing.

We followed her gesture to the treetops above, where two dragons were flying toward us. Even with the distance, their familiar shapes told me immediately that it was Quietus and Askal.

"Where did they come from?" I asked.

"I think they were here all along," Samuel said. "Maybe that Nameless One kept them somewhere nearby."

"You mean, imprisoned?" Ruth asked.

"I think he wanted to talk to me first," I said. "Now that he's had his say, we're free to do what we want."

Both dragons landed on the far side of the lake. I wondered why they didn't land closer, but I realized I had left all my stuff over there, anyway. We walked along the lake until we reached the other side. I grabbed my belt, putting it on, along with putting on my jacket and picking up my pack.

I went to stand in front of the dragons. Something about the both of them looked haggard and worn. They'd had to fly hundreds of miles.

Forgive me, Elekim, Askal said as I stood before him. *The Nameless One prevented me from speaking to you until now.*

I know, I said. *It's good to see you, but I thought you were at the battle.*

The rest of the Elekai *are, but the real battle is here. Even as they flew west, I flew north.*

I'm glad you came, I said. *Because we need your help to get to the Crater.*

I turned to Quietus, whose movements were slow and lethargic. Her white eyes didn't seem as bright as usual. Her large wings wilted, dragging against the ground. She closed her eyes, as if in pain.

Quietus?

Yes, Elekim?

Are you alright?

Her eyes seemed to look deeply into mine, filled with a pain that was haunting to see. It was hard to believe that Quietus, before she had become *Elekai,* was a creature of violence. Now, she was a gentle giant.

I...just returned from the Crater. Askala, of course, knows you're here, and I barely managed to escape once she discovered me. Before that, I succeeded in convincing her to send much of her swarm to the battle, so it is too late for her to recall them. She is proud, Elekim. *She believes that you will never make it to the Two Seas. Askal and I can at least see you as far as the Crater.*

The Two Seas?

Yes, Quietus said. *The Two Seas lie in the deepest part of the Warrens, far below the surface. At their joining is the Point of Origin, the entrance to Askala's sanctum.* Quietus looked at me, sadly. *I would take this cup from you, but I believe you shall drink it in full, in due time. I could not bear the hypocrisy of telling you that you will win. There is little to no hope,* Elekim. *Despite my persuasion, great monstrosities still lurk in the shadows of Ragnarok – Askala's most dear pets, raised with a cruel love only she can instill. It is best not to comprehend such darkness,* Elekim – *but you will know this darkness better than even I, Quietus, who endured it for untold eons. You must ask – is it worth it? If you understood even a fraction of this question's implications, you would cower in fear.*

I could say nothing in response. Maybe the only reason I could go on was because I didn't know what I had to face. I couldn't imagine what I was risking, or the pain I would feel.

But I couldn't turn back. Not now. Too many had died to get me here. I had to fight, no matter the cost.

"We've come too far," I said. "Whatever happens to me...I need to be at the Crater. It's what I'm supposed to do."

Then come, Quietus said. *Askal and I will fly you to Ragnarok, to the deepest darkness of the world.*

I turned to my friends, looking each of them in the eye. Makara. Samuel. Anna. Ruth. And finally, Michael.

"This is our last chance," I said. "Our final battle. Nothing but death or worse is ahead. There's no turning back. There's no one I'd rather be here with than you. Without all of you, I would have never made it this far. We'll need each other every step of the way. We lost Julian today. We'll lose more. I can almost guarantee that. This might sound weird, but...it might be best if we consider ourselves dead already. When we go down into the Crater, there'll be no coming back up."

"If we are dead," Anna said. "We have nothing more to lose. There's nothing more Askala can take from us."

"I have no regrets," Ruth said. "Let's get moving."

"For Julian," Michael said.

"For Julian," Makara agreed.

"Let's not forget Ashton, too," Anna said, "and Grudge, and everyone who has died to get us here."

"This is the moment," Samuel said. "I know none of us asked for this. When we first found the Black Files, I never imagined our road would lead here. Some doors, once opened, can never be closed. Our only choice is to go through them. And right now, we're walking through the wide-open door of Hell. Whatever may be said of us, if anyone lives to tell our stories – it's been a hell of a ride. All of us should have died a long time ago." He cracked a rare smile. "Maybe we can surprise ourselves one more time."

It was time to get moving. The longer we dragged this out, the harder it would be. Everyone became focused, determined, maybe even defiant.

"Anna and I can take Askal," I said. "Everyone else can go on Quietus. She'll be able to carry four easily."

Everyone agreed, so Anna and I went to mount Askal. He lowered his wings as we climbed onto his back. Meanwhile, Samuel, Makara, Ruth, and Michael got on Quietus. Each of them had plenty of room, occupying a different spot between Quietus's spikes, the spikes themselves serving as natural handholds.

When everyone was seated, I gave the order.

Go.

As Askal lifted into the air, the grove below dropped away. The wind cooled as we rose up into the sky, leaving the grass, forest, and pond behind. From above the grove, I could see the bright light shining from deep within the pool. I wondered if the Nameless One was watching us.

It wasn't long before we had passed out of the hills and over the surface of the Great Blight. The morning sky was surprisingly clear – still red, but the clouds weren't so thick. In the distance, I could see the northern perimeter of the xenoforest. It was hard to believe we had run all that distance through the night. Even now, I was weary, and could have fallen asleep on Askal's back if I had wanted to.

Anna wrapped her arms around me more tightly.

"How are you feeling?"

I took her hands, sheltering them within my own.

"I don't know. I think I'm just ready for all this to be over."

She held on, saying nothing.

"I guess it will be, soon," she said.

"It's hard to see a happy ending coming out of this," I said. "I'm trying to think about it as just another task, without emotion."

"You can't keep your emotions out of something like this," Anna said. "Without emotions, without love, you have nothing." She paused. "It's not over, yet. Nothing has ended the way we expected. Why should this be any different?"

I had no idea how to answer her.

"We *need* to believe there's a happy ending," Anna said. "Not just for the world, but for ourselves. How else are we to go on? If we don't believe that, there's not much point to this. Even if we die, maybe life will go on for us, afterward. At least, that's what I hope."

Those words brought me back to what the Nameless One told me. If I defeated Askala, it meant there was life after death, but not in any human sense of the word.

I couldn't think about that, though. At this point, I didn't even know if I was going to make it to Askala alive, to the Two Seas and the Point of Origin.

I had no idea what came after that, so all I could do was keep going.

Chapter 20

As the day brightened, we flew directly south over the xenoforest. The trees were a blaze of orange and pink, glimmering in the crimson morning. The forest ended on the horizon, the land rising toward a jagged line. I couldn't see beyond that line, but I knew it was the beginning of the Crater. As the minutes passed, the line became bolder, but I still couldn't see over its edge.

In time, that line moved and I could see into the Crater itself. Its size took me aback, because it was so much larger than I had expected. I knew Ragnarok Crater was about one hundred miles wide, which meant the whole thing couldn't be seen in its entirety. All the same, I could see the curvature of the rim, wrapping from horizon to horizon. To the south, there was no way I could see the other side. A thick haze blanketed the Crater's interior, making it impossible to look far within. It was probably large enough to have its own weather patterns. From what I could see of its descending slope, nothing grew inside it – not even xenofungus.

The rim fell away in a sheer cliff, dropping thousands of feet into the cloudy murk: sheer, deadly, impassable. There was no way down except by air. Even if we had managed to get here on foot, we would have had to go through *that*. I thought of the meteors destroying our ship – maybe they had been Askala's way of keeping out unintended visitors.

Looking down into the Crater, I wondered how Askala's monsters even got out. There must be tunnels that led from the Crater to the surface.

A meteor as large as Ragnarok had been would have struck deeply into the Earth's crust. Visibility was clear for the first mile or two into the Crater, but anything further was lost in reddish haze. Depending on how deep the Crater went, the atmospheric pressure would be greater than on the surface. If it went down for even a few miles, the pressure would be substantially greater.

Askal and Quietus flew side by side, bearing us over the rim of the Crater. We began our descent. No movement or sound came from the surrounding haze.

Askala and Quietus glided downward in silence, rarely beating their wings. I looked behind and saw that the Crater's edge was fading through the miasma. We were far below the edge by now.

The air warmed as we continued to descend. Soon, all we could see was the haze – I couldn't see the sky above, or the ground below, and the cliffs had been left behind. This journey was nowhere near over.

The minutes passed in silence. The air thickened and became hotter, until sweat collected on my skin. The air reeked of sulfur. And still, we descended. All was silent save for the flapping of Quietus's and Askal's wings.

The heat became altogether sweltering, and the air thick and difficult to breathe. In time, through the haze, the ground itself appeared – black, scarred, and cracked. Thick smoke billowed from vents. We passed right over one, sending me into a fit of coughing. Askal did his best to avoid the smoke, but this was impossible at points.

A red glowing abyss materialized in the distance. *This* was the entrance we were looking for. Fissures had cracked away from the opening, smoldering with molten heat. Smoke hissed from the vents, adding to the thick atmosphere and oppressive heat. Heat waves riddled the air, and the thick, red clouds clung to the ground.

If there was a Hell on Earth, we'd just found it.

Over the opening of the abyss, several dragons spread their wings, rising in the hot updrafts. The hellish *Radaskim* glowed red from the light of the magma below. Their high-pitched shrieks shot through the air, piercingly loud.

For now, the dragons seemed unaware of our presence. We had to get out of this heat and find refuge underground, hopefully in a dark passageway. Otherwise, we'd be cooked alive.

Askal and Quietus, however, didn't seem to mind the heat. They flew at the same speed and with the same intensity as they had been. About halfway from our position to the fiery edge of the abyss, a dark tunnel opened into the ground.

Land there, I said to Askal.

Askal changed trajectory, flying toward the opening. Quietus followed suit.

"We're going in there?" Anna asked.

"Yeah. Getting out of the heat is the number one priority."

As the ground neared, it became even hotter. The heat, I realized, was being reflected from the rocks. This entire crater was a heat trap. The atmosphere was thick, so any heat that entered would never escape.

When Askal landed, I jumped onto the ground immediately. I stripped myself of my jacket, leaving it on the Crater's floor. As everyone else rid themselves of unnecessary garments, the heat rose in waves from the cracked rocks. Smoke and haze curled from cracks, and the molten glow of the abyss lit the ground in the distance, about half a mile ahead.

I turned to the dragons, addressing both of them.

Askal...Quietus...thank you. We have to go the rest of the way on our own.

Be careful, Elekim, Askal said. *We will help you, such as we can.*

I had no idea what the dragons had in mind. All I knew was that we had to get moving.

You are entering a dark place, Elekim, Quietus said. *Be on your guard, and choose your path wisely.*

"I'll do what I can, Quietus. Stay safe. Save yourselves."

The dragons merely watched, not taking flight, as I turned to the others.

We drank deeply from our canteens. Everyone's skin was reddened from the heat.

Then, we ran toward the tunnel, the heat from the rocks penetrating the soles of my boots. I remembered that my watch had a temperature setting. I switched the display until a number came up, too large to even be believed.

"One hundred and seventy-two," I said.

I could only hope that it was cooler underground. Even if it were one hundred degrees, which was still unbearable, it would be a vast improvement.

As we crossed the Crater's floor, Askal and Quietus took to the air, keeping watch on our progress.

A few minutes later, we had reached the dark tunnel entrance. Cooler air emanated from its depths, a welcome relief. We entered the tunnel, the descending slope so steep that we practically slid our way down. Where the slope evened out, we stood. Samuel and Makara retrieved their flashlights. When they clicked them on, it revealed a twisting, angular path ahead.

"Be ready for anything," Makara said.

She started forward, the rest of us following her into the darkness.

***

The tunnel twisted in tight angles, tending to go down rather than up. As we descended, the air cooled somewhat, though it was still stifling.

After about ten minutes of our navigating the tunnel's strange angles, it forked into two paths. The right definitely seemed to be the easier path, continuing the same course we were on. The other tunnel, however, was little more than a hole in the floor, its slope steep. Only one person could fit through it at a time.

"Here comes the fun part," Makara said.

"How do we know which way to go?" Ruth asked.

Samuel shook his head. "We don't. We have to guess."

"Well, I know which way I'd rather go," Makara said.

"We should go with the one that has the coolest air," Anna said.

I went to the passageway to the right, lifting a hand to test the air. "This one feels the same. Warmer, if anything."

"That leaves this one," Makara said, kneeling down. She placed her hands over the opening. "Can't really tell."

"Let me go in," I said, stepping forward.

Makara held up a finger. "No."

I paused, watching Makara sit at the edge of the opening. She shone her flashlight down.

"It goes down a good ways," she said. "It's not a complete drop-off. There's a slope, but it's very steep. I'll have to climb down to see anything more."

"Let's just keep going," I said. "Might be hard to climb out of that if we run into trouble."

"I agree," Samuel said.

"Straight, then?" Michael asked.

"It's as good as anything else," I said. "We can always come back if we change our minds."

No one could argue with that, so we proceeded down the tunnel.

It twisted a few more times, dropping in elevation as we arrived at yet another crossroads. This time, there were *three* different directions: left, center, and right. A molten glow bathed the walls of the right tunnel, while darkness shrouded the other two.

"Maybe we can at least *see* what's on the right," Anna said. "If it leads to that fiery chasm we saw on the way here."

"Sounds like a *great* idea," Makara said.

I ignored Makara and picked the right tunnel, at Anna's suggestion. I wanted to see if it led to the abyss as well. If it did, I could get a good look to the bottom and see how much farther we had to go down.

We walked on. The tunnel ascended in a long, straight line, brightening as we went along. About one hundred feet ahead, the tunnel ended, the light red and fiery. As we walked, the temperature shot up. We'd have to turn back eventually, but there would be no harm in seeing what lay beyond the opening. Probably.

At last, we reached the end of the tunnel and stepped onto an overhang overlooking the blazing abyss below. Looking up, the surface wasn't far – perhaps a couple of hundred feet. Looking down, however, there was a drop of at least a full mile before the abyss ended in bright, glowing magma. Countless tunnels, like the one we'd just left, opened into this abyss at various points above, below, and around us. Pathways had even been carved into the sides, zigzagging from tunnel to tunnel. I felt like this was some sort of connection hub. For now, it was empty, but if more of Askala's swarm were here, this place would probably be humming with life.

Whether or not that was the case, we probably needed to head back. We were too exposed out here, not to mention being subjected to the incredible heat blasting from the magma below.

Above, several dragons flew over the opening of the abyss.

"Back!" I said.

Everyone recognized the danger, stepping back into the tunnel, running along it until we reached the intersection we'd left behind. Even if the dragons had seen us, there was no way they could have followed us.

Now, there were two tunnels to choose from.

"Number one," Anna said. "Or number two?"

"If this happens much more, we'll become hopelessly lost," Makara said.

"We should mark which ones we choose," I said. "In case we have to come back."

"Good idea," Samuel said.

He searched the ground a moment, until he picked up a hard, sharp rock. He went to the leftmost passageway.

"Does this one work?" he asked.

I shrugged. "Sure."

He scratched a huge arrow on the wall, pointing left toward the tunnel. He stepped back, inspecting his handiwork.

"Good," he said. "Backtracking shouldn't be an issue, now."

We went down the left tunnel. This one dropped steeply, at a nearly a forty-five-degree angle. The drop in elevation was a good sign.

The air was quite cool now; we were far from the magma of the abyss and the stifling air of the surface. The tunnel leveled out, and we found ourselves on a path that was crisscrossed by another. Looking back, I saw there were two other tunnels, besides the one we had exited.

"Sam, mark the one we just left," Makara said.

As Samuel got to work, Makara strode toward the intersection. She paused at the crossroads, shining her light in each direction.

"Well, this'll be tricky."

I stepped forward to see what she was talking about. Whichever way she flashed her light, it revealed the same view – a long tunnel leading in a straight line.

"What do you think?" Makara asked.

I stared down each corridor, trying to notice anything that would lead me to pick the right one. For all I could see, all three were identical.

"The best thing I can see is to choose one and see where it leads," I said. "We can always turn back."

"I'm just wondering why it's so quiet," Anna said.

"You wish it wasn't?" Michael asked.

"I like to know what I'm up against," Anna said.

"We'll head left," I said.

After Samuel had finished scrawling his arrow, I followed the left tunnel. We had been walking only five minutes when we arrived at an intersection identical to the first. On our left was a chamber with three tunnels, leading outward. On our right, a straight tunnel, and ahead, our current path continuing.

I chose going straight. Again, after another five minutes, we arrived at a similar intersection.

"It's repeating," Anna said.

"There might be a pattern," I said. "Let's keep our eyes open."

A distant shriek sounded in the dark halls, bringing us to a stop. Everyone retrieved their weapons. We waited for the shriek to fade to silence.

"What was *that?*" Ruth asked.

"The welcoming committee," Makara said.

"Took them long enough," Anna said.

Ruth shook her head. "Speak for yourself..."

I listened intently, but it was impossible to tell where the sound had come from. It could be near, far, from ahead or behind.

If this thing was following us, then it might be good to mix things up a bit.

"Let's go right," I said.

We turned right into the new tunnel. It was only when we'd been walking for a minute or so that I realized what the pattern was.

"It was going in a circle," I said.

"What was?" Makara asked.

"That tunnel we just left. It was so slight that the turning was pretty much imperceptible. Each tunnel branching right will have a central meeting point. The layout is like the spokes of a wheel. At least, that's what I'm thinking."

"Which means?"

"We're heading for the center. Something important is bound to be there."

"Let's hurry, then," Samuel said.

We started to run. Even though we had been pushing ourselves hard, I felt strangely energized. I realized if the atmosphere was thicker down here, then there would be more oxygen in the air. We were running harder and faster than what seemed possible.

All the while, the inhuman screams came louder, closer…

"Something's up ahead," Makara said.

The tunnel opened into a giant chamber, in the center of which was a shaft, leading straight down into the earth. Mist spilled from its opening, and a sticky, pink substance climbed over the tunnel's edge, covering the ground around it.

"Fungus," I said.

The shriek came from behind, much closer. I stared back into the tunnel, but the darkness hid whatever was tailing us.

"We need to go down there," I said.

That was easier said than done. We ran to the mist-shrouded tunnel. I couldn't see a thing down there, and the walls were perfectly vertical. There was no telling how far the drop was.

"You're *not* jumping," Anna said.

"None of us are," I said. "There's fungus lining the sides. We can use it as handholds on the way down."

"You can't be serious," Makara said.

"He is," Samuel said. "And he's right. It's the only way down."

There was no time to lose, so I knelt at the edge and swung my legs around, facing the wall. I planted my feet into the fungus, finding that it held surprisingly well. I tested its strength by putting my full weight on it. It was slightly elastic, but nowhere near ripping.

"We're good," I said. "Come on."

I began my descent into the mist, everyone following after me. Again, another shriek sounded from the tunnel, just seconds away.

I picked up the pace. The mist thickened as we descended, and after a minute of going down, my feet hit solid ground. Well, it wasn't exactly solid. The spongy quality immediately told me I was standing on yet more fungus. It was like we had entered a living thing.

I tried to dash that thought from my mind.

I peered up into the mist, seeing the shapes of everyone climbing down. From the top of the shaft came another piercing shriek. It didn't seem like whatever was chasing us could follow us down.

Everyone now stood beside me. The fungus glowed, providing enough light to proceed. The mist reduced visibility to ten feet or so, the air was warm and wet, like breath.

After we had walked for a minute or so, I stopped short. There was...*something*...hanging down from the ceiling. It was like a vine, pink in color. Similar vines hung nearby, filling the space by the dozens, like an inverse forest.

"Gross," Anna said. "Should I cut them down?"

"No," I said. "I don't think we should touch them."

"Try to go around?" Makara asked.

I nodded. "Yeah. Let's hang back a bit. Find another way through."

We walked along the edge of the vines, but they never thinned.

"Keep going straight," I said. "Don't touch anything."

We made our way forward slowly, making sure not to touch the vines. It proved to be almost impossible, and took some creative acrobatics. I wondered, as we went on, whether I was freaking out over nothing. The vines were still, and seemed harmless.

Ruth stumbled behind me; crying out in alarm, she fell into a large vine. Instantly, the vine stiffened and threw her backward onto the spongy turf. This caused her to brush into yet two other vines, both of which came alive and began attacking her. She groaned in pain, rolling away, only to touch *another* vine. Every time she touched one, it lashed out and sent her careening into another.

Anna withdrew her katana, cutting at the nearest vine. The blade cut through, slicing it in half. A geyser of pink slime gushed from the vine, the cut section writhing on the ground. By this point, the rest of the vines had wakened and had begun to attack.

A vine went for me, wrapping around my right arm. I grabbed my knife and cut it halfway through. Immediately, I felt its grip weaken, and I used the chance to free my arm, grab the vine, and slice the rest of it off. The bottom half of the vine fell to the floor, and I readied myself to face other threats.

Ruth had been wrapped by three vines – two smaller ones for each leg, and a larger one constricting her lower abdomen. With her free hand, she drew her own knife and sawed at the constricting vine. Pink blood spewed from the laceration, the vine splitting as the knife cut deeper. At last, the vine went limp, and Ruth began working on the ones around her ankles.

At that moment, another vine lashed out and wrapped around Ruth's right arm, yanking on it and constricting tightly. She screamed, dropping her knife to the ground.

Samuel was fighting off his own vines, ripping them from the ceiling with his bare hands. They tumbled to the ground, coiling like ropes as they fell. He fought his way to Ruth.

As a vine tightened around my torso, I followed Samuel's example and yanked really hard on it. There was some resistance, but after I pulled for a few seconds, the vine snapped from its roots. As the vine fell, I stepped out of the way to avoid getting hit.

Everyone had figured out the same trick. Makara and Anna worked together, heaving on a particularly large vine, using their combined body weight to snap it from the ceiling. Samuel, using both hands, pulled at the two vines that had wrapped Ruth's legs, yanking them both down. A pink rain fell from above, soaking us with pink slime.

Ruth, at last, managed to cut the last vine from her arm. She shook it off as Samuel helped her up. We made a circle, facing out, but the entire area had been cleared of vines. The floor was piled with their dead.

I noticed, toward our right, the ceiling was free of vines, forming a straight path. I hadn't noticed it before, which made me think that the vines there had left. Perhaps they had retracted into the ceiling, somehow.

"Let's head that way," I said. "It's leading somewhere."

"Where?" Makara asked.

"We're about to find out."

Chapter 21

After a few minutes, we passed the hanging vines and found ourselves standing at a precipice. We peered down; the bottom was lost to the mist. There was no way around. We couldn't climb down, as we had before, because fungus didn't line the sides. The sides were of smooth rock the entire way down, with no handholds.

"What now?" Ruth asked.

"Throw something down there," Makara said. "See if it hits anything."

Samuel looked at the rock he'd been using to mark our tunnels. He shrugged, and tossed it into the hole.

We waited, the seconds passing by, but there was no sound.

"Great," Makara said.

"Turn back?" Ruth asked.

I didn't like the thought of having to go through that hell again.

"We need other options," I said.

"Well, there's Cthulhu's forest behind us, or the Pit of Doom ahead," Ruth said. "Pick your poison."

"If we go back through those vines, we'd have to climb back out and backtrack," Anna said. "Should we try climbing down the abyss?"

"What do you mean?" Makara asked. "This *is* an abyss."

"The fiery one, not the infinite one," Anna said.

"The only way down this hole is jumping," Makara said. "And that would be supremely idiotic."

"Supremely?" Michael asked.

"Yeah. *Supremely.*"

"No one's jumping," I said. "We'll have to turn back."

Still, I couldn't shake the feeling that this was where we were supposed to be, that somehow there *was* a way down there. We just hadn't found it yet.

"Alright," Anna said. "Where to?"

I stood at the precipice, still looking over the edge. Trying to climb down would be suicide.

There was nothing but to turn back.

But as I turned, the ground gave a sudden lurch beneath my feet. I cried out, falling backward. Anna grabbed my arm, but I had too much momentum. As I fell into the hole, she tumbled over the edge with me.

We screamed and fell through the misty air. The seconds stretched for what seemed forever, and I saw nothing but the white mist.

And then, something elastic pushed against my back. The pressure increased until I was no longer falling, but was now going *up*. I sailed high into the air before falling back down, landing on the springy substance.

After a couple more bounces, Anna and I came to a stop. At seeing what had stopped us, I wanted to scream. It was those vines again, only they seemed to be coming from the walls, forming a tangled web stretching horizontally across the hole.

High up above, the muffled voices of our friends echoed downward.

"Alex! Anna!"

"We're okay!" I yelled.

"Okay" was a relative term. We weren't dead, but we were also stuck at the bottom of a hole with no way out.

But a way out appeared soon enough. The vines retracted into the walls, and Anna and I screamed once again as we fell. Above, the vines reformed their web, blocking us from communicating with the others.

It was just a few seconds before Anna and I splashed into cold, dark water. The shock of it sent my heart into overdrive. I swam upward, and when I broke the surface I sucked in a lungful of air. Anna emerged beside me.

My main fear wasn't for my own safety, but whether the others would jump after us. I looked above, but whatever was up there was lost in the mist.

"We need to get out of this water," Anna said, teeth chattering.

I looked around, but the fog obscured everything. There was nothing for it but to pick a direction and go.

Anna swam straight ahead, and I followed her through the fog. It looked like we were separated from the others for now. We had to continue our journey alone.

Thankfully, a shoreline materialized in the foggy darkness. It was hard to tell where the light was coming from, but it seemed to be shining from the walls themselves. Without it, we would have been completely lost.

My feet found the bottom, so I stood and walked to the shoreline. Anna emerged beside me. Everything was soaked – our clothing, our boots, and our packs.

"We need to keep moving," I said.

We walked ahead, leaving the water behind. The thick fog obscured everything, but it was still bright enough to see, making flashlights unnecessary. Fungus coated the floor, emitting a pink, ethereal glow. Our boots squished on the ground.

After a few minutes of steady walking, the mist thinned. At some point, we entered a tunnel. I looked back, only to see fog. There was a deadening of all sound. The tunnel continued straight, veering slightly downward.

A few minutes more, and the tunnel opened up into a small chamber, the walls of which gave off a slight glow. A perfectly circular pool of pink, glowing ichor sat in the center, perhaps ten feet in diameter. There were no other entrances or exits.

Somehow, I knew we had to go in that pool.

I stepped forward, but Anna pulled me back.

"Alex..."

I looked her full in the face, holding her hands. "That's the way out," I said. "Together?"

She hesitated, but nodded after a moment.

We went to stand at the ichor's edge. As we peered down into that pink, clear liquid, it seemed as deep as infinity.

I tried to calm myself, but I couldn't. I was afraid, even with Anna standing right there next to me.

"If we get separated, how do I know where to find you?" Anna asked.

I paused, thinking for a moment.

"Just call. I'll hear you. We'll need to hold on tight. I think this stuff might take us somewhere. Whatever happens, nothing can hurt us as long as we're together."

I didn't know if that was true, but in that moment, it seemed true enough.

"Alright," she said.

"I'm going to count to three. Then we jump."

I waited a moment, feeling my nervousness rise.

"One. Two. *Three.*"

We jumped and were swallowed by the pink liquid. The warmth engulfed me, and for a moment, we floated beneath the surface. Before we even had the chance to move, the pool sucked us down.

I held Anna tightly as we sunk deeper and deeper. We lurched through twists and turns, my lungs burning for air. When I felt I couldn't hold my breath much longer, we began to ascend.

A moment later, we broke the surface. I gasped for air as the ichor pushed us onto a bed of fungus.

After we lay there for a moment, catching our breath, I struggled to my feet and helped Anna up. The ichor receded from my body and clothing, retreating into the glowing pool from which we had emerged. The shape of this pool was exactly the same as the one we had jumped in – a perfect circle.

"You alright?" I asked.

Anna nodded. "Yeah. I think so."

"Let's keep moving."

We walked ahead, the tunnel curving and seemingly coming to a dead end. But as we neared, I could see the path had merely narrowed to a thin crack in the wall, just wide enough for one person to squeeze through.

I decided to go first. I turned myself sideways, wriggling myself between the two walls. At the narrowest point, it became so tight that I had to release all the air in my lungs just to squeeze through. I fell to the other side, landing on the fungus. I scrambled up and peered back through the crack.

Only, it had completely closed.

"Anna!"

No sound came through that wall. If she was yelling, too, I had no way of hearing it.

I dug my fingers into the fungus covering the wall, where the opening had once been, trying to rip it apart. It was no use; the fungus held firm.

Alex?

I heard Anna's voice in my mind.

Anna...are you there? Are you alright?

I'm stuck over here. It just...closed.

I didn't know it was going to close like that. If I had, I wouldn't have gone through.

She was waiting for this, for the chance to separate us.

No. We're not separated. We'll find a way. We have to get this wall open.

Let me try to cut my way through. The walls themselves didn't close. The fungus just grew between them.

I stared uncertainly at the wall. I didn't think that would work, but it was better than trying nothing.

I waited another moment, staring at the wall and willing it to open. Of course, it wasn't going to obey me. The fungus was controlled by the *Radaskim* version of the xenovirus.

I wondered, though...could I perhaps *convert* it? If the *Elekai* version dominated the *Radaskim* version, then if I could somehow infect this fungus, I could command it to open. I didn't even know if such a thing was possible, but if it was, how exactly would I do that?

It was worth a shot. I had nothing else to go on.

I reached out and touched the fungus lining the wall. I closed my eyes, feeling the soft, spongy substance beneath my fingers. It was warm, at first, but felt strangely cool as my hand kept contact. Soon, my fingers began to feel numb. I did not remove them, willing the fungus to change, emptying my mind and trying to establish contact.

Then, my fingers began to burn.

I gritted my teeth and kept my hand there. I could only hope that *something* was working. I cleared my mind, finding the void in my consciousness, the place where I could distance myself from pain and watch it from afar. Stabs of pain from the fungus continued to enter my hand, spreading through my arm and chest.

I connected to the *Radaskim* xenofungal network, and at every moment, more of it entered my awareness. I knew Askala might be able to find me, so I needed to work quickly.

I saw immediately that it would take a lot of my strength to permanently convert the fungus surrounding the crevice, but it would take significantly less if I only temporarily took control. That was what I opted to do.

Change, I thought. *I just need ten seconds.*

Nothing happened at first, but slowly, feeling returned to my hand, warmth outspreading from my fingers. A wave of brightness radiated outward from my fingers on the fungal surface. It began to glow brightly and hum.

I'd done it. It only awaited my command.

Open. Now.

The fungus unfolded, revealing Anna at the other end of the crevice, hacking with her katana. Her eyes widened upon seeing me.

"*Run!*" I shouted.

She ran into the crevice, turning her body to squeeze through the narrow bit. The fungus now fought back against my mind, wanting to crush Anna in the crevice. The attack on my mind came suddenly, and my control nearly slipped – it was as if the fungus *knew* how vulnerable Anna's position was. I fought with everything I had, my mind straining with the effort. Just as I was about to black out, she dove to the other side. I allowed the opening to seal shut. I collapsed to the ground next to Anna, my vision dimming.

"Alex?" Anna asked. "Alex, get up. No, don't close your eyes. Please! Get up."

My eyes *had* closed – I didn't remember when, or how, I had lost consciousness. I forced my eyes open. Anna's face above me swam in waves. All I could do was breathe, one slow lungful after another. For one brief moment, I had been a part of the *Radaskim* collective consciousness, and its energy was like poison.

Anna knelt beside me, talking, but I couldn't understand her words. My hearing had somehow been affected, and all I could feel was my heart beating, my pulse pounding in my ears.

Then, water splashed on my face. With that sensation, my paralysis seemed to melt. I sat up, and Anna handed me her canteen. I took a couple swallows.

"You alright?"

I nodded, pushing the canteen away. I held Anna close, both of us on the ground.

"Wasn't expecting that," I said.

"How did you open it?"

"I connected to the *Radaskim* consciousness, somehow," I said. "I didn't even know if it would be possible."

"It fought back?"

I nodded. "Yeah. Like hell. It almost closed on you, but I held it open, just long enough. It burned my hand."

I looked at my right hand. It didn't appear hurt or any different than usual, but it might as well have been on fire touching that fungus.

"If controlling the fungus is this hard, I can't even imagine controlling Askala."

"Don't think about that," Anna said. "What matters is we made it."

Anna helped me up, and we continued down the tunnel. There were no more obstacles for now, only an oppressive watchfulness that seemed to mark our every move.

We were getting close. I felt it. If Askala didn't know where we were before, she definitely knew now, and so far, things had not gone according to her plan.

I knew that she would have plenty of opportunities to change that, all too soon.

***

We entered a new cavern, so large that it was like an entirely new world. The glittering ceiling rose at least a thousand feet above, from which glowing stalactites hung. Stalagmites rose from the ground, covered by xenofungus. Ichor dripped from the ceiling, forming pools among the rock formations. There were no tunnels, no doors – just this vast maze.

We climbed a large stand of rocks, putting ourselves above the cavern floor. In every direction, shining pools, twisted rocks, and earthen pillars spread for miles. This vast, underground realm seemed to be empty of *Radaskim* life. On one side of the cavern, a lake of magma glowed red in the distance. In the opposite direction, through twisting tunnels and jagged rock walls, stretched a flat expanse filled with small pools, boulders, and rock formations. A similar underground landscape spread in the other two directions.

"Lava Lake," Anna said, "or the Endless Plain of Icky Ichor?"

"Both sound like lovely options."

I sat down on a flattened boulder, staring at the magma lake. Through all the twists and turns on the cavern floor, getting there would be tricky. Not that I had a mind to go that way.

"I think that might be the bottom of the abyss," I said. "If it is, that probably isn't the right way."

Anna oriented herself as if she had come from that direction. "We can rule out the right, because we came from that way. Which leaves straight, or left."

We were thinking in terms of the four directions, but really, there were much more down here. The entire cavern was gigantic, and its directions weren't limited to the four points of the compass. For all we knew, we could have missed our turn already.

Anna turned in the direction of the magma lake. Her eyes widened.

"Down!"

I dropped to the ground while Anna fell behind a boulder. I crawled until I was hidden with her. I heard the flap of wings, enough of a reason to keep my face and body to the ground. A moment later, the dragon swooped overhead. I only dared to look when it had gone a good distance.

The dragon was huge, already obscured by shadow. It continued beating its wings and gaining distance. It flew in a direct line, never turning.

I realized what we had to do.

"We need to follow it.'

Anna nodded, understanding. "You think it's going to her?"

"I'm not sure," I said. "But I think so."

I looked in the direction of the magma lake to make sure no more dragons were coming. Once I was sure the coast was clear, I stepped from the safety of the boulder, facing the direction the dragon had flown. By now, it had been completely swallowed by the darkness.

"A straight line in this place is going to be hard," I said.

"We'll have to climb some rocks every now and then to make sure we're going the right way," Anna said. "We can look back to this formation to orient ourselves. It's the tallest thing around."

"And after that?" I asked.

"We'll figure it out as we go."

We made our way down the outcrop, taking care not to fall. Even so, the descent was difficult. I placed my right foot down on a hold. It fractured, and I slipped, falling toward the edge. Anna grabbed me by the shoulders, pulling me back to the rock wall.

"Careful," she said.

From then on, I tested each and every step, not letting myself relax until we were on the cavern floor. We began walking in the direction the dragon had flown.

"The trouble will be staying on track," Anna said.

"Easy," I said. "Every fifteen minutes, we can climb something to reorient ourselves."

"You mean *I* can climb," Anna said. "No more climbing for you."

"You could fall just as easily as me."

"Yeah," Anna said, looking at me pointedly. "My life isn't as valuable, though."

"That's not true."

She shook her head. "No use arguing. Besides, I'm lighter on my feet than you."

I knew she had me there.

We navigated the twists and turns of a jagged canyon. The rock was porous and black, but there were areas where surfaces glinted, with edges as sharp as a blade.

"Obsidian," I said. "Watch where you step."

Anna nodded.

Five minutes later, we took our first break. Anna climbed a promising rock formation, only going halfway before peering into the distance.

"We're still good," she said. "Keep going."

"You see anything different over there?"

"Much the same. There's an entire world under here."

"The Underworld," I said.

"I guess that's fitting."

Anna climbed down and we continued on, entering a chasm that cut between two rising plateaus. Somewhere in this place, Askala lurked. Quietus had said she was at the meeting of the Two Seas, wherever that was. I hadn't seen anything down here resembling a sea, except maybe the magma lake, and it was a stretch to call that a sea of any sort. We just had to keep following the line the dragon made.

I was just grateful this place was empty, because there was evidence of its once being full of life. We passed molted chitin shells and dark burrows carved into the rocks. This must have been where the *Radaskim* swarm had laired.

"This entire place was filled with them," Anna said. "What did they *eat?*"

That question was answered as soon as the chasm ended, placing us before a large pool glowing with ichor. Along the banks of the pool grew a thick layer of xenofungus.

"Here," I said.

"It's hard to imagine those nasty monsters being vegans," Anna said.

"They'll eat anything they can get nutrition from. The fungus is their main source of food, but they wouldn't shy away from a kill, either."

"Gross."

We walked past the pool, patches of fungus, empty barrows, and jagged spires. Occasionally, Anna would climb on top of a large rock or plateau and straighten our course. Checking my watch, I was surprised to see that it was evening. We'd been up all day, all night, and all through the day again. I thought we would have found Askala by now, but this place was far larger than I had ever imagined.

We stopped again, and I decided that we needed to take a rest. We hadn't slept the previous night, and there was no way we could face Askala in such a state. Even Anna was moving lethargically. She stopped halfway up her climb, staring into the distance. She stayed there longer than usual.

"What is it?" I asked.

"There's something over there," she said. "Like a long, pink line on the horizon. The rocks end there."

"Whatever it is, we'll have to face it tomorrow. You're going to fall asleep on your feet."

She climbed down, sliding down the last twenty feet. Once she'd reached the cavern floor, she dusted herself off.

"Let's find someplace safe to lie low," I said.

We looked along the side of the cliffs, finding an empty hole that had probably been a burrow for crawlers, not so long ago. We walked by several of the holes, taking a pass because most of them smelled horrible. Hopefully, we'd be able to find a burrow that hadn't been used.

After another minute, we were in luck. We found a small burrow, slightly hidden behind a stand of rocks, and the best part was that it had no smell.

We ducked inside, settling into the corner farthest from the opening. We set down our packs, digging out what little food we had: basically just some fruit we had picked from the grove. It didn't take us long to eat it.

"Should one of us keep watch?" I asked.

Anna shook her head. "We didn't sleep last night. If either of us goes without, it will be bad. This place is empty, so I think we'll be fine."

I didn't have a mind to argue, especially now that I had sat down for a few minutes. I closed my eyes, and it wasn't long before sleep took me.

Chapter 22

When I awoke, I could barely bring myself to move, I was so tired. I drained what was left of my canteen before closing my eyes again.

Anna's breathing was even. I wrapped my arms around her, but she didn't stir. I drifted off again.

It was some time before I heard her voice.

"Alex."

I opened my eyes, still heavy with exhaustion. She was already standing, pack on her shoulders.

I checked my watch. It was 05:30, which meant we had gotten eight hours of sleep. It felt nowhere near enough.

"We'll have to conserve our energy," she said. "There's no more food, and before long, no more water."

"I'm out," I said.

"I know. I still have a container left, so we'll have to be sparing."

A couple of minutes later, we were walking through the canyon. The thick, jagged walls leaned on either side, the paths branching at random angles between the cliffs. Anna repeated her routine of climbing the rocks from time to time.

"We're off course," she said. "Head right."

As we continued, the chasms narrowed and the plateaus on either side grew taller. The overhanging tops almost formed a tunnel, blocking out most of the light of the bioluminescent ceiling. We came to a fork, finding the right completely submerged in pink, bubbling ichor. It was the direction we needed to go, yet we had no choice but to head down the left path.

Anna climbed again at our next juncture. The cliffs were climbable in places, but they were higher than they had been, and it made me nervous to watch her climb.

"A lot of them are flooded," she said from above, standing on the precipice. "And it only gets worse the further we go. Probably because..." She paused. "Well, maybe you should see this for yourself."

I scrambled up the rocks, my right foot slipping on a non-secure foothold. A rain of rock showered into the chasm below, but I quickly shifted my right foot to another hold to avoid falling. Anna looked down at me, her face tense.

"I'm only ten feet up," I said. "It's okay."

"Even ten feet can kill you if you land wrong. Take it slowly."

I wanted to point out that she hadn't taken it slowly, but then again, she was better at climbing than me.

"Stretch your right leg, and put it on that hold, there..."

Anna instructed me the rest of the way up. After another couple of minutes of patient climbing, I reached the top. Anna pulled me onto the flat expanse on the plateau. I made myself stand, and I surveyed the level area that made up this plateau. It stretched in all directions, before being cut off by a narrow chasm a hundred feet away. A series of mesas, rock towers, and plateaus rose above the cracks.

I stood, looking in the direction we were heading. I could see what Anna was talking about: the fissures glowed pink from being flooded with ichor. But what caught my attention lay *beyond* the plateaus and mesas.

The pink line Anna had mentioned yesterday had revealed itself as a vast, underground sea of pink ichor. It was probably two miles away, spreading seemingly forever toward the glowing line on the horizon. The collective light of that sea bathed our skin and the surrounding rocks. This *had* to be one of the Two Seas Quietus had mentioned. But where was the other one?

"That's where our buddy was headed," Anna said. "I'm sure of it."

"Quietus said Askala was at the meeting of the Two Seas," I said. "I'm only seeing one."

"We're not there, yet," Anna said. "Maybe we'll have to follow the shore."

"Askala might live in there," I said. "In that ichor."

Anna looked at me. "You think so?"

"I don't know," I said. "Just an idea."

"If that's true, what do we do when we get there? Swim?"

"I hope it doesn't come to that."

We walked across the plateau, descending on its opposite side. Thankfully, the canyon below was clear of ichor. We continued traveling, and after a few more twists and turns, we met the ichor that submerged the rest of the chasm, forcing us to climb once again. We soon found ourselves on top of a long plateau heading in the direction of the sea. We followed it toward its end, still about half a mile away.

"What do we do when we get there?" Anna asked.

I honestly didn't know. We were close enough now to the sea that I could make out its finer details. It even had waves. To the left and right, the sea came to an end in either direction after a few miles each way, curving around again to meet the glowing horizon. I supposed this technically made it a large lake. A miasma of light hung over its surface, reflecting off the dazzling ceiling perhaps a quarter of a mile above. The shoreline was hidden by craggy cliffs, where the plateaus dropped off and met the sea.

Maybe we would have to swim, in the end, but I was afraid that the *Radaskim* ichor would be hostile, and would maybe even lead us far from where we wanted to go.

Anna's hand stiffened, and she pulled me to the ground. Before I could ask, she pointed ahead.

I squinted my eyes against the wavy lines of the sea. I saw nothing at first. But after a moment, the shadow of wings materialized in the distance. It was a large dragon, flying straight toward us.

We crawled away from the edge, trying to find a safe place to descend and hide in the chasms. Glancing back one more time, I realized we didn't need to hide.

Quietus?

I watched her approach over the cliffs, the ones above the sea. Anna came to stand by me, touching my arm. All was silent as Quietus flew the last of the distance to the plateau. She glided downward, extending her legs and landing in front of us lightly.

I had no idea how she had gotten down here, but what she said was even more unexpected.

Your friends fight for their lives beyond the Sea of Destruction.

Anna and I looked at each other. There was no time to stand here and ask for details.

It was only after Anna and I were mounted and Quietus taking to the air that I started to ask questions.

What's happening? Where are they?

She knows you are here, but she is looking in the wrong place, Quietus said. *She thinks you are with your friends. Askal is there, too, fighting with them.*

Then there's no time to lose, I said.

***

We flew over the Sea of Destruction, as Quietus had called it, leaving the black cliffs far behind. The waves danced and crashed a couple of hundred feet below us. A warm updraft rose from the surface – Quietus barely had to flap her wings to keep aloft. It felt as if we were floating.

Soon, we were miles from the mainland, and the cliffs and chasms were far behind. I focused intently on the distance, keeping my eye out for any sign of land.

"We came a long way," Anna said. "Much farther than I would have ever guessed."

"They must have been going the opposite way," I said.

I could only hope that we weren't too late.

As we flew farther away, a dark line materialized on the horizon. The opposite shore wasn't far away. The dark line spread in the distance, its boundary with the sea squiggly. If that was land, it was like no land I'd seen before.

Behold, Quietus said. *The Sea of Destruction.*

I thought we were over the Sea of Destruction, I thought.

No. This is the Sea of Creation. The black sea is the Sea of Destruction. They meet in the middle, forming the Point of Origin. That is where Askala lairs. You will see it, soon. That is not our destination for now. There is land on the other side of the Sea of Destruction, and that is where your friends are. It's also where the worst of Askala's monsters are.

As Quietus spoke, I looked at the meeting of the two seas in the distance. While the Sea of Creation was pink and bright, the Sea of Destruction was dark as night. Very little light reflected from its dull surface, but I could see it roiling far in the distance, much more violently than the pink Sea of Creation. Right in the center of the two seas was a molten, brilliant line, and in the middle of that line, a colossal whirlpool of interweaving pink and black swirling downward to a single point of light as bright as the sun. As we neared, the whirlpool became larger. We were far from it, but high enough that I could look down into its funnel. I couldn't see the bottom – not only because it was too deep, but it was so bright that I had to avert my gaze.

She's in there?

Yes, Quietus said.

I tried not to think about *entering* that whirlpool. But wasn't that what Quietus had said? We would find Askala where the Two Seas joined, at the Point of Origin.

We left the whirlpool behind, and now we flew fully over the black Sea of Destruction. On the horizon, I could see the beginnings of dry land, made of wicked, jagged spires wreathed in black smoke. Fiery rivers descended from the heights, meeting the Sea in streams of molten red. That area looked far more inhospitable than where we had left.

As we neared, I could see three dragons swirling above a ridgeline not far from the black ichor. Two *Radaskim* dragons were fighting against one *Elekai*. I knew immediately that *Elekai* dragon was Askal.

Hurry, I said.

I'm flying as fast as I can, Elekim. *We will be there soon.*

True to her word, Quietus seemed to fly more swiftly. The cliffs fast approached, and as they got nearer, I saw human forms fighting among the rocks, while horrible, twisted monsters closed in from the periphery. Horrifying screams filled the air, but thankfully none of them were human. Gunshots echoed off the rocks.

At last, we left the blackened sea behind and made straight for the ridgeline. Now, I was close enough to make out the finer details. One of the figures – Samuel, I think – turned in our direction, pointing and shouting. All of them had gathered together, their backs to us, firing into the mass of monsters. Among them were crawlers, but also other horrible creatures I'd never seen before. There was a giant centipede that might have been forty feet long with thousands of tiny legs, which might have been a smaller version of the giant worm that had attacked the army. Its chitin was completely black, and its wide mouth opened to reveal rows of needle-like teeth. Another monster, standing as tall as a Behemoth, made its way on six legs, reptilian in nature. It had two scythed arms jutting from its torso, opening and closing like a pair of pincers. Its many white eyes glowed from its face, where a large mouth snapped open and shut.

Everyone was running out of room to maneuver, and they were being pushed toward the cliff. It was easily a five-hundred-foot drop to the sea below. Askal let out a high shriek, changing course to free himself from fighting the *Radaskim* dragons.

"Quietus..."

Hold on, Elekim, she said. *We're going to pick them up.*

Just as soon as I'd tightened my grip, Quietus went into a short dive, fanning out her wings. The two dragons that had been fighting Askal went straight for Quietus. Their white eyes burned with hatred, and they opened their wide jaws and let out twin, horrible shrieks.

Meanwhile, Askal maneuvered closer to the cliff. Everyone had run out of room to back up. The monsters closed in, forming a ring, ready to drive the final nail in the coffin.

Askal hovered at the edge of the cliff. Everyone rushed to get on – Ruth first, followed by Michael.

Samuel and Makara continued to fight while Michael and Ruth held tightly to Askal.

Quietus gave a sudden turn, narrowly dodging the dive of a dragon. Makara and Samuel were waving for Askal to fly away. Michael and Ruth were shouting something, but that didn't stop Askal from spreading his wings, gliding down toward the Sea of Destruction.

"No!" I said.

Quietus then went into a dive. At the same time, the frontrunners of the monsters lurched at Makara and Samuel. Quietus drew even with the cliff, just feet away from the precipice. She spread her wings, slowing down. Though she was slowing, Quietus was still going incredibly fast.

But it would be Samuel's and Makara's only chance of rescue. Without hesitating, they both turned and sprinted for the cliff, jumping into the air, the monsters charging into the vacated space. Makara and Samuel seemed to fly through the air in slow motion.

It wasn't far enough. With horror, I watched as they both dropped.

"No!" Anna screamed.

And then, Quietus tilted to the left, so that both Makara and Samuel landed in the center of her left wing. Quietus tightened the wing, causing Makara and Samuel to both roll down it, toward us.

Anna and I braced ourselves to catch them. Makara rolled right into me, but my back pushed against the lower part of one of Quietus's spikes. Quietus screamed in pain when the spike bent slightly. But she had come to a stop, and was now safe.

Samuel ran into Anna, and pushed her toward the other side of the dragon. Anna screamed, grabbing on the bottom of a spike with one hand.

I reached out with my other hand, grabbing Anna by the hand. She caught herself with her feet on Quietus's side. Her hand was so sweaty that I was terrified it would slip. But Samuel grabbed Anna by the other arm, and together we pulled her up until she was behind me. She held on to me tight, her entire body shaking.

Quietus was still dropping in elevation. She shrieked as she spread her wings, stopping our mad descent right before we crashed into the black sea, the waves of which stretched upward, as if trying to reach us.

As Quietus flapped her wings, rising above the surface of the sea, we sat there, panting, shaken, but safe. Quietus wheeled away from the cliffs, gaining altitude above the Sea of Destruction. I sat there in silence, disbelieving what had just happened. Everyone was alive.

Askal joined us at our side. Ruth and Michael were both sitting safely on his back, holding on tightly. They both looked over at us with wide eyes.

"Everyone alright?" I asked.

Neither of them answered, and I didn't blame them. We were heading for the meeting of the two seas: the Point of Origin. With dread, I realized our time was near.

By some miracle, all of us had survived and had been reunited. We'd made it through the Warrens, the monsters, and every other obstacle we had to face in getting here.

Askala was waiting.

Chapter 23

We didn't make immediately for the Point of Origin. There was nothing between us and Askala, and I thought it would best if we could recoup a bit and get our bearings.

A jagged island rose from the Sea of Destruction, perhaps halfway from the shoreline to the Point of Origin.

Go there, I said to Quietus.

Quietus complied, switching her course toward the island.

Makara's eyes were closed – both she and Samuel were uninjured, but both were utterly exhausted. I wouldn't have been surprised if they hadn't gotten any sleep last night, which would have made for two nights in a row. Anna gave them the rest of the water from her canteen, but even that did little to revive them.

At last, both dragons glided toward the black rock rising above the ichor. There was only one flat area – at the very top – that was large enough for both dragons to land on. Even then, they landed gingerly, not having much room to maneuver.

Once they landed, I was the first one off. Soon, everyone followed me, immediately lying down on the black rock, closing their eyes. They were past the point of exhaustion.

"Um...should we wake them?" Anna asked.

I looked out at the Point of Origin, watching the Two Seas meld into one. A beam of light shot straight up, illuminating the ceiling far above. It was like a beacon, leading me to my final destination.

"They haven't slept," I said, turning to face Anna. "It's a miracle they're even alive."

Anna looked at the light beaming upward. I saw it reflected in her eyes. I just watched her for a moment, completely taken by her beauty.

She looked at me. "I guess we have a chance to relax, too."

"Relax," I said. "Yeah, right."

Makara stirred, forcing her eyes open. "We...we need to..."

"Go to sleep, Makara," I said. "It's alright. Really."

She nodded slowly, closing her eyes.

Anna turned to face the land. It was far away, and I couldn't see anything moving over there. The dragons hadn't followed us out here.

Maybe even *they* were afraid of her.

For now, though, I felt like nothing was watching us. It was strange, to be this close and to not have to worry about anything attacking us.

"Alright," Anna said. "We can keep watch. But we can't stay too long."

I looked over at everyone again. They were all so still. If I had come upon them like this, I would have thought they were dead.

Both of the dragons sat on their haunches quietly. Quietus fluttered her wings, giving a loud snort.

Are you alright? I asked.

I am well enough for a place as evil as this. She looked in the direction of the Point of Origin. *She watches us, even now. She waits for you,* Elekim.

How did you and Askal get down here, anyway? I asked.

I know every passage, every path in this labyrinth, Quietus said. *It helped that most of them were empty. I knew, if you were ever to reach Askala, you would need our help. I thought that Askala would direct you to the Sea of Destruction, it being far more dangerous. So, that was where Askal and I began our search. We found everyone else, but you and Anna were nowhere to be found. We searched the Destruction shore, until Askal suggested I bring my search to the other side.*

We saw you, I said. *We saw you flying above us, yesterday, but we didn't know it was you.*

Yes, Quietus said. *That was me, arriving for the first time. I searched, on my way to the Twin Seas, but I didn't believe you were going to be there, so I didn't stay long. Much time could have been saved.*

It doesn't matter, Anna said. *We're all safe now.*

Elekim.

I looked at Askal.

I feared you were dead.

Yeah. Me too.

And now we are near the end.

I smiled grimly. *Don't remind me.*

I want you to know…you won't be fighting alone.

What do you mean?

We've decided, Elekim…*we are coming with you, as far as we can. Even into the Point of Origin.*

What?

We will follow you as far as we can, Askal said. *There might be a time where we can no longer follow…but until that time, we will stand by your side.*

There's no need for everyone to die, just for my sake.

It has already been decided. We fight together. We Elekai *live and die together.*

Anna touched my hand. "We can *help* you. Remember with the writhe? Without me, you would have died. Can you imagine how much stronger Askala will be?"

Anna had a point, but I'd already set myself up as the sacrificial lamb. I didn't want everyone else to die with me. At the same time, though, they had to watch *me* die. Why would they do this, when there was a still chance they could save themselves?

"There's a chance we can defeat her, Alex," Anna said. "But we all have to work together."

"One thing's for sure...when we enter the Point of Origin, there won't be any coming back. We *all* die, not just me."

"Askal is right," Anna said. "This is how we do it. This is how we win."

I remained silent. I didn't want to be the one to tell them it was okay to die when it might serve no purpose.

"The Nameless One told me what I have to do. I...have to join my consciousness to Askala. Such a thing would mean I'd *become* her, in a sense."

I turned, looking at Anna. I wasn't sure what was she was thinking, though I could tell she hadn't expected that.

"Winning means immortality," I said. "Forsaking my humanity. Dying would be so much easier, but my sacrifice will be more than that. I have to live forever."

Anna didn't speak for a long time – out of shock, more than anything.

"Why didn't you say anything?"

"I don't know. Because I feel like there's nothing we can do it about it. It's the price I have to pay."

"No, it's not," Anna said. "Is that what you *want?* You would live forever. Forever is a long, long time."

"If you have another solution, I'd love to hear it," I said. "This is all we have. Even the Wanderer said I had to sacrifice myself, and the Nameless One said the same thing." I looked at Anna. "What greater sacrifice is there than to become your own enemy, to live forever and give up your humanity? I'd die in a second if that was all it was, and I know all of you would, too."

"We have to fight back," Anna said. "I won't let you do this. I've said that, over and over. The others...we talked, before the battle, about how we were going to do it together. Either we all do this together, or not at all. That's how it happens. Something tells me you're not going to make it very far without us, even in there." Anna pointed to the whirlpool, churning between the Two Seas.

She waited for me to respond, and suddenly, I knew Anna was right. We had to do this together. I couldn't explain it, but I felt a sense of peace about it.

"You're right," I said, finally.

Anna grabbed my hands, pulling me to face her. "Of course I'm right. And I wouldn't have cared what you said, yes or no. We were going to do this, anyway."

I smiled. "Good thing I agreed, then." Quickly, my smile went away. "What will it be like, though? Do we die, the minute we enter that whirlpool?"

Anna couldn't answer that question, so I turned to Quietus and Askal. It was Quietus who provided an answer.

The Point of Origin is the meeting of the physical world and the world of the Radaskim *consciousness. When you enter, yes, you die to this world, and your minds will enter the consciousness. It…is a strange place, far different from the physical world. Within the* Radaskim *mind, you must find Askala and join with her consciousness*

She doesn't exist physically? I asked.

No, Elekim, Quietus answered. *Otherwise, she could merely be destroyed. But you cannot destroy that which has no physical manifestation. You must conquer her mind, and that can only be done by entering the Point of Origin.*

And all of us can enter it? I asked.

Yes, Quietus said. *It would be death for anyone who did not have the xenovirus, but the virus will allow you to enter the* Radaskim *mind.*

Even as an Elekai?

Yes. Even as an Elekai. *There are deeper rules, deeper realities, within the melding of consciousness. An* Elekai *may exist among the* Radaskim, *but a* Radaskim *may not exist among the* Elekai.

This has to do with the dominance of the Elekai *virus?*

Yes, and it is also why a Radaskim *can never learn the Secrets of Creation, which are housed within the consciousness of the* Elekai. *If ever a* Radaskim *entered that consciousness, they would immediately become* Elekai.

And that's what will happen, when we enter the Point of Origin?

Quietus paused. *It is not so simple. Askala will be fighting on a familiar front, a front that is unfamiliar to you or any of the* Elekai. *Her greatest strength would have been in destroying you before you ever arrived here. You have evaded her so far,* Elekim...*but it isn't over, yet. The* Radaskim *consciousness is like a maze, and you would do well with a guide.* Quietus paused. *That is why I'm going with you, along with Askal.*

You're both going with me?

Askal looked at me intently. It seemed like everyone, dragons included, would be fighting with me once we passed through the Point of Origin.

Now sleep, Elekim, Quietus said. *Askal and I will keep watch. I do not think she will attack you – not here. Besides, the* Radaskim *fear you, and they will cling to the safety of the Destruction Shore. Rest, for where we are going, you shall need it.*

***

Despite Quietus's ominous tone, I fell asleep as soon as I lay down. It was a long time before I stirred, and when I opened my eyes, it felt as if I were in a dream. The swirling black Sea of Destruction crashed against the rocks far below.

I sat up, focusing on the Point of Origin. It looked the same as it had before, but it still awed me with its immensity and power. The Two Seas, Creation and Destruction, fell into the maelstrom, melding into one. I couldn't see the very center, hidden by the tumultuous waves, but I knew that was my end point. It wouldn't be long until we were all entering it.

Around me, everyone else was waking. Everyone stood, stretched, and looked over the edge of the rocks at the roiling sea below.

"Crazy," Michael said. "I wonder what Julian would think of all this."

"Or Ashton," Anna said.

"Jesus," Michael said. "I can't believe they're gone."

"I just want you guys to know," I began, "that you don't have to do this. I know you have people waiting for you, up above. I have nothing there. Everything I have is right here." I paused, trying to collect my thoughts. "If anyone decides to take one of the dragons to the surface…no one will judge you for it."

Everyone was silent for a long time.

"There's no shame in turning back," I said. "Michael, I know you have a family…"

"I'm this far," Michael said. "I'm not turning back. I'm here until the end, wherever that is. I'm doing this to protect my family, and you'll need me, Alex. I'm not backing down now."

The others nodded. I looked at Makara, Samuel, and Ruth.

"I'm with you," Makara said. "This is the moment I've been waiting for."

Ruth didn't say anything, only giving a slow nod.

"We're all in this together," Samuel said. "As we all agreed earlier."

As one, we turned to face the whirlpool, watching its swirling ichor fall toward the center.

"If everyone is ready…"

"Let's just stand here, for a little bit," Makara said. "I have stuff to say." It was a moment before Makara continued. "Whatever happens down there…it's been good, fighting with you guys. I have no idea if it all ends right here. It probably does. But I couldn't have asked for a better crew, and I would never have imagined we'd be standing here, like this. We made it a lot farther than I ever thought we would. The fact that we're standing here, at the center of it all, is an amazing achievement." She turned, looking at each of us. "Don't forget that."

We continued to watch the Point of Origin. Finally, I had a few words to say.

"I was planning on doing this on my own, as much as possible. But I learned a valuable lesson. When you try to do everything on your own, everything proves to be impossible. Just knowing I don't have to face this alone...it makes it easier. And a part of me thinks we have the strength to do this. The Wanderer told me a prophecy. Though a thousand worlds will fall, one will remain." I looked at everyone. "I think that's *our* world. We won't let our world fall, and we won't stop until the *Radaskim* have been defeated. Like Quietus, they're imprisoned in there. But we have the power to free them. Even Askala. I can defeat her, but I will need your help to do it."

"We're all with you," Makara said.

"I know. There might be a time, though, where there's something that only *I* can do. If that time comes...then watch my back. Make sure I do it. It still all hinges on me, and there's a time where I'll have to go the final distance alone. If there is...promise me. Promise you'll stay back, and get out, if possible. That's my condition. That's the only way you get to come with me."

It was a long time before anyone else spoke. I had no idea where those words came from, but I felt, deep down, that there was some element of my needing to do something alone. I was *Elekim,* and in a sense, to be *Elekim* was to be alone. Only I had the power to infect Askala, and none of my friends could help me with that.

At last, Anna nodded. "We'll go as far as we possibly can. But make us a promise as well: don't go on alone unless you absolutely have to."

"I won't," I said.

Everything had been settled. There was nothing more to say. We were all in agreement, and we all knew what we had to do, so far as we could ever know.

With that realization, I said the two fateful words.

"Let's move."

We mounted our dragons, Anna and I taking Askal while the rest climbed on Quietus. I felt a sense of both dread and peace, a strange combination. Dread, for what was about to come. Peace, because I knew it was the only thing that I could do. That it was what I was *supposed* to do.

It was my destiny as *Elekim*.

After we had settled, I connected minds with Askal.

Ready?

In truth, no. But we must do what we must do.

Then let's go, I said. *To the Point of Origin.*

A moment later, Askal kicked off the ledge, spreading his wings. Before we fell too far, he glided over the surface of the black ichor. Quietus and the rest followed close behind, and both dragons flapped wings in tandem.

The tall rock was left behind, and the Point of Origin advanced all too quickly, growing larger in my vision. We would be over it within a couple of minutes.

Anna held on tightly, knowing we would only have a few more moments in the physical world with no guarantee of return. I knew for sure I wouldn't be returning, so I cherished Anna's touch, the feel of her face on my neck. It was something I would never experience again.

"I love you," I said. "Never forget that."

"I won't," she said. "I couldn't forget that, even if I tried."

"Without you, I could have never done this," I said. "You're everything to me, Anna. Because of you, I have no regrets."

Anna was quiet. A great hiss filled the air as we neared the whirlpool, just a minute away from crossing its horizon. The wind gusted heavily.

"There was so much more we had to do," Anna said. "So much more we had to see."

"We can't think about that," I said.

"I know," Anna said. "Just...hold on to me, when we go in there."

"I will," I said. "I promise."

We passed over the horizon. Below, the light of the Point of Origin shone upward, bright as the sun. I shielded my eyes as Askal sank lower and lower. We were now even with the ichor of the Two Seas, and still we sank lower into the whirlpool. Both dragons' wings were outspread, spiraling toward the single bright point.

As we neared, the world faded. Images swam before me, but still, I felt Anna holding on. I grabbed both of her hands tightly, using only my legs to stay on Askal's back. My vision failed, and my hearing became filled with white noise, until it was almost the entirety of my senses. Still, I felt Anna's hands, and that feeling let me know that I was okay, that she was okay.

We kept falling, falling, until it was so bright and hot that I felt as if I was burning alive. We were suddenly pulled down. Askal had disappeared beneath me completely.

I shot downward, incredibly fast, feeling my body disintegrate and fade into the maelstrom. Though my body was now gone, my thoughts continued, struggling for something to grasp onto. But there was only the surrounding whiteness, a great nothing extending in all directions.

And in time, even that nothing faded, until I could experience no more.

Chapter 24

My first thought when I came to my senses was that this was far too beautiful to be anything created by the *Radaskim*.

Wide silvery trails arced from my position in miasmic streams. An infinite white mist spread in every direction. Points of light floated in the air, nodes toward which the silver streams flowed. I looked down, seeing that I was floating in the air, the mists descending for what seemed forever. It was like looking onto a galaxy of stars.

I focused on one of the nearby nodes of light, toward which one of the streams flowed in a cascade of molten silver. I needed to go there. As soon as that thought entered my mind, I flowed across the stream, like electricity along a wire, until I connected with the node. I looked around at my new surroundings. There were thousands upon thousands of these nodes, just floating in the mist like stars.

I'd have to search among these nodes for the others. I transferred myself to the next node. Movement was easy; all I had to do was think of the neighboring node and will myself to travel there, and I could do this so long as the nodes were connected by a silver stream. As I became used to this new state, I was flying from one point of light to the next in a flurry of movement.

After five minutes, I'd lost all sense of direction. Here, there was no down or up, east or west. There wasn't even gravity. This place had its own rules, and I had to be careful since I didn't know them.

I had just paused to collect my thoughts when I saw an orb of pink light racing along the streams. It bounced back and forth between the starry nodes, incredibly fast. I knew it had to be someone else. If we'd all entered by the same place, it would make sense that we were all in the same area. At least, that was what I hoped.

I made my way toward the moving pink orb, which had paused on a node below me. I directed my attention there, finding the quickest path.

The orb was still. I was only one connection away. If I wanted to move on, I needed to occupy the same space.

So, I raced along the stream, connecting to the node, joining with the energy. When I did, I found that I was not alone. Somehow, I knew I had come upon Ruth.

Alex? Is that you?

Yeah. It's me. This place is really weird.

I know. Have you seen the others?

No. They have to be around, somewhere...

There were these black lights chasing me a while ago, but I think I got away. They...sort of looked like you, only black.

Like an orb?

I guess, Ruth said. *I don't know what they are, but I don't think they're on our side. We should keep moving. Find the others.*

I watched the surrounding nodes and connecting streams, but saw nothing of these black orbs. I was thankful they weren't here now, but they could show up any second.

I decided to turn back in the direction I'd come from. If Ruth had come from the other direction, then that was probably where these black orbs were. We traveled together, shooting from node to node as a single entity. Joined together, it seemed as if we were going faster than when I'd just been on my own. We sped faster and faster until our original area had been left behind entirely. Beyond the streams and glowing nodes, a thick constellation lit the distance, its collective glow radiant and mesmerizing. All the streams seemed to lead there.

Maybe we should go there, I thought.

Look.

My attention was drawn below. A bright pink orb shot along the silver streams as three black orbs gave chase.

We changed our direction to head straight down, following the chaos of streams so fast that everything passed in a blur. The three black orbs had converged on a single node. Apparently, they *also* had the ability to join, and with that joining, the black orb brightened considerably, shooting off toward the pink orb at a much higher speed. It seemed like when orbs joined, they became brighter and faster. This applied to both the black orbs and the pink ones.

We raced downward, seeking to cut off the path of the pink orb. That light was brighter than when I had seen Ruth, but it wasn't as bright or fast as the black orb. This made me think there were two people sharing that energy. If that was the case, then if Ruth and I could intercept, it would be our four against the black orb's three. Hopefully, that would be enough to tip the scales in our favor.

The black orb was only two nodes behind the pink one. There was a node that the pink orb was heading toward, the only clear spot where we could intercept it.

That node, I said. *That's where we meet them.*

We were just a few nodes away. We flowed from stream to stream, connecting to the target node. At the same instant, the pink orb fused with Ruth's and mine's.

At first, I felt only shock. Then, I became aware of Michael and Askal's presence.

Alex? Michael's voice said. *Ruth?*

Yeah, it's us, I said. *We need to move.*

The approaching black orb, was only one node away. It hesitated, trying to decide if this was a fight it would take.

We are too strong for it, Askal said.

The black orb flowed away, as quickly as it had come.

Sweet, Michael said.

They'll be back, I said. *And next time, they'll have more. We still have to find the rest.*

We saw some of them, over toward that group of really bright lights, Michael said. *But those black lights chased us away.*

Then we need to go back, I said. *Everyone keep an eye out. We're definitely not out of this yet.*

***

With all four of our energies fused together, we were able to go faster than ever before. We raced toward the thick, interlocking nodes in the distance, on our way seeing a pink orb. It was about as bright as Michael and Askal's had been, leading me to believe it was two people. We were missing Anna, Makara, Samuel, and Quietus.

But as we raced along the streams, the mist darkened. The only light came from the streams themselves and our own emitted aura. Black orbs flowed from every direction, all heading for the node where the lone pink orb stood its ground.

Hurry, I said.

We raced along the streams, but not before one of the black orbs attacked the pink one. The pink orb shot from the node, right toward us, as if knocked back. We moved to intercept it, connecting on the same node. I became aware of both Makara's and Samuel's presence.

Alex! Makara said. *It's just me and Samuel.*

We need to find Anna, I said. *Quietus, too.*

Right now, we need to run, Samuel said.

I saw Samuel's point. Already, many of the black orbs were converging, forming an orb that would far overpower ours. It was time we left.

I oriented our orb toward the constellation of lights, glowing in the distance. We flowed along the streams at breakneck speeds, able to outpace the black orbs still converging. Soon, they would be fast enough to follow us, and we did not know these paths as well as they did. We needed Quietus to show us the way to Askala's consciousness.

Even though Quietus was the one we needed, finding Anna was more important to me. I could only hope that the two of them had found each other, somehow. I couldn't bear the thought of Anna being alone in this hostile place.

As we shot toward the constellation, the nodes and interconnecting streams were so close and tangled that it was dizzying to even look at them. Quietus was right; this place was a maze, and without her guidance, we would surely be overtaken by the black orbs sooner or later. In the overwhelming amount of lights, I searched for any pink orbs flowing along the streams. So far, I hadn't seen any. There were too many streams, too many nodes...

There, Ruth said.

My attention focused on where Ruth was looking. And there it was. A pink light, navigating interlocking streams at incredible speed. It was as bright as Makara's and Samuel's. Hopefully, that meant Quietus and Anna were together.

Behind, the black orbs had regrouped, chasing us along the silver pathways. I watched the pink orb, twisting and turning through the silver conduits, getting closer and closer. I realized that *they* were coming to *us*. As much as I wanted to stand my ground to make it easier for them, we had to get moving – the black orbs would reach us before they did.

So, I directed our energy along random pathways, hoping to confuse our pursuers. Several of the black orbs fanned out on alternate paths; to my dismay, some of them even shot ahead of us. I angled downward, only to find several more black orbs rushing to block our retreat.

We had been completely penned in.

It was at that moment that Quietus's and Anna's pink light occupied the node I was about to connect with. A black orb filled the neighboring node, just an instant away from striking at Quietus and Anna.

Thankfully, I got there first. As soon as I became aware of Quietus's and Anna's presence, a huge shock reverberated throughout my mind, followed by a monstrous scream. My vision darkened, before returning to me, revealing the black orb shooting away at incredible speed down the streams. Within moments, it was out of sight.

Anna... I thought.

I'm fine, she said. *Quietus was telling me that we're almost there.*

Quietus took control of our orb, weaving it through the labyrinth of streams and nodes. Dozens of black orbs followed the paths, seeking to trap us, and more yet joined from the periphery. But Quietus always knew which way to go – if there were five different routes blocked, she would find a sixth one.

She worked our orb through the various streams, heading deeper into the central constellation. A single bright light occupied the center. I knew *that* was our target.

We reached a node that only had two possible paths, but each path led to a node occupied by a black orb. Several more orbs tailed us from behind, closing off the possibility of backtracking.

Quietus suddenly turned us toward the right, directly at one of the orbs. As soon as we connected, we were met with strong resistance.

Command it, Elekim!

I had no idea what that meant, but I reached out with my mind, seeking to make a connection.

Let us pass!

One life...

Let us pass! Now!

One life...

I realized what it was asking. It wanted one person to stay behind.

I'll...I'll stay, Makara said. *The rest of you go on.*

Makara, no...

Elekim, there is no time! Quietus said.

Alex, listen to me. We are not getting out of this unless I stay here. Alright? Now move.

Makara... Samuel said.

No arguing! Go now! Do what you have to do, Alex.

Behind, the black orbs were fast advancing. There was no time to think, no time to do anything but what Makara had told me.

I'll stand my ground here, she said. *Go, Alex. All of you...protect him. The price I'm paying now will be small compared to what he'll go through.*

Makara...

Go! Don't hesitate!

I turned my attention back to the black orb.

You give her soul? the black orb whispered.

I didn't hesitate; I did just as Makara had told me.

Yes.

Instantly, I felt Makara's consciousness depart. And like that, she was gone, her life snuffed out like a candle. I wanted to scream, but I couldn't. I couldn't think *anything* as we were allowed to go by, Quietus leading us along the pathways now clear of black orbs. I looked back, but we were already too far away.

I'm sorry, I thought.

You did nothing wrong, Anna said. *There was no other way.*

She died well, Samuel said. *She died a warrior.*

That was who Makara was. A warrior. It seemed a travesty that I couldn't cry in this place, couldn't scream or grieve. I just felt an emptiness that went beyond words. Makara, who had saved my life countless times, had saved it one, final time...and it had cost her own life.

There were no more nodes – just a single, long pathway leading to the point of brightness in the far distance.

And then, we were brought to a stop on a final, hidden node. Nothing but white brightness extended ahead.

It was terribly quiet. No one said anything, and I couldn't help but feel that this was the final door...a door which only I could pass through.

I have to go on alone, I said.

No, Anna said.

You promised me, I said. *If there was a point where I had to go on alone, you would let me.*

Then I'll break that promise, gladly. You can't fight her alone, Alex.

She'll only let me in, I said. *I'm sure of that.*

We will defend you here, Quietus said. *For as long as we can.*

Alex, no! Anna said.

Anna...I'll always love you. Remember that. Please...I have to go.

We've done as much as we can, Samuel said. *All we can do is hold the line.*

No one said anything for a long while. I just waited for Anna to say something. But she didn't. I was afraid I would never hear her voice again.

And then, she spoke. *Alex...please come back. I don't know how you can find a way out, but please, find a way...*

If there is any way, I'll find it. But I have to do what I came here to do. You know that. And no matter what happens, nothing will ever stop me from loving you.

You must go now, Elekim, Quietus said.

The black orbs were fast approaching, just several nodes away. I turned my attention to the central point of light, the nexus of Askala's consciousness.

If there's a way out, I said to Quietus, *please use it.*

Time seemed to slow, and the black orbs moved at a crawl.

I made a promise to myself, Anna said. *I promised I would go with you, to the end. And I meant the very end. Not the last door. The rest of them can leave. But me...I'm coming with you.*

Before I could say anything more, the black orbs lit the nodes directly bordering ours.

Go, Elekim! Quietus said.

There was no time, so I turned toward the bright light, willing myself to move forward.

But somehow, Anna had caught hold of me, riding along.

Anna!

She didn't answer – we were both pulled toward the great white light.

Chapter 25

I awoke to find myself in darkness, the brightness gone and replaced with a featureless void. Everything felt cold.

Then, I remembered being pulled away from the others – and that Anna had somehow attached herself to me.

Anna?

There was nothing but blackness, no light for guidance. I walked forward – this place felt physically *real*. The air was so heavy that it felt like walking through water. I touched my arms, my face.

Askala's voice entered my mind in a soft hiss.

Elekim...

I then felt myself being pulled toward the left, as if by gravity. I was falling, faster and faster, until a burst of light filled my vision, as bright as a star. I was racing toward it, my speed ever-increasing. The coldness faded and was replaced by a sickly warmth that grew increasingly hotter. It would only be moments until I entered that star.

Anna!

She cannot help you now, Elekim.

In an overwhelming flood of light, the star burst. I felt myself ripped apart from the blast of energy, disintegrating into nothing. I screamed, and all went dark.

***

After a long while, I felt my consciousness return, and with it came Askala's voice.

You've come to destroy me, Askala said. *But you haven't the slightest idea how. I must say, though, I am impressed. You walk where no* Elekim *has walked before.*

Where's Anna?

Askala cackled. *And why would I tell you that,* Elekim? *You are already dead, and so is the girl. I will destroy you, again and again, until you are broken and mad.* She paused. *I would hear you beg now.*

I beg nothing, I said.

Did you think you could enter my world and control it? Pitiful fool. You will join the ranks of the other champions, maddened beyond identity. Askala chuckled. *You will break, in the end. Make no mistake,* Elekim...*I will* break *you.*

I stood in the darkness. Askala seemed to have disappeared, leaving me in a vast, empty nothingness.

Anna?

I had to find her, if it was the last thing I did. I ran, never seeming to tire, looking for some change in this emptiness.

I couldn't say how long I ran, but surely for hours, if there was such a thing as time in this place. Maybe even *that* didn't exist here. Turning in each direction, I found nothing but a black void. I looked up, down, left, and right, but there was no escape, no indication of where I should go.

I was alone.

Anna?

What if she *wasn't* here? What if Askala wanted me to *believe* Anna was here, but only to make me go insane? I would never know for sure. The only thing I knew was that I was supposed to infect Askala with the *Elekai* xenovirus. But I had to find Anna first. Unlike me, she wasn't *Elekim*. She wouldn't have the same ability to fight Askala.

I reached out with my mind, seeking her consciousness in the void, increasing my scope farther and farther in every direction. And then...it suddenly became very difficult to concentrate. I realized what this was: Askala was weakening my ability to focus. I redoubled my efforts – no matter how much power Askala had here, she couldn't take away my mind.

Anna, however, might not have the same luxury, which made it all the more important to find her.

The scope of my awareness enveloped hundreds of miles in each direction, an ever-widening sphere. Hours passed, with still no sign of Anna. Even Askala's influence seemed to ebb, with time, as I became surer of my abilities and the freedom of my mind – but I never let my guard down in case Askala decided to unleash a new attack.

Alex?

There she was. I could scarcely believe it.

Anna? Where are you? Anna, I...

Alex, help me...

Hold on. I'm coming.

She's going to kill me, she said. *She'll kill me if you fight her...*

Stay there. I'm coming.

I'm...too far gone, Alex. She's won. She's...

And like that, Anna was gone. Tears formed in my eyes as I searched madly to find her voice again.

This happened, came Askala's voice, hideous. *You could not save her, Alex. She is mine, now.*

No.

A horrible, grating laughter reverberated in my mind. It only grew louder, driving me to madness.

***

...and suddenly, there was light. There was feeling. There was warm air on my skin.

I opened my eyes, a pink light filling my vision.

And I heard voices.

"He's coming to."

"Ma...Makara?"

"Stand still. We got it off you, but you were still passed out for a good while."

I coughed – my throat was incredibly dry and...*slimy*.

"Makara..." I said. "I thought you were..."

"Dead?" She chuckled. "I couldn't die in that place. It wasn't real, Alex."

I frowned. Though there was pink light, that was all there was. I couldn't see anything, just hear the voices, feel the clothes on my skin and the firmness of the ground beneath me.

"Where is this?" I asked. "What happened? Got *what* off me, exactly?"

"There was a tube, going into your right ear," Makara said. "We all got separated when we entered the whirlpool, and..."

"None of this was real?" I asked. "The orbs...you died, Makara, saving us. I went to fight Askala, and..."

I pulled myself up. I felt as if I were in a dream. I didn't know where I was, and all I cared about was reaching Anna. But still, I couldn't see anything – nothing but the pink in front of my vision.

"Anna. Where's Anna?"

Neither Makara nor Samuel answered.

"Where's Anna?" I repeated.

Again, silence. A sickening dread twisted my stomach.

"I don't care what the answer is!" I yelled. "I need to know. *Now!*"

With mounting horror, I realized that this wasn't real. Makara was still dead. The others, probably dead as well. This was just one of Askala's tricks to twist my mind, and my battle with her was far from over.

With this realization, all went dark.

***

Did you enjoy that, Elekim?

My heart still raced, and I still felt sick to my core.

This is only the beginning. I will make you see their faces, again and again. I will make you forget that they are dead, only to kill them again in front of your eyes. Imagine this pain for the rest of time. I have that power, Elekim. *It can all end in sweet oblivion, blessed annihilation, if only you surrender your power to me.*

Never.

Your friends are all dead. Yes, even the girl. That is why you cannot find her. Her memory is like a mirage, beyond the horizon. A sweet dream, never to be recaptured. You are alone, Elekim...*well and truly alone.*

I don't believe you. I refuse to believe you.

Then you must learn. I have an eternity to teach you.

With each passing second, I felt myself grow smaller. Still, I wasn't going to back down or give up. Not if this *took* an eternity.

I would always have my mind, and I would always have the ability to choose what to believe. I resolved to never believe a word Askala said to me. I had to assume it was all a lie, every single word, or eventually she *would* win.

So in that darkness, in that smallness, I remembered what the Wanderer had told me, my original purpose for being here: I was supposed to infect Askala with the *Elekai* version of the xenovirus. I had thought this infection would be physical, but this was a battle of wills.

Even here, in this darkness, there must be some line to the real world. I had to *believe* it was there, or I would never find it.

I closed my eyes, and listened for anything that *wasn't* Askala's voice. Still, she whispered, sometimes several things at once. I had to expand my awareness beyond that, and let the whispers pass me by.

This continued for a long while. The whispers became more insistent, more permeating, and more difficult to ignore. I refocused myself, remembering why I was doing this. I had no power here, so my only chance was finding a source of power that went beyond this horrible place.

And then, I heard it: the Eternal Song of the *Elekai*. It was faint, but it was there, existing far beyond the confines of this Hell. It wasn't a mirage or a dream, but entirely real. Even Askala would not have had the ability to profane its notes in imitation – the Eternal Song was not something that could be copied.

So, I embraced it in full, until it became louder, drowning out Askala's fell whispers. They no longer had any power over me – and what's more, I realized that they never did. For the first time, I detected a new emotion in Askala's consciousness.

Fear.

Her new attack became unrelenting, brutal, even panicked. And like that, the song was dashed from my mind. The darkness returned, along with my fear, my sickness, my helplessness.

Desperately, I reached for the Song again before Askala's assault could continue. It was still there. And I knew: whatever Askala tried, she could never silence it. The Song had found me, even in this place.

Fool, she whispered. *You have no power here.*

I remembered my resolve to not believe a word she said, so I believed the opposite. The Song had *all* the power here.

Listen, I told her. *Listen to the Song.*

Before she could silence the Song again, I became a conduit for it. Somehow, I started to sing its notes – reproducing it perfectly, channeling its beauty to fill this dark void with a bright, spreading light. In a nova-like burst, the light expanded outward. Askala screamed, long and horrible, as the darkness departed and ceased to be.

There was nothing but the light, the Song, the cleansing of Askala's consciousness. There was nothing here that was hers – no memory, no thoughts or intents; everything had been wiped clean. This consciousness, this world, was mine now.

I opened my eyes to the whiteness, not believing that it was over. The oppressive air had been lifted. Askala was truly gone.

"Anna?" I called out.

Nothing responded in the following silence. I realized then, now having full access to this consciousness, that Anna wasn't here. She never had been. Askala had only led me to believe that.

I reached out, beyond the consciousness, seeing the outside world for the first time. Every creature, every plant, every cell under the dominion of Askala reverted to my control, to the control of the *Elekai*.

Far beyond, on the plateau, by some miracle, a few thousand men stood back to back, fighting the legions of crawlers and swarms of dragons.

I commanded those creatures to stop. And they did. I could see, through their eyes, the terrified faces of the legionaries. I switch perspectives, until I was looking down from above, at Augustus himself, staring dazed out into the vast field of corpses – of men, of crawlers, of monsters.

The battle was over. We had won.

All at once, I commanded the creatures to retreat, to fall back into the Great Blight. They were all *Elekai,* now, the commands and directives of their former master completely forgotten.

So, as one, I issued a new command.

Askala is dead, I said. *All of you are free, and all of you are* Elekai. *Live according to the tenets of the Eternal Song. Meditate on its precepts. It was what you were born to do.*

There was agreement among all the new *Elekai*. A thousand different voices flooded my mind, all incomprehensible when taken together. In that mass of voices, I only cared about one thing – the fate of my friends. They had all entered the whirlpool with me, and I had to know if Quietus had led them to safety.

And I had to know if Anna was alive.

But a great weariness overcame me, one that I could not explain. I remembered the Wanderer, and when he released his power, how it had only taken a few minutes for him to pass.

I knew that was now happening to me.

Anna...

My mind was beginning to fade – soon there would be nothing at all.

But before that eventuality arrived, I heard the most important thing I could ever hear.

Alex...

Anna...you're alive?

Quietus kept me from following you...

I'm...just glad you're okay.

Alex...where are you?

I'm...fading, Anna, I said. *But all is well. I have a feeling eternity won't be so bad after all.*

Alex...no. You can't go. You have to come back...

...I can't.

Makara...she never came, either. We were all there, on the shoreline, but she was gone...

I felt my consciousness slipping away. A sense of peace filled my entire being.

I will see her soon, I said. *But go now. Live your life. Remember what happened here. Remember how hard we fought. Never let anyone forget what happened this day, but not for my sake. The* Radaskim *will return in four hundred years. You can't let the world forget. I...might not be able to protect them next time.*

Alex...I won't. God, you can't leave me.
Where are you now?
We're all standing here, watching the sea. Wondering if you or Makara will come back.
She's home now. And when your time comes...it will be your home, too. Live your life, Anna. There is so much for you to do, so much for you to see, and a new, safer world for you to live in.
I don't want to live in it, she said. *Not without you.*
I'll always be with you, I said. *I promise.*

And then, I saw her face with the tears streaming down, tinted pink from the light of the Sea of Creation. It was all one sea, now, just as we were both one – one in purpose, one in life, one in love.

And then, all went quiet. All went white. I faded into that which was eternal, the song of the universe.

The music was waiting for me.

Epilogue

As I stood on the edge of the Sea of Creation, somehow I knew he wasn't coming back. He was lost somewhere beyond that line, and always would be lost to this world. He had gone to join another.

I remember someone placing a hand on my shoulder – Ruth, I think – and we lifted off on dragons' wings, never to return to this haunted place.

After it was all over, no one knew how we had gotten out. Quietus found a way, I guess, just as Alex told her to. The Sea of Creation remade our bodies, and we emerged from it without a single shred of clothing or weapon to our names.

None of that mattered, though. Alex was dead and gone, along with Makara, and Julian. We waited on the shore of the Sea for hours after Alex stopped speaking with me, but I knew the truth.

I was alone, now.

We flew out, returning to the army, naked, cold, and hungry. We were clothed, and fed, but even so, we remained empty. Even with the Radaskim *stopped and our world saved, at least for another four hundred years, there would always be a void in our hearts that couldn't be filled, and I think in mine most of all.*

Death is natural, but it feels unnatural. There's a sense of fairness in our mind that says death should never be. And yet, there it is. There, it always will be. I can only remember Alex, what he did, and how I loved him.

Not an hour, not a minute, goes by when I don't think of him, knowing he lives eternally in a place I can never go to – not until my dying day. I said I'd follow him, and I suppose this wish will be granted, in time.

Days, then weeks, passed. We lived. We rebuilt. We went on, because that's what people do. And nine months later, I was given something to remember my husband by.

I had a son. Of course, I named him after his father. He has his eyes and his face, and even as a child, he has that same courage and fearlessness, that ability to brighten one's day simply by being there, a quiet courage that values actions rather than words.

My husband will never be with me, but because of my son, Alex, some part of him will live on. I'd like to think that he's watching over me, watching over us...just as he promised. Sometimes, I get the sense that he's there. At times, I see him in dreams. These are becoming fewer, as the years pass.

Augustus now rules in the Wasteland, and the rule of the Black Reapers is no more. Samuel is one of the Emperor's most trusted advisors, and he and Ruth are married, now. They have two children, a son and a daughter. They live in Los Angeles with Michael and Lauren, who have also had more children.

A curious thing happened, after the Radaskim *fell.* The clouds began to go away. It was slow, at first, but it became more discernible with time. The land warmed, and the rain returned, cleansing the dry land. Green things began to grow – in small amounts, but the warmer weather meant more food for all. I suspect, by the time I'm gone, the Wasteland will not be a wasteland for much longer. Perhaps dry, as it had been in the Old World, but with more water and warmth than before.

The Blights have receded, but are not gone. The dragons, both Radaskim *and* Elekai – but I guess I should say they are all *Elekai,* now – continue to live and thrive. It turns out that they do *need each other.* The Radaskim *are female, and the* Elekai *are male, and they are having baby dragons. I think it's possible for them to originate without that, but this seems a more natural way. Either way, I suppose* the Elekai *and humanity will have to learn to live with each other. The dragons don't visit us much, sticking to their Blights, but sometimes I'll go to see them – though these visits have become fewer as I've grown older. It's hard to relive the past.*

After the battle, we tracked the retreating converted Radaskim *to Ragnarok Crater, and watched them disappear into the Warrens. We haven't heard from them since. No one goes that way – not even me. Something tells me a darkness is still rooted down there, but mostly I don't go because there are too many painful memories. I've learned that the pain doesn't go away with the years. We just make more space for it.*

Not to say I'm unhappy. I will always carry my sorrows, but seeing my son grow up is my greatest joy. I live among friends and lead as peaceful a life as I can manage. I have my friends, my son, and we all spend a lot of time together. There's less shooting, less killing, and more talking, food, and wine. Augustus is always sure to send us a cask every Xenofall to celebrate. That's what they're calling the anniversary, now, and it will probably be celebrated every year for a long time. Though Xenofall is a holiday for most, it's hard for me to celebrate, for understandable reasons. All the same, it's good that Augustus remembers us.

As far as Carin– he died in the battle. I know how hard he fought, but I can't help but be glad. He destroyed so many lives, and in the end, it's hard to imagine him ever being redeemed for it. But at least he died doing something good, and that's all I have to say about the matter.

I suppose it's impossible for there to be a completely happy ending, when we have lost so much. Even though I've lost Alex, I don't believe that happiness is impossible. How could I not be happy, when I have so much to be thankful for and a world free of the Radaskim? *My thoughts always return to my son, and when I look into his eyes, I see* him, *and I know that he's watching over me.*

I guess he was right, in the end. He would always be with me. We are all Elekai, *still, all bound together with something deeper than friendship, something deeper than love. It's our common humanity, our common purpose, our common dreams. Alex, Makara, Ashton, and Julian are all gone, and they are all honored, but none so much as Alex. For generations, people will learn about him.*

There are so many reasons I love him, and will continue to love him, until the day I die. Forgetting would be impossible, and much more, unwanted. After saving this world, after losing so much, we need a new purpose, or humanity will fight amongst itself again. I lost almost everything of who I was, and I suppose I'll have to find a way to live with that sadness.

I still wish I could have gone down with him. But then I look at my life, at my son, at every good thing I possess, and know that he was right. This is better.

And a curious thing has happened. It seems as if our children are going to become Elekai *as well. They all have the same abilities we do, so whatever change the virus made to us was genetic. I don't know what that means for our future, but at least for now, it means that the children enjoy visiting Askal and the others whenever we get the chance.*

I know, in the end, when I close my eyes for the final time, I'll go to meet him. But until then, I'm content to live, raise my son, and teach him about his father, the man who gave himself up to save the world, the man who is alive, even today, watching over us all.

We on Earth are the only ones who were able to stop the Radaskim. *Some might say it was luck, but I believe* he *was the reason. I can only hope we can build a world that respects his sacrifice – a world without war. So far, this has been a lasting peace...but I know how easy it is to forget what everyone fought and died for.*

That's why I tell his story to anyone who will listen. In a sense, it's all of our stories, and if we ever forget what happened here, it will be to our peril. The Radaskim *will return, and it's up to us to begin*

planning for that...even now.
Until then, we'll watch, and we'll wait...
...and we'll never forget.

THE END

A Note

After that ending, I almost don't want to write anything here. It was sad for me, because this series that has grown with me for almost two years. The characters feel real, like people I know.

A lot of people have been asking if this is the end of *The Wasteland Chronicles*. Yes, this is the end of the main series, but don't despair just yet. I'm writing a follow-up series, set four hundred years after the events of the first books. As Anna's words hinted, the story isn't completely over, but it will be up to people growing up in a very different world to put up their own fight.

In a way, Anna and the others are passing the torch to future generations – but that will come with its own set of difficulties, as you will soon see.

I have no idea what this new series will be called – maybe *Xenoworld*? Regardless, I'm planning on three books. I've already written the first 10,000 words. Assuming I can cobble the thing together without messing everything up, I think you guys will love it. It's going to have all the trademarks of this series – a very intricate world, lots of action, characters you can root for, and of course, dragons and a host of other creatures.

For those of you hoping for a completely new series – I'll get to that sort of stuff some day. I have more ideas than I know what to do with. For now, though, I'm working on my next series. From what I've developed so far, the history will be fascinating in its own right.

The final thing I have to say is that I'm incredibly humbled by your support. The possibilities for the future are exciting. I hope you guys can continue to spread the word.

Of course, let me know what you think. Head to contact section below. My email is always open, and you can follow me on Facebook, Twitter, or keep up with my blog. I plan on blogging about more of my thoughts about the end, so be sure to check that out.

Acknowledgements

I just wanted to take a page to thank everyone who's helped me to get to this point. There were *a lot*. It was amazing to see people supporting me, even from the very beginning.

The first person I'd like to thank is my dad. He's always the first person to read a rough version of the book, and he's really good at finding logical inconsistencies and his suggestions have definitely made the series better.

My mom has also helped a ton, especially on *Darkness,* which was probably the hardest one for me to write. She had some great developmental insight that really saved the beginning of the book. She also did some excellent proofing work. Actually, I'm incredibly lucky to have such supportive parents. I can't remember them ever discouraging me from writing, and that encouraged me to keep going.

I've had a host of people offer to beta and proofread throughout the series. I don't think everyone's done it for every book (except my dad), but as far as I can remember, and hopefully I'm not forgetting anyone, special thanks to Nich Spragg for excellent proofing for my past five books, and more recently, Cindy McKenzie and Joy Finkle. Athena Delgado and Holly Searls also did some beta reading, *way* back in the day, so I also thought I'd mention them. Hopefully I haven't forgotten anyone.

Special thanks to Mel Odom. He was my professor at the University of Oklahoma. He taught me a lot about writing and has always been a *huge* support to me (as he is with all of his students).

A lot of things might have been different if he had not stepped in and taught me something new. He also did some editing for *Apocalypse* (on his own time, I might add – I wasn't even his student anymore.)

Similarly, I'd like to thank Ron Rozelle, who was my creative writing teacher in high school. Even though it was a while ago, sometimes you just have that teacher who sticks just because of how they inspired you. That's definitely the case for him. I remember him telling me, before I left for my senior year, that I shouldn't give up and keep writing. For some reason, I listened, and I didn't give up. He was always a great support, and I'm lucky to have had such a good teacher.

I could go on. I've had a lot of friends who have inspired me along the way, but sometimes, it takes a writer to understand a writer. In that vein, thanks to Jelani Sims for listening to my ideas.

Last of all, thanks to my readers (that is, you) for reading this far. It's hard to believe I've written something that's almost two thousand pages and almost half a million words. Amazingly, thousands of people have read the series, and there were a lot of times where I thought only a few people would.

Again, thanks. It's been an incredible journey and I'm looking forward to writing my next book!

About the Author

Kyle West is the author of *The Wasteland Chronicles*. From a young age he has always been a voracious reader of sci-fi and fantasy. He graduated from the University of Oklahoma with a degree in Professional Writing. When not writing, he might be running, crafting the perfect breakfast burrito, playing various RPG's, or reading an overly large book. He writes full-time and resides in the bustling metropolis of Oklahoma City.

Find out immediately when his next book is released by signing up for The Wasteland Chronicles Mailing List, found at eepurl.com/A1-8D. Be sure to follow him on Facebook for updates, book giveaways, and general shenanigans.

Contact

[Facebook](#)
[Twitter](#)
[Goodreads](#)
[Blog](#)
kylewestwriter[at]gmail[dot]com

Glossary

10,000, The: This refers to the 10,000 citizens who were selected in 2029 to enter Bunker One. This group included the best America had to offer, people who were masters in the fields of science, engineering, medicine, and security. President Garland and all the U.S. Congress, as well as essential staff and their families, were chosen.

Alpha: "Alpha" is the title given to the recognized head of the Raiders. In the beginning, it was merely a titular role that only had as much power as the Alpha was able to enforce. But as Raider Bluff grew in size and complexity, the Alpha took on a more meaningful role. Typically, Alphas do not remain so for long – they are assassinated by rivals who rise to take their place. In some years, there can be as many as four Alphas – though powerful Alphas, like Char, can reign for many years.

Askala: Askala is the *Radaskim* Xenomind dwelling in Ragnarok Crater.

Batts: Batts, or batteries, are the currency of the Wasteland and the Empire. They are accepted anywhere that the Empire's caravans reach. It is unknown *how* batteries were first seen as currency, but it is rumored that Augustus himself instigated the policy. Using them as currency makes sense: batteries are small, portable, and durable, and have the intrinsic quality of being useful. Rechargeable batteries (called "chargers") are even more prized, and solar batteries (called "solars," or "sols") are the most useful and prized of all.

Behemoth: The Behemoth is a great monstrosity in the Wasteland – a giant creature, either humanoid or reptilian, or sometimes a mixture of the two, that can reach heights of ten feet or greater. They are bipedal, powerful, and can keep pace with a moving vehicle. All but the most powerful of guns are useless against the Behemoth's armored hide.

Black Reapers, The: The Black Reapers are a powerful, violent gang, based in Los Angeles. They are led by Warlord Carin Black. They keep thousands of slaves, using them to serve their post-apocalyptic empire. They usurped the Lost Angels in 2055, and have been ruling there ever since.

Black Files, The: The Black Files are the mysterious collected research on the xenovirus, located in Bunker One. They were authored principally by Dr. Cornelius Ashton, Chief Scientist of Bunker One.

Blights: Blights are infestations of xenofungus and the xenolife they support. They are typically small, but the bigger ones can cover large tracts of land. As a general rule of thumb, the larger the Blight, the more complicated and dangerous the ecosystem it maintains. The largest known Blight is the Great Blight – which covers a large portion of the central United States. Its center is Ragnarok Crater.

Boundless, The: The Boundless is an incredibly dry part of the Wasteland, ravaged by canyons and dust storms, situated in what used to be Arizona and New Mexico. Very little can survive in the Boundless, and no one is known to have ever crossed it.

Bunker 40: Bunker 40 is located on the outer fringes of the Great Blight in Arizona. It is hidden beneath a top secret research facility, a vestige of the Old World. Many aircraft were stationed at Bunker 40 before it fell, sometime in the late 2050s.

Bunker 108: Bunker 108 is located in the San Bernardino Mountains about one hundred miles east of Los Angeles. It is the birthplace of Alex Keener.

Bunker 114: Bunker 114 is a medical research installation built about fifty miles northwest of Bunker 108. Built beneath Cold Mountain, Bunker 114 is small. After the fall of Bunker One, Bunker 114, like Bunker 108 to the southeast, became a main center of xenoviral research. An outbreak of the human strain of the xenovirus caused the Bunker to fall in 2060. Bunker 108's fall followed soon thereafter.

Bunker One: Bunker One was the main headquarters of the Post-Ragnarok United States government. It fell in 2048 to a swarm of crawlers that overran its defenses. Bunker One had berths for ten thousand people, making it many times over the most populous Bunker. Its inhabitants included President Garland, the U.S. Senate and House of Representatives, essential government staff, and security forces, along with the skilled people needed to maintain it. Also, dozens of brilliant scientists and specialists lived and worked there, including engineers, doctors, and technicians. The very wealthy were also allowed berths for helping to finance the Bunker Program. Bunker One is the location of the Black Files, authored by Dr. Cornelius Ashton.

Bunker Six: Bunker Six is a large installation located north of Bunker One, within driving distance. It houses the S-Class spaceships constructed during the Dark Decade – including *Gilgamesh,* the capital ship, and three smaller cruisers – *Odin, Perseus,* and *Orion.* While *Gilgamesh* and *Odin* are under Cornelius Ashton's care, *Perseus* and *Orion* are still locked inside the fallen Bunker.

Bunker Program, The: The United States and Canadian governments pooled resources to establish 144 Bunkers in Twelve Sectors throughout their territory. The Bunkers were the backup in case the Guardian Missions failed. When the Guardian Missions *did* fail, the Bunker Program kicked into full gear. The Bunkers were designed to save all critical government personnel and citizenry, along with anyone who could provide the finances to construct them. The Bunkers were designed to last indefinitely, using hydroponics to grow food. The Bunkers ran on fusion power, which had been made efficient by the early 2020s. The plan was that, when the dust settled, Bunker residents could reemerge and rebuild. Most Bunkers fell, however, for various reasons – including critical systems failures, mutinies, and attacks by outsiders (see **Wastelanders**). By the year 2060, only four Bunkers were left.

Chaos Years, The: The Chaos Years refer to the ten years following the impact of Ragnarok. These dark years signified the great die-off of most forms of life, including humans. Most deaths occurred due to starvation. With mass global cooling, crops could not grow in climates too far from the tropics. What crops *would* grow produced a yield far too small to feed the population that existed. This led to a period of violence unknown in all of human history. The Chaos Years signify the complete breakdown of the Old World's remaining infrastructures – including food production, economies, power grids, and the industrial complex – all of which led to the deaths of billions of people.

Coleseo Imperio: *El Coleseo Imperio*, translated as the Imperial Coliseum, is a circular, three-tiered stone arena rising from the center of the city of Nova Roma, the capital of the Nova Roman Empire. It is used to host gladiatorial games in the tradition of ancient Rome, and serves as the chief sport of the Empire. Slaves and convicts are forced to fight in death matches, which serves the dual purpose of entertaining the masses while getting rid of prisoners and slaves who would otherwise be, in the Empire's eyes, liabilities. Ritual sacrifices routinely take place on the arena floor.

Crawlers: Crawlers are dangerous, highly mobile monsters spawned by Ragnarok. Their origin is unclear, but they share many characteristics of Earth animals – mostly those reptilian in nature, although other forms are more similar to insects. Crawlers are sleek and fast, and can leap through the air at very high speeds. Typically, crawlers attack in groups, and behave as if of one mind. One crawler will, without hesitation, sacrifice itself in order to reach its prey. Crawlers are especially dangerous when gathered in high numbers – at which point there is not much one can do but run. Crawlers can be killed, their weak points being their belly and their three eyes.

Dark Decade, The: The Dark Decade lasted from 2020-2030, from the time of the first discovery of Ragnarok, to the time of its impact. It is not called the Dark Decade because the world descended into madness immediately upon the discovery of Ragnarok by astronomer Neil Weinstein – that only happened in 2028, with the failure of *Messiah,* the third and last of the Guardian Missions. In the United States and other industrialized nations, life proceeded in an almost normal fashion. There were plenty of good reasons to believe that Ragnarok could be stopped, especially when given ten years. But as the Guardian Missions failed, one by one, the order of the world quickly disintegrated.

With the failure of the Guardian Mission *Archangel* in 2024, a series of wars engulfed the world. As what some were calling World War III embroiled the planet, the U.S. and several of its European allies, and Canada, continued to work on stopping Ragnarok. When the second Guardian Mission, *Reckoning,* failed, an economic depression swept the world. But none of this compared to the madness that followed upon the failure of the third and final Guardian, *Messiah,* in 2028. As societies broke down, martial law was enforced. President Garland was appointed dictator of the United States with absolute authority. By 2029, several states had broken off from the Union.

In the last quarter of 2030, an odd silence hung over the world, as if it had grown weary of living. The President, all essential governmental staff and military, the Senate and House of Representatives, along with scientists, engineers, and the talented and the wealthy, entered the 144 Bunkers established by the Bunker Program. Outraged, the tens of millions of people who did not get an invitation found the Bunker locations, demanding to be let in. The military took action when necessary.

Then, on December 3, 2030, Ragnarok fell, crashing into the border of Wyoming and Nebraska, forming a crater one hundred miles wide. The world left the Dark Decade, and entered the Chaos Years.

Elekai: The *Elekai* are the peaceful counterpart to the *Radaskim*. They seek the harmony and growth of all life, even if that means that the universe will eventually one day end. The *Radaskim* take the opposite viewpoint – that the destruction of all life is a fair price in exchange for controlling the destruction and reconstruction of the universe, called the Universal Cycle:

Eternal War, The: The Eternal War has spanned hundreds of thousands of years across the cosmos. The *Radaskim* seek to infect and conquer every life-bearing world. The *Elekai* are always with them and fight the *Radaskim* at every turn. However, the *Radaskim* are more numerous and have always won on every world. The Wanderer and the *Elekai* hope to reverse this on planet Earth.

Exiles, The: The Exiles are led by a man named Marcus, brother of Alpha Char. The Exiles were once raiders, but were exiled from Raider Bluff in 2048. Raider Bluff faced a rival city, known as Rivertown, on the Colorado River. A faction led by Char wanted to destroy Rivertown by blowing up Hoover Dam far to the north. Marcus and his faction opposed this. The two brothers fought, and in his rage, Marcus threw Char into a nearby fireplace, giving him the severe burns on his face that Char would live with for the rest of his life. For this attack, the Alpha at the time exiled Marcus – but in solidarity, many Raiders left to join him. For the next twelve years, the exiled Raiders wandered the Boundless, barred from ever returning farther west than Raider Bluff. The Exiles at first sought to found a new city somewhere in the eastern United States, but the Great Blight barred their path. Over the next several years, they hired themselves as mercenaries to the growing Nova Roman Empire. Now, they wander the Wastes, Marcus awaiting the day when his brother calls upon him for help – which he is sure Char will do.

Flyers: Flyers are birds infected with the xenovirus. They fly in large swarms of a hundred or more. They are only common around large Blights, or within the Great Blight itself. The high metabolism of flyers means they cannot venture far from xenofungus, their main source of food. They are highly dangerous, and cannot be fought easily, because they fly in such large numbers.

Gilgamesh: *Gilgamesh* is an S-Class Capital Spaceship constructed by the United States during the Dark Decade. It holds room for twelve crewmen, thirteen counting the captain. Its fuselage is mostly made of carbon nanotubes – incredibly lightweight, and many, many times stronger than steel. It is powered by a prototypical miniature fusion reactor, using deuterium and tritium as fuel. Its design is described as insect-like in appearance, for invisibility to radar. The ship contains a bridge, armory, conference room, kitchen, galley, two lavatories, a clinic, and twelve bunks for crew in two separate dorms. A modest captain's quarters can be reached from the galley, complete with its own lavatory. Within the galley is access to a spacious cargo bay, where supplies, and even a vehicle as large as a Recon, can be stored. The Recon can be driven off the ship's wide boarding ramp when grounded (this capability is the main difference between *Odin* and *Gilgamesh*...in addition to the cargo bay boarding ramp, *Gilgamesh* also contains a passenger's boarding ramp on the side, that also leads into the galley). The porthole has a retractable rope ladder that is good for up to five hundred feet. *Gilgamesh* has a short wingspan, but receives most of its lift from the four thrusters mounted in back, thrusters that have a wide arc of rotation that allows the ship to fly in almost any direction. The ship can go weeks without needing to refuel. As far as combat capabilities, *Gilgamesh* was primarily constructed as a reconnaissance and transport vessel. That said, it has twin machine gun turrets that open from beneath the ship. When grounded, it is supported by three struts, one in front, two in back.

Great Blight, The: The Great Blight is the largest xenofungal infestation in the world, its point of origin being Ragnarok Crater on the Great Plains in eastern Wyoming and western Nebraska. Unlike other Blights, the Great Blight is massive. From 2040-2060, it began to rapidly expand outside Ragnarok Crater at an alarming rate, moving as much as a quarter mile each day (meaning the stretching of the xenofungus could actually be discerned with the naked eye). Any and all life was conquered, killed, or acquired into the Great Blight's xenoparasitic network. Here, the first monsters were created. Animals would become ensnared in sticky pools of purple goo, and their DNA absorbed and preserved. The Great Blights, obeying some sort of consciousness, would then mix and match the DNA of varying species, tweaking and mutating the genes until, from the same pools it had acquired the DNA, it would give birth to new life forms, designed only to spread the Blight and kill whoever, or whatever, opposed that spreading. As time went on and the Xeno invasion became more sophisticated, the Great Blight's capabilities became advanced enough to direct the evolution of xenolife itself, leading to the creation of the xenovirus, meaning it could infect species far outside of the Blight – including, eventually, humans.

Guardian Missions: The Guardian Missions were humanity's attempts to intercept and alter the course of Ragnarok during the Dark Decade. There were three, and in the order they were launched, they were called *Archangel, Reckoning,* and *Messiah* (all three of which were also the names of the ships launched). Each mission had a reason for failing. *Archangel* is reported to have crashed into Ragnarok, in 2024. In 2026, *Reckoning* somehow got off-course, losing contact with Earth in the process. In 2028 *Messiah* successfully landed and attached its payload of rockets to the surface of Ragnarok in order to alter its course from Earth.

However, the rockets failed before they had time to do their work. The failure of the Guardian Missions kicked the Bunker Program into overdrive.

Howlers: Howlers are the newest known threat posed by the xenovirus. They are human xenolife, and they behave very much like zombies. They attack with sheer numbers, using their bodies as weapons. A bite from a Howler is enough to infect the victim with the human strain of the xenovirus. Post-infection, it takes anywhere from a few minutes to a few hours for a corpse to reanimate into the dreaded howler. Worse, upon death, Howlers somehow explode, raining purple goo on anyone within range. Even if a little bit of goo enters the victim's bloodstream, he or she is as good as dead, cursed to become a Howler within a matter of minutes or hours. How the explosion occurs, no one knows – it is surmised that the xenovirus itself creates some sort of agent that reacts violently with water or some other fluid present within the Howlers. There is also reason to believe that certain Howlers become Behemoths, as was the case with Kari in Bunker 114.

Hydra: A powerful spawning of the xenovirus, the Hydra has only been seen deep in the heart of Bunker One. It contains three heads mounted on three stalk-like necks. It is covered in thick scales that serve as armor. It has a powerful tail that it can swing, from the end of which juts a long, cruel spike. It is likely an evolved, more deadly form of the crawler.

Ice Lands, The: Frozen in a perpetual blanket of ice and snow, the northern and southern latitudes of the planet are completely unlivable. In the Wasteland, at least, they are referred to as the Ice Lands. Under a blanket of meteor fallout, extreme global cooling was instigated in 2030. While the glaciers are only now experiencing rapid regrowth, they will advance for centuries to come until the fallout has dissipated enough to produce a warmer climate. In the Wasteland, 45 degrees north marks the beginning of what is considered the Ice Lands.

L.A. Gangland: L.A. Gangland means a much different thing than it did Pre-Ragnarok. In the ruins of Los Angeles, there are dozens of gangs vying for control, but by 2060, the most powerful is the Black Reapers, who usurped that title from the Lost Angels.

Lost Angels, The: The Lost Angels were post-apocalyptic L.A.'s first super gang. From the year 2050 until 2055, they reigned supreme in the city, led by a charismatic figure named Dark Raine. The Angels were different from other gangs – they valued individual freedom and abhorred slavery. Under the Angels' rule, Los Angeles prospered. The Angels were eventually usurped in 2056 by a gang called the Black Reapers, led by a man named Carin Black.

Nova Roma: Nova Roma is the capital of the Nova Roman Empire. It existed Pre-Ragnarok as a small town situated in an idyllic valley, flanked on three sides by green mountains. This town was also home to Augustus's palatial mansion – and it was around this mansion that the city that would one day rule the Empire had its beginnings. Over thirty years, as the Empire gained wealth and power under Augustus's rule, Nova Roma grew from a small village into a mighty city with a population numbering in the tens of thousands. Using knowledge of ancient construction techniques found in American Bunkers, Augustus employed talented engineers and thousands of slaves to build the city from the ground up. Inspired by the architecture of ancient Rome, some of the most notable construction projects in Nova Roma include the *Coleseo Imperio,* the Senate House, the Grand Forum, and Central Square. An aqueduct carries water over the city walls from the Sierra Madre Mountains north of the city. The city grows larger each passing year, so much so that shantytowns have overflowed its walls, attracted by the city's vast wealth.

Nova Roman Empire, The: The Nova Roman Empire (also known as the "Empire") is a collection of allied city-states that are ruled from Nova Roma, its capital in what was formerly the

Mexican state of Guerrero. The Empire began as the territory of a Mexican drug cartel named the Legion. Through the use of brutal force, they kept security within their borders even as other governments fell.

Following the impact of Ragnarok, many millions of Americans fled south to escape the cold, dry climate that permeated northern latitudes. Mexico still remained warm, especially southern Mexico, and new global wind currents caused by Ragnarok kept Mexico clearer of meteor fallout than other areas of the world. At the close of the Chaos Years, Mexico was far more populous than the United States. Many city-states formed in the former republic, but most developed west of the Sierra Madre Mountains. Language clashes between native Mexicans and migrant Americans produced new dialects of both Spanish and English. Though racial tensions exist in the Empire, as Americans' descendants are the minority within it, Americans and their descendants are protected under law and are entitled to the same rights – at least in theory. The reality is, most refugees that entered Imperial territory were American – and most refugees ended up as slaves.

Of the hundreds of city-states that formed in Mexico, one was called Nova Roma, located inland in a temperate valley not too far east of Acapulco. Under the direction of the man styling himself as Augustus Imperator, formerly known as Miguel Santos, lord of the Legion drug cartel, the city of Nova Roma allied with neighboring city-states. Incorporating both Ancient Roman governmental values and Aztec mythology, the Empire expanded through either the conquest or annexation of rival city-states. By 2060, the Empire had hundreds of cities in its thrall, stretching from Oaxaca in the southeast all the way to Jalisco in the northwest. The Empire had also formed colonies as far north as Sonora, even founding a city called Colossus at the mouth of the Colorado River, intended to be the provincial capital from which the Empire hoped to rule California and the Mojave.

Because of its size and power, the Empire is difficult to control. Except for its center, ruled out of Nova Roma, most of the city-states are autonomous and are only required to pay tribute and soldiers when called for during the Empire's wars. In the wake of the Empire's rapid conquests, Augustus developed the Imperial Road System in order to facilitate trade and communication, mostly done by horse. In an effort to create a unifying culture for the Empire, Emperor Augustus instigated a representative government, where all of Nova Roma's provinces have representation in the Imperial Senate. Augustus encouraged a universal religion based on Aztec mythology, whose gods are placed alongside the saints of Catholicism in the Imperial Pantheon. Augustus also instigated gladiatorial games, ordering that arenas be built in every major settlement of his Empire. This included the construction of dozens of arenas, including *El Coleseo Imperio* in Nova Roma itself, a large arena which, while not as splendid as the original Coliseum in Old Rome, is still quite impressive. The *Coleseo* can seat ten thousand people. By 2060, Augustus had accomplished what might have taken a century to establish otherwise.

Oasis: Oasis is a settlement located in the Wasteland, about halfway between Los Angeles and Raider Bluff. It has a population of one thousand, and is built around the banks of the oasis for which it is named. The oasis did not exist Pre-Ragnarok, but was formed by tapping an underground aquifer. Elder Ohlan rules Oasis with a strong hand. He is the brother of Dark Raine, and it is whispered that he might have had a hand in his death.

Odin: *Odin* is an S-Class Cruiser Spaceship built by the U.S. during the Dark Decade. It is one of four, the other being *Gilgamesh*, the capital ship, and the other two being *Perseus* and *Orion*, cruisers with the same specs as *Odin*. Though *Odin's* capabilities are not as impressive as *Gilgamesh's*, *Odin* is still very functional. It contains berths for eight crew, nine counting the captain. It has a cockpit, armory, kitchen, galley, two dorms, one lavatory, and the fusion drive in the aft. A cargo bay can be reached from either outside the ship or within the galley. Unlike *Gilgamesh,* it is not spacious enough to store a Recon. It contains a single machine gun turret that can open up from the ship's bottom. *Odin,* in addition to being faster than *Gilgamesh,* also gets better fuel efficiency. It can go months without needing to refuel.

Praetorians, The: The Praetorians are the most elite of the Empire's soldiers. There are one hundred total, and they are the personal bodyguard of Emperor Augustus. They carry a long spear, tower shield, and gladius. They wear a long, purple cape, steel armor, and a white jaguar headdress, complete with purple plume. They are also trained in the use of guns.

Radaskim: The *Radaskim* seek to conquer all life in the universe in their quest to discover the Secrets of Creations, Secrets which the *Radaskim* believe are the key to recreating the universe. Whether this is even possible is unknown, but all *Radaskim* motives are based on this idea. They have conquered hundreds of worlds and are in the process of conquering Earth. The *Radaskim* on Earth are led by the Xenomind, Askala.

Raider Bluff: Raider Bluff is the only known settlement of the raiders. It is built northeast of what used to be Needles, California, on top of a three-tiered mesa. Though the raiders are a mobile group, even they need a place to rest during the harsh Wasteland winter. Merchants, women, and servants followed the Raider men, setting up shop on the mesa, giving birth to Raider Bluff sometime in the early 2040s. From the top of the Bluff rules the Alpha, the strongest recognized leader of the Raiders. A new Alpha rises only when he is able to wrest control from the old one.

Ragnarok: Ragnarok was the name given the meteor that crashed into Earth on December 3, 2030. It was about three miles long, and two miles wide. It was discovered by astronomer Neil Weinstein, in 2019. It is not known *what* caused Ragnarok to come hurtling toward Earth, or how it eluded detection for so long – but that answer was revealed when the Black Files came to light. Ragnarok was the first phase of the invasion planned by the Xenos, the race of aliens attempting to conquer Earth. Implanted within Ragnarok was the xenovirus – the seed for all alien genetic life that was to destroy, acquire, and replace Earth life. The day the Xenos arrive, according to the Black Files, is called "Xenofall." The time of their eventual arrival is completely unknown.

Ragnarok Crater: Ragnarok Crater is the site of impact of the meteor Ragnarok. It is located on the border of Wyoming and Nebraska, and is about one hundred miles wide with walls eight miles tall. It's the center of the Great Blight, and it is also the origin of the Voice, the consciousness that directs the behavior of all xenolife.

Recon: A Recon is an all-terrain rover that is powered by hydrogen. It is designed for speedy recon missions across the Wastes, and was developed by the United States military during the Dark Decade. It is composed of a cab in front, and a large cargo bay in the back. Mounted on top of the cargo bay is a turret with 360-degree rotation, accessible by a ladder and a porthole. The turret can be manned and fired while the Recon is on the go.

Secrets of Creation, The: The Secrets of Creation are the name given to the knowledge the *Radaskim* must have in order to destroy the universe and remake it in the exact same way it had been created – allowing the universe to exist indefinitely.

Skyhome: Skyhome is a three-ringed, self-sufficient space station constructed by the United States during the Dark Decade, designed to house two hundred and fifty people. Like the Bunkers, it contains its own power, hydroponics, and water reclamation system designed to keep the station going as long as possible. Skyhome was never actually occupied until 2048, after the falls of both Bunker One and Bunker Six. Cornelius Ashton assumed control of the station, along with survivors from both Bunkers, in order to continue his research on the xenovirus which had destroyed his entire life.

Universal Cycle, The: The Universal Cycle is a *Radaskim* prophecy stating that the universe has been destroyed and reborn an infinite number of times, only because the *Radaskim* discovered the "Secrets of Creation" in every manifestation of the universe in time to recreate it. The rebirth of the universe depends on the *Radaskim* discovering these secrets, and it involves acquiring all known life in order to discover the knowledge that might unlock the Secrets – whatever they are.

Voice, The: The Voice is the name given to the collective consciousness of all xenolife. It exists in Ragnarok Crater – whether or not it has a corporeal form is unknown. However, it is agreed by Dr. Ashton and Samuel that the Voice controls xenolife using sound waves and vibrations within xenofungus. The Voice also sends sound waves that can be detected by xenolife while off the xenofungus. The Voice gives the entire Xeno invasion sentience, and is a piece of evidence pointing to an advanced alien race that is trying to conquer Earth.

Wanderer, The: A blind prophet who wanders the Wasteland. He is also the Xenomind who leads the *Elekai,* the alien faction that wants to stop the *Radaskim* from conquering all life.

Wastelanders: Wastelanders are surface dwellers, specifically ones that live in the southwestern United States. The term is broad – it can be as specific as to mean only someone who is forced to wander, scavenge, or raid for sustenance, or Wastelander can mean anyone who lives on the surface Post-Ragnarok, regardless of location or circumstances. Wastelanders are feared by Bunker dwellers, as they have been the number one reason for Bunkers failing.

Wasteland, The: The Wasteland is a large tract of land comprised of Southern California and the adjacent areas of the Western United States. It extends from the San Bernardino

Mountains in the west, to the Rockies in the east (and in later years, the Great Blight), and from the northern border of Nova Roma on the south, to the Ice Lands to the north (which is about the same latitude as Sacramento, California). The Wasteland is characterized by a cold, extremely dry climate. Rainfall each year is little to none, two to four inches being about average. Little can survive the Wasteland, meaning that all life has clung to limited water supplies. Major population centers include Raider Bluff, along the Colorado River; Oasis, supplied by a body of water of the same name; and Last Town, a trading post that sprung up along I-10 between Los Angeles and the Mojave. Whenever the Wasteland is referred to, it is generally not referred to in its entire scope. It is mainly used to reference what was once the Mojave Desert.

Xenodragon: The xenodragon is the newest manifestation of the xenovirus. It is very much like a dragon – reptilian, lightweight, with colossal wings that provide it with both lift and speed. There are different kinds of xenodragons, but the differences are little known, other than whether they are large or small. A particularly large xenodragon makes its roost on Raider Bluff.

Xenofall: Xenofall is the day of reckoning – when the Xenos finally arrive on Earth to claim it as their own. No one knows when that day is – whether it is in one year, ten years, or a thousand. It is feared that, when Xenofall *does* come, humans and all resistance will have been long gone.

Xenofungus: Xenofungus is a slimy, sticky fungus that is colored pink, orange, or purple (and sometimes all three), that infests large tracts of land and serves as the chief food source of all xenolife. It forms the basis of the Blights, and without xenofungus, xenolife could not exist. The fungus, while hostile to Earth life, facilitates the growth, development, and expansion of xenolife. It is nutrient-rich, and contains complicated compounds and proteins that are poison to Earth life, but ambrosia for xenolife. It is tough, resilient, resistant to fire, dryness, and cold – and if it isn't somehow stopped, one day xenofungus will cover the entire world.

Xenolife: Any form of life that is infected with the xenovirus.

Xenomind: A Xenomind is an ancient sentient being, evolved over the eons by the xenovirus and xenofungus. They are split into two factions – the *Radaskim* and the *Elekai*. The *Radaskim* are warlike and want to conquer all life in the universe – a seemingly impossible aim. The *Elekai* want to stop the *Radaskim* from achieving this. So far, on every world the Eternal War has been fought, the *Elekai* have lost.

Xenovirus: The xenovirus is an agent that acquires genes, adding them to its vast collection. It then mixes and matches the genes under its control to create something completely new, whether a plant, animal, bacteria, etc. There are thousands of strains of the xenovirus, maybe even millions, but most are completely undocumented. While the underlying core of each strain is the same, the strains are specific to each species it infects. Failed strains completely drop out of existence, but the successful ones live on. The xenovirus was first noted by Dr. Cornelius Ashton of Bunker One. His collected research on the xenovirus was compiled in the Black Files, which were lost in the fall of Bunker One in 2048.

Also by Kyle West

The Wasteland Chronicles
Apocalypse
Origins
Evolution
Revelation
Darkness
Extinction
Xenofall

Watch for more at kylewestwriter.wordpress.com.

Printed in Great Britain
by Amazon